EARRINGS

Other Books by Eric Koch

FICTION

THE FRENCH KISS
McClelland & Stewart, Toronto, 1969

THE LEISURE RIOTS
Tundra Books, Montreal, 1973
German paperback version, Die Freizei Revoluzzer, Heyne Verlag,
Munich

THE LAST THING YOU'D WANT TO KNOW
Tundra Books, Montreal, 1976
German paperback version, Die Spanne Leben, Heyne Verlag, Munich
(Both German versions were reissued together in 1987 under the title C.R.U.P.P.)

GOOD NIGHT, LITTLE SPY
Virgo Press, Toronto and Ram Publishing Company, London, 1979

KASSANDRUS
Heyne Verlag, Munich, 1988
Liebe und Mord auf Xananta Eichborn, Verlag, Frankfurt, 1992

ICON IN LOVE: A NOVEL ABOUT GOETHE
Mosaic Press, Oakville, 1998
Noblepreis fur Goethe, Fischer Tachenbuch 14536, Frankfurt, 1999

THE MAN WHO KNEW CHARLIE CHAPLIN
Mosaic Press, Oakville, 2000

NON-FICTION

DEEMED SUSPECT
Methuen of Canada, Toronto, 1980

INSIDE SEVEN DAYS
Prentice Hall of Canada, Toronto, 1986

HILMAR AND ODETTE
McClelland & Stewart, Toronto, 1996

THE BROTHERS HAMBOURG
Robin Brass, Toronto, 1997

EARRINGS

a novel by Eric Koch

mosaic press

National Library of Canada Cataloguing in Publication Data

Koch Eric, 1919-
    Earrings: a novel set in Baden-Baden

ISBN 0-88962-775-4

    I. Title.

PS8521.O23E27 2001   C813'.54   C2001-901945-9
PR9199.3.K6E272001

Published by Mosaic Press, offices and warehouse at 1252 Speers Road, Units 1 and 2, Oakville, Ontario, L6L 5N9, Canada and Mosaic Press, PMB 145, 4500 Witmer Industrial Estates, Niagara Falls, NY, 14305-1386, U.S.A.

Mosaic Press acknowledges the assistance of the Canada Council and the Department of Canadian Heritage, Government of Canada for their support of our publishing programme.

Le Conseil des Arts | The Canada Council
du Canada | for the Arts

MOSAIC PRESS, in Canada: MOSAIC PRESS, in U.S.A.:
1252 Speers Road, Units 1 & 2,   4500 Witmer Industrial Estates
Oakville, Ontario   PMB 145, Niagara Falls, NY
L6L 5N9   14305-1386
Phone/Fax: 905-825-2130   Phone/Fax: 1-800-387-8992
mosaicpress@on.aibn.com   mosaicpress@on.aibn.com

Acknowledgements

I would like to thank my publisher, Howard Aster, for rejecting the first draft of this novel. He understood far better than I did that all along I had really wanted to write this final version.

The book is based on the daily issues of the *Badeblatt der Grossherzoglichen Stadt Baden-Baden*, August and September 1883.

Thanks are due to two histories of Baden-Baden which provided much invaluable information, Klaus Fischer, *Baden-Baden erzählt*, 1985, Keil Verlag, Bonn, and Rolf Gustav Haebler, *Geschichte der Stadt und des Kurortes Baden-Baden*, 1969, Dr. Willy Schmidt Verlag.

I am particularly grateful to Klaus Fischer whom I met in Baden-Baden in May 2000 and who enlightened me on many of the finer historical points.

Dostoyevsky's *cri de coeur* to Appolon Maykov, dated August 16, 1867, is loosely based on a letter published in *The Complete Letters of Dostoevsky, Vol. 2, 1860-1867*, Ardis, Ann Arbor, 1989, p. 351.

The portrait of Duchess Marie of Hamilton and the drawings from Louis Katzau's guest book are reproduced with the kind permission of the Stadtarchiv Baden-Baden, Inv. # 89/367 and D10 respectively.

Finally, a word of thanks to my daughter Madeline whose perceptive observations during our visit to Baden-Baden were invaluable and who later corrected innumerable errors and infelicities in the text.

Eric Koch

Robert Koch

Preface

In 1883, my grandfather Robert Koch won the favour of the elderly Duchess of Hamilton on a visit to Baden-Baden, the summer capital of Europe. She launched him on his way to become one of the most eminent jewellers of Europe.

I was curious to find out how he made this conquest but this proved to be impossible. Therefore, in order to tell the story, I had no choice but to embroider established historical facts about time and place with the way I wanted it to have happened.

Eric Koch

The Duchess of Hamilton

THE HOUSE OF BADEN

The Grand Dukes are underlined.
Only persons relevant to the story are listed.

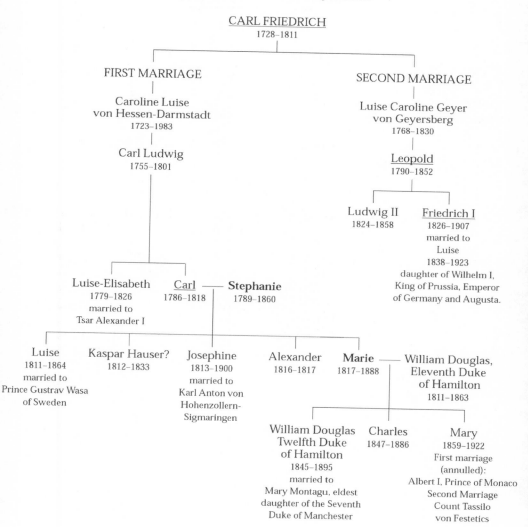

CARL FRIEDRICH
1728–1811

FIRST MARRIAGE

Caroline Luise
von Hessen-Darmstadt
1723–1983

Carl Ludwig
1755–1801

SECOND MARRIAGE

Luise Caroline Geyer
von Geyersberg
1768–1830

Leopold
1790–1852

Ludwig II
1824–1858

Friedrich I
1826–1907
married to
Luise
1838–1923
daughter of Wilhelm I,
King of Prussia, Emperor
of Germany and Augusta.

Luise-Elisabeth
1779–1826
married to
Tsar Alexander I

Carl
1786–1818

Stephanie
1789–1860

Luise
1811–1864
married to
Prince Gustrav Wasa
of Sweden

Kaspar Hauser?
1812–1833

Josephine
1813–1900
married to
Karl Anton von
Hohenzollern-
Sigmaringen

Alexander
1816–1817

Marie
1817–1888

William Douglas,
Eleventh Duke
of Hamilton
1811–1863

William Douglas
Twelfth Duke
of Hamilton
1845–1895
married to
Mary Montagu, eldest
daughter of the Seventh
Duke of Manchester

Charles
1847–1886

Mary
1859–1922
First marriage
(annulled):
Albert I, Prince of Monaco
Second Marriage
Count Tassilo
von Festetics

THE BONAPARTE FAMILY

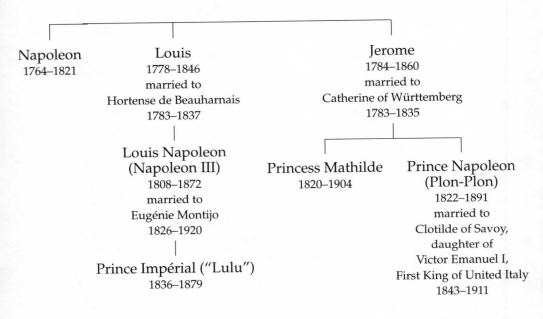

Napoleon
1764–1821

Louis
1778–1846
married to
Hortense de Beauharnais
1783–1837

Louis Napoleon
(Napoleon III)
1808–1872
married to
Eugénie Montijo
1826–1920

Prince Impérial ("Lulu")
1836–1879

Jerome
1784–1860
married to
Catherine of Württemberg
1783–1835

Princess Mathilde
1820–1904

Prince Napoleon
(Plon-Plon)
1822–1891
married to
Clotilde of Savoy,
daughter of
Victor Emanuel I,
First King of United Italy
1843–1911

THE BEAUHARNAIS CONNECTION

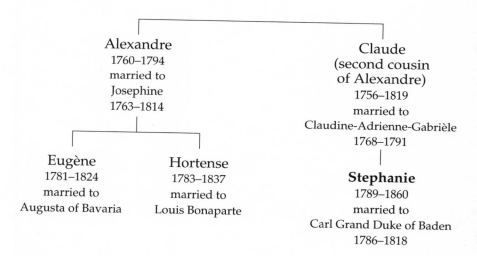

Alexandre
1760–1794
married to
Josephine
1763–1814

Claude
(second cousin
of Alexandre)
1756–1819
married to
Claudine-Adrienne-Gabrièle
1768–1791

Eugène
1781–1824
married to
Augusta of Bavaria

Hortense
1783–1837
married to
Louis Bonaparte

Stephanie
1789–1860
married to
Carl Grand Duke of Baden
1786–1818

The Scene

Baden-Baden is an ancient spa in the Black Forest, surrounded by seven heavily wooded mountains. It is close to the Rhine in the valley of the Oos River, not far from Strasbourg. The hot waters gushing out of the depths, 110,000 gallons a day, with their content of chloride of sodium, lithium and arsenic, were known to the Romans who called them *Aquae Aureliae*. At the time of Martin Luther, it was said that Baden-Baden was the place "where cardinals, bankers and courtesans were rubbing shoulders."

It was Baden-Baden to distinguish it from two single Badens, one near Vienna, which was Beethoven's occasional summer resort, and the other near Zürich.

It was already an important resort in the early nineteenth century. At the *table d'hôte* in the hotels, inns and taverns tourists made friends with strangers. A number of renowned literary men assembled there, attracted by the dark romantic forests and the nearby ruins, which they eloquently praised in songs and ballads. Among these were the storyteller Berthold Auerbach, the medical doctor Justinus Kerner and the Shakespeare translator Ludwig Tieck. On August 20, 1812, the playwright Johann Peter Hebel ate at the Badische Hof, with one hundred and eighty other guests, and reported that he had been "in an entirely different world, a world of glamour, of leisure, with kings and princes, counts, professors, Jews, and comedians." Goethe made one abortive attempt to visit Baden-Baden, but his coach collapsed on the way. He carefully avoided it in future, remaining loyal to his resorts in Bohemia.

Later, in 1844, the poet Nikolaus Lenau met the last great love of his life, the daughter of a Frankfurt senator, at the *table d'hôte* in the Holländische Hof. Shortly after she agreed to marry him, the "happy-unhappy poet descended into the night of madness."

In 1883, Baden-Baden had ten thousand inhabitants. Every summer, sixty thousand guests came to enjoy the natural beauties of the town and its surroundings, the social scene, the baths and the many cultural delights.

Robert Koch deliberately arrived at the peak of the season that year. He knew that in August and September Baden-Baden was celebrating the twenty-fifth anniversary of the horse races in nearby Iffezheim.

Chapter 1

Wednesday, August 22, 1883, was a warm day. The time was three o'clock in the afternoon. There was not a vacant room in the hotels. Edward, the Prince of Wales, was expected to arrive in Baden-Baden in an hour's time. In the coming week, the festivities would reach their peak with a costume ball on Tuesday, opera performances and the famous *Blumen-Corso*, the flower parade along the Lichtentaler Allee. In ten days' time, on September 2, the Prince was to leave for Bad Homburg.

Louis Katzau, the Hungarian owner of Boutique Number Five in the Promenade in Baden-Baden, had the same whiskers as his Kaiser Franz Joseph. His customers cheerfully paid extra for his famous charm and wit when they bought his extravagantly priced souvenirs, his tortoise shell, mother-of-pearl and ivory knick-knacks, rococo mirrors, Hungarian folk pottery, multi-coloured Venetian glass, fat-bellied pots, English silver, French cameos, German pewter, Swiss cuckoo clocks, large varieties of bric-a-brac, chinoiseries, and genuine and imitation antiques from five continents. The store was located across from the nerve centre of Baden-Baden, the Conversationshaus.

Louis Katzau had just sold a silver-gilt wine cooler to Frau Königsberg, whose husband built ships, and a Dutch gold-and-enamel goblet to Frau Grunau, a banker's wife. Both ladies came from Hamburg. These purchases had enabled them to make good use of the money they had won last night in their hotel at a game of whist. Regrettably, the Casino, which had attracted thousands of visitors to Baden-Baden every summer, had closed in 1872, like those in other German spas, after the Prussian victory over the French and the subsequent German unification, because they had been run by French operators and were considered French enclaves on German territory.

Both ladies were staying at the Hotel Stephanie-les-Bains. They wore brightly coloured long silk dresses with skirts that were narrow and clinging and hampered them while they walked. More than a decade earlier, such skirts had superseded the crinoline, which had now vanished, as had the casinos, after the end of the *belle époche* when Baden-Baden was virtually a suburb of Paris.

"Johann Strauss is undoubtedly a little odd," Louis Katzau, a pink rose in his buttonhole, told the two ladies from Hamburg. He spoke Hungarian in every language—German, French, Italian or Russian. "But I only found out how odd he was when I persuaded him to conduct a concert here. That was eleven years ago. He had never performed in Baden-Baden before, but he returned in 1876, staying at your hotel, *mesdames*. I had scored an unprecedented coup. 'Johann Strauss conducts in Baden-Baden!' *Mon Dieu!* The people over there"—he pointed to the Conversationshaus—"were speechless with admiration. I had succeeded where many others had failed."

"You say you 'persuaded' him, Herr Katzau," Frau Königsberg observed. "How did you manage that? Did you know him?"

"Of course, I had met the waltz king a few times before, in Vienna. I always told him he was the only king I knew—and I knew many—whose throne was not built on sand."

"So what was so odd about him?" Frau Grunau asked.

"A week before the concert," Louis Katzau ignored the question, "I had distributed portraits of *Hofballmusikdirektor* Johann Strauss all over town, to be displayed at the baths, at every tap in the Pump Room, in every hotel lobby, in every store window, on every lamp post. Two days later he sent me a telegram informing me that he was unfortunately unable to come. He gave no reasons. The mayor almost fainted when I told him.

I immediately took a train to Vienna to grab him by the scruff of his high collar and bring him back with me. When I arrived in Vienna, I discovered that somebody had told him there was cholera in Baden-Baden. I explained that the story was absolute nonsense and reminded him that I had promised him two thousand francs for the concert. So he relented."

"So far, not very odd," Frau Königsberg observed dryly.

"True. But wait. I rented a royal coach, a royal coachman and two royal horses. We were in high spirits when we began our trip. But after two hours the coach had to climb a hill. So Strauss shouted to the coachman 'Stop! I'm getting out!' To me he explained, 'I cannot abide hills or mountains. I'm going to return to Vienna.'"

The two ladies from Hamburg had to admit this was a little odd.

"'Perhaps you would like to have a look at a map of Austria and South Germany,' I told him. 'You will see that it is not easy to travel from Vienna to Baden-Baden without climbing a mountain. But it can be done. All one has to do is find the Rhine and then go up the Rhine towards the North Sea.' I sent a telegram to book two rooms at a nice inn I knew in Sulzbach just south of Freiburg, where we were going to spend the night. They gave him a splendid room on the first floor, and a tiny cell for me on the third. After settling down, before I could go down to meet him in the dining room for dinner, there was a knock at the door. It was the owner of the inn. I was to come down to the *Hofballmusikdirektor's* room at once. 'I will not stay here for one more minute,' Johann Strauss announced fortissimo, not at all in three-quarter time. 'Look out of the window!' I did. Across the street I saw, at one side, a hospital and, on the other, the crosses of a cemetery. 'I will not be reminded of illness and death. Get me another room!' So I had to find another inn, much smaller, making sure that his room did not face a hospital, a cemetery or a mountain. He liked it so much that the next morning he did not want to leave. You do not think, my ladies, that is a little odd?"

They conceded the point.

"In Baden-Baden, did he conduct *The Blue Danube*?" Frau Königsberg asked.

"Yes, he did. It was only five years old. Naturally, the concert was a sensation. The Grand Duke promptly awarded him the Order of the Red Eagle. But when Strauss heard that he had to go the Neue Schloss to receive it and discovered that the Neue Schloss was on top of a hill, he arranged to have it sent to him by courier. We subsequently became bosom friends. He always called me 'sKatzerl.'"

"I think I should find something for Hans." Frau Grunau had heard enough about Johann Strauss. "Too bad he doesn't smoke. I like these cigarette cases."

"What about a golden watch chain?" Frau Königsberg suggested.

Frau Grunau shook her head. "He's already got three. Who is this?" She picked up a lithograph of a handsome middle-aged woman with black hair parted in the middle and an intelligent, pensive face. "I see her picture everywhere."

"That is the lady who symbolized Baden-Baden in her most splendid years—the Grand Duchess Stephanie."

"After whom our hotel is named," Frau Königsberg remarked.

"Exactly. Napoleon's daughter."

"What?" Both ladies exclaimed in unison. "Herr Katzau!" Frau Grunau shook her finger at him. "You're being very naughty. You know perfectly well that Napoleon did not have a daughter. Not a legitimate one, anyway."

"This one could not have been more legitimate." Katzau was in his element. "I should have said adopted daughter. Actually, she was the cousin of his wife Josephine's first husband. Adopted or not, Stephanie adored Napoleon. She may even have been more than a daughter to him."

"What do you mean?" The ladies pretended to be horrified.

"Oh, there was some gossip. Personally, of course I would not believe it for a minute. The story did the rounds that soon after they first met, when Stephanie was fourteen, after flirting with him shamelessly, to Josephine's distress—it seems Josephine was quite jealous of her little relative—they spent a little time alone together. Not much, because he was very, very quick. May I add that, there was no minimum age in the *Code Napoleon* for—what shall I call it?—sexual congress. That congress took place in 1803. Then, eight years later, at the end of December 1811 or early January 1812, after Stephanie's first child was born, they may have had another congress, at a time when Napoleon needed a little distraction after marrying his second wife, Marie-Louise, who had just presented him with a son, the King of Rome. This was the time when he tried to persuade his father-in-law, the Kaiser of Austria, and the King of Prussia, both of whom he had recently defeated, to send troops to help him in his forthcoming military campaign against his former friend Tsar Alexander I, who happened to be Stephanie's brother-in-law by marriage."

"Stop!" The ladies simultaneously clapped their hands over their ears. "Please, Herr Katzau," Frau Königsberg insisted, "just give me the answer to one simple question. How did the lady who you said was Napoleon's adopted daughter get to Baden-Baden?"

"Delighted, *madame*. Put yourself in Napoleon's place. The time is February 1806. A little more than a year ago you crowned yourself emperor. That was in December 1804. You are almost the master of Europe, but not quite. You still had to defeat England and Austria. An invasion would easily take care of England. And a military campaign would crush Austria. Child's play, obviously. But first you have to consolidate your power. What better way to do it than to place your siblings on a few thrones? One of the German states it would be nice to have is the duchy of Baden, on the other side of the Rhine. The prince in line of succession, Carl, is conspicuously unmarried. You might make it impossible for him to refuse to marry a sister of yours. But by now your three sisters are already queens. And, as you said a minute ago, you have no daughter."

"No legitimate daughter," Frau Grunau corrected him.

"Exactly, *madame*. The situation is serious but by no means hopeless. Your wife, Josephine, has a perfectly good daughter, Hortense, who would have served the purpose admirably. But she is now Queen of Holland, wife of your brother Louis, who was crowned King of Holland last June. So what to do? Fortunately, Josephine's first husband, the Vicomte Alexandre de Beauharnais, who happened to have been guillotined in 1794, had a second cousin whose name was Claude who had a daughter, Stephanie."

"The name of our hotel," Frau Grunau said.

"Exactly." Katzau smiled. "In 1806 she was seventeen. She could be procured for the purpose. Josephine had told you some time ago that an English woman, Lady Bath, was paying for Stephanie's education in an exclusive convent, run by Madame Campan, who had been lady-in-waiting to Marie Antoinette. You are a Corsican. You are well known for your strongly developed sense of family. There is little doubt that you already demonstrated your sense of family by committing incest with at least two of your three sisters, Caroline and Pauline. It is unacceptable to you that the education of a relative of your wife's guillotined husband is being paid for by, of all people, Lady Bath, an English aristocrat. So you summon Stephanie to the Tuileries. Your wife is enchanted. Stephanie calls her 'Tante Josephine.' A year later you crown yourself emperor. You invite her. In the picture that Jacques-Louis David paints of your coronation in Notre Dame, Stephanie is on the balcony just above your mother and your sisters, immortalized, above your mother, whom David thought expedient to include in the picture even though she did not approve of your coronation and refused to attend.."

"So Stephanie married the Prince of Baden?" Frau Grunau asked.

"She did. But first Napoleon adopted her. Otherwise it would not have worked."

"And she was happy ever after?"

"She was not. For one thing, she did not like the Prince. He was fat. He did not like her either. He slept on a sofa outside the bedroom. He soon learned to console himself with stable boys. Stephanie was well educated and used to the glitter of

Paris at its most glittering. Now the poor girl, who of course was Catholic, was cold-shouldered by petty-minded, Protestant, ignorant and boorish provincials whose ancestor was none other than Count Hermann von Zähringen, who died in 1074. They considered her adoptive father a nobody—no, worse than a nobody because he was spreading all kinds of dangerous ideas about liberty, equality and fraternity. Only the old Grand Duke Carl Friedrich was nice to her. He knew what he was doing. He had already profited immensely by becoming a satellite of this subversive revolutionary nobody. Thanks to him Baden's territory had increased four times, and its population five times."

"Not bad," Frau Königsberg commented.

"Yes, not bad," he agreed. "Five years passed. By 1811, Carl had got tired of his stable boys and Stephanie had changed her mind and opened the bedroom door. Nine months later their first daughter was born. By then the old man had died and Carl and Stephanie were Grand Duke and Grand Duchess of Baden. Excuse me, please."

A perspiring young man in a sporty brown checkered suit had come in, wiped his forehead with a red handkerchief and impatiently drummed his finger on the top of one of the glass show-cases.

It was Paul Arnheim, a clerk at the International Club, the Jockey Club of Baden-Baden.

The two Hamburg ladies took their leave, saying they would be back tomorrow to hear the rest of Stephanie's story.

"I know it's a little late," Paul Arnheim said. "But our president wishes to send a suitable welcoming gift over to the Palais Hamilton for the Prince of Wales. He said you were sure to have the right thing."

Katzau went to the back and returned with a baroque tankard.

"Made in Nuremberg in 1691. Your president will consider it more than appropriate."

He put it in a blue carton and handed it to the clerk.

"There is another matter," Arnheim said. "Our president asked me to pick your brains."

Katzau knew the sort of thing that was coming. It happened all the time. He was known as a living *Almanac de Gotha*. Anybody with a title who wanted to avoid a *faux pas* considered it prudent to consult him when in doubt. No dowager duchess in Baden-Baden, however venerable, knew more about who was related to whom—they were almost all related, one way or another—what their respective ranks were and what was the correct mode of address.

"At the banquet the Club is giving on Friday night to honour the Prince, the President will of course drink a toast to His Royal Highness. Prince Hermann of Saxe-Weimar will also speak." He looked at the rococo clock over the door. "Aha. Four-thirty. I think Prince Hermann is welcoming the Prince at the station at this very moment. Together with the Mayor. Now, in his toast the President wishes to quote Goethe. He would be most grateful to you, Herr Katzau, if you would tell me whether Goethe's patron, the Duke Carl August of Saxe-Weimar, was Prince Hermann's father or grandfather."

"Neither," Katzau replied without hesitation. "Prince Hermann belongs to a different line. That's all he has to know."

"I'll pass this on," Arnheim said. "Many thanks."

He took the blue carton and, as he turned to rush back to the Club, bumped into Louis Katzau's good friend, the thirty-one-year-old Georg, the sixth duke of Leuchtenberg, who, at the same time, in his capacity of being his mother's son—his mother having being the Grand Duchess Marie Nicolaievna, the oldest daughter of Tsar Nicholas I—also carried the title Prince Romanowsky—he was the seventh grandchild of Josephine's son Eugène Beauharnais and Augusta, the daughter of the King of Bavaria's seventh child. Katzau had already read in the Fremdenliste, the list of visitors printed daily in the Badeblatt der Stadt Baden-Baden, that His Imperial Highness was staying at the Englische Hof. The Prince of Wales was only His Royal Highness. (The editor of the *Badeblatt*, incidentally, was Baden-Baden's "music tsar," Richard Pohl, an enthusiastic promoter of the "New Music" by Richard Wagner, Franz Liszt and Hector Berlioz.)

"Louis," Georg, the sixth duke of Leuchtenberg, said in a tone that left it open whether he was serious, "I have an important, highly confidential message for you from the Duchess's *Haushofmeister*." The Duchess could only have been Marie, the Duchess of Hamilton, Stephanie's youngest daughter, now sixty-six. The Prince of Wales was her guest. The *Haushofmeister*, a native of Wimbledon who was head of her domestic staff, was Edmund Jenkins, whom Louis Katzau knew well. "It can't be so important," Katzau said, "that you cannot first sit down, like a normal human being, and tell me how you are."

Georg sat down. "I'm fine, thanks. Not complaining. Glad I don't have to worry about any horse of mine running at Iffezheim. I can relax and enjoy the races."

Now what was it, Katzau tried to remember, that I wanted to tell Georg when I saw him again? Oh yes, a French doctor named Dr. Pierre Simoneau, *très sympathique,* had recently come in, bought a silver tray, and told him he was writing a book about Georg's great grandmother's, the Empress Josephine, specifically about her intimate life. He had unearthed a number of delicate matters usually discussed only in men's baths.

Dr. Simoneau had closely examined the memoirs of Josephine's confidantes and ladies-in-waiting. Did Katzau know Georg well enough to tell him about these discoveries?

"I suppose you have collected quite a library of books about Josephine," he ventured, hoping to set the right tone for the revelations to come. "Have you read them all?"

"Of course," Georg said. "I'm very proud of her. Not everybody has an ancestor like her."

"And like your grandfather Eugène, a truly honourable man, mild-mannered and self-effacing."

"Quite true," Georg agreed. "As a matter of fact, Louis, it was my grandfather who first brought Napoleon and Josephine together. He was fourteen at the time. He demanded that the men of the Committee of Public Safety who had guillotined his father, the Vicomte Beauharnais, return his sword to him. Napoleon had just been appointed General of the Army of the Interior. He witnessed the scene and was so touched by the son's affection for his dead father that he wanted to meet the mother of so loyal a son. When they met, Josephine invited the newly appointed general to her next little reception in her little house in the rue de Chantereine. Josephine was six years older than Napoleon, you know."

"A residence," Katzau added, "known for its many mirrors. Your refined great grandmother treasured her beauty and was generous in her affections."

Georg let that go. "Evidently," he continued, "at first she found the young general's uncouth appearance and clumsy manners quite unappealing. He had not learned at his military school in Brienne how to please women. With the exception of a short affair with his sister-in-law Désirée Clary, he'd had experience only with prostitutes, whom he detested."

"Yes. It was all quite dramatic." Katzau tried to find the right words for what he was about to say. He told his friend about his visit from the French doctor. "Dr. Simoneau set himself the task to analyze the elements that quickly aroused Napoleon's passions to a state of red-hot frenzy."

"My great grandmother had a lovely, smooth, velvety voice," Georg said dreamily.

"Everyone remarked on it."

"And used delicious perfumes and had a bath every morning of her life. Except when she was in prison in *Les Carmes*, waiting to be guillotined. But even there she and two other ladies were given special washing privileges."

"Yes, Dr. Simoneau also knew about that. He said that as a girl she had got into the habit of bathing in the streams on the family's plantation in Martinique."

"Napoleon had a very sensitive nose," Georg went on. "I've read that for that reason he rejected many beautiful women who made themselves available to him."

"And"—Katzau now approached dangerous territory—"Josephine had mastered the invaluable art of charming men, an activity in which she excelled in spite of her bad teeth, and in spite of her nose, which was too long and too pointed. But everyone who met her remarked on how lovely she looked and how gracious and kind she was. You see, the fashions of the *Directoire* made it easy for her to bare her shoulders and display her figure. She possessed genuine, languorous *volupté* that men immediately sensed and found irresistible. I've heard that physical love in all forms made your great grandmother shiver with pleasure. Hence her many infidelities even while she was married to Napoleon. She learned to enjoy love early, in the springtime of life, with her first husband, and many others. The Vicomte did not believe in marital fidelity for either party. He was probably not the father of Hortense, Josephine's second child. As a type, your great grandfather, the Vicomte Alexandre de Beauharnais, has been compared to the seducer Valmont in *Les Liaisons Dangereuses*. She was sixteen when she married him. He was eighteen."

Katzau studied Georg's face. Had he gone too far?

"None of this is really new to me." Georg's voice was subdued. "I am not shocked. Is there more to come?"

"I don't know," Katzau took a deep breath, "how many of the intimate details about their love-making are generally known and, in particular, whether Dr. Simoneau was the first scholar to examine the implications of Napoleon's extraordinary speed. Stendhal reported he had heard the average time was three minutes, followed by immediate deep sleep. The emperor also gobbled down his food in record time, Dr. Simoneau told me, and in an imperial procession he once used his sceptre to prod a cardinal who was walking ahead of him too slowly. Talleyrand, who limped, always had trouble keeping up with him. As I say, speed and impatience characterized Napoleon's behaviour, including his love-making. So naturally, Dr. Simoneau found, Josephine had to learn to live with that and, as well, get used to the idea that his mind was usually on something else. To please him, she occasionally simulated pleasure when she felt none, though most likely she did not need to bother because her responses were a matter of complete indifference to him."

"Which," Georg observed, "did not mean that he did not love her. He most certainly did."

"Of course. But to Napoleon a wife, however loved—and

there's no doubt that Josephine was the great love of his life—was her husband's property."

Louis Katzau hesitated before taking one more risk.

"By the way," he swallowed hard, "Napoleon was known for conspicuously lacking manual dexterity in every field of human activity, including the manipulations women often need in the early stages of the act. To enable Josephine to shiver genuinely, without having experienced any lubricating preliminaries, she encouraged him to engage first in unorthodox practices such as to kiss her *forêt noir,* a practice to which Napoleon referred several times in love letters written during the Italian campaigns. These letters Dr. Simoneau examined carefully. Quite a different Black Forest from the one we've got here in Baden-Baden, wouldn't you say?"

The Prince of Leuchtenberg shared Katzau's mild amusement.

"Also," Katzau continued, "Dr. Simoneau found some evidence that occasionally she satisfied him while he was fully dressed, a sword at his side, standing up or sitting down. In those instances, presumably, he rarely went to sleep immediately afterwards. Apparently, having learned to play the harp as a young girl in Martinique, her manual touch, in contrast to his, was remarkably sensitive. It should be added that she was available to him any time. Usually, she wore no *culottes.* In her best days she owned five hundred dresses and three *culottes.* These she put on when she had to go on horseback. If she was thrown off, considerate as always, she did not want to be the cause of embarrassment."

Josephine's great-grandson barely concealed a smile.

"I am delighted," Katzau concluded, "you braved all this with the gallantry for which your house is rightly famous."

"Thank you, Louis. I look forward to adding Dr. Simoneau's book to my library when it appears. Now, may I tell you why *Haushofmeister* Jenkins has given me a message for you?"

"Please go ahead."

"The Duchess came back from Marienhalden yesterday, with her daughter."

The Duchess was Marie, the Duchess of Hamilton, Stephanie's youngest daughter and, therefore, by adoption Josephine's granddaughter. Marienhalden was her estate on Lake Constance. Her daughter was also called Marie, although she was usually called Mary, and was the wife of the Hungarian Count Tassilo Festetics of Tolna. Mary's first husband was Prince Albert I of Monaco.

"The Duchess," Georg continued, "only gave herself one day to prepare for the arrival of Edward, Prince of Wales."

"I understand. By the way, why is he staying with her?" Katzau stroked his whiskers in deep thought. "They're not related. For the moment I can't think of a single instance, during the last thousand years, when a Hanoverian or Saxon-Gotharian married a Badenser. Can you?"

Georg laughed. "If you can't, Louis, nobody can. The answer is quite simple. He has a horse running at Iffezheim. So has his friend William."

William was the Duchess's older son, the twelfth Duke of Hamilton.

Georg turned serious. "When the Duchess came home yesterday she was shocked to discover that in her absence someone had broken into her living quarters, opened the safe and stolen the jewels she treasured most of the many she possesses—two ruby earrings of Josephine's that she had inherited from her mother. The ones she wore at her coronation in Notre Dame. The thief had left the rest of the jewellery alone."

"I see." It took a moment for Katzau to digest the news. "I remember them well. She wore them in that marvellous painting of David's in the Louvre. It's of that magical, unforgettable, magnificently theatrical, fairy-tale moment when Josephine received the crown from her husband, the Emperor. She was kneeling. She already wore a tiara—he placed the crown on top of it. His own crown he had just gently but firmly taken out of the Pope's hands and put on his head. The symbolism could not have been clearer. Young Stephanie was watching from the balcony."

He paused, savouring the glorious scene in his mind.

"And why," he resumed irritably in the sordid here-and-now, "did the *Haushofmeister* ask you to convey this absurd piece of news to me?"

"Because he did not want to go to the police. He thought you're a shrewd man who might have some idea what to do next. The Duchess is extremely upset and worried. This could not have happened at a worse time, with the Prince coming to-day for the races, and with all the festivities she has to attend."

Katzau frowned.

"I really have no time for this. I wish these people would leave me alone. I'm not a detective."

Georg von Leuchtenberg smiled, knowing full well, as did Katzau himself, that the *Haushofmeister* could not have chosen a better man to solve the Duchess's problem.

Chapter 2

Edward, Prince of Wales, arrived in Baden-Baden on Wednesday, August 22, 1883, at four-thirty in the afternoon, in the company of Lord and Lady Charles Beresford, the Duchess of Manchester, Christopher Sykes and Henry Chaplin, as well as his personal staff of seven persons headed by his adjutant Tyrwith Wilson. One of the people he looked forward to seeing in Baden-Baden was his old friend Louis Katzau.

The Prince and part of his retinue stayed in the Palais Hamilton, on the Leopoldsplatz at Sophienstrasse 1, guests of the Duchess of Hamilton and her son William. The Prince's other companions were invited by friends to stay in their villas in Baden-Baden or stayed in hotels.

Robert Koch came alone, an hour later than the Prince of Wales. He took a small room in the Pension Luisenhöhe, Werderstrasse 12, run by Fräulein Gertrud Fröhlich, an pleasant elderly amateur pianist who had been the governess of Clara Schumann's seven children when the composer's widow, herself a famous pianist, had a chalet in nearby Lichtental. Apart from a letter of introduction to Louis Katzau from Katzau's supplier, Friedrich Breul, Junior, Frankfurt am Main, Zeil 61, he carried with him an assortment of pieces designed by himself—two emerald broaches, one pearl necklace, three diamond rings, one onyx bracelet and two pairs of sapphire pendants, each in a green leather case. He asked Fräulein Fröhlich to lock them up in a safe in a back room. He only kept one of the emerald broaches and put it in his pocket.

Robert was determined to improve his fortunes dramatically and decisively. A first-class jeweller's objective had to be any location where there was a productive relationship between love and money. Robert's store on the Zeil in Frankfurt, in close proximity to Friedrich Breul's, was not doing at all well. His wife's Uncle Gustav, without whose help he could not have opened it four years ago, was going to ask for his money back any day.

Robert was thirty-one, twelve years younger than Katzau. He had dark hair, a high forehead, a round face, bright, expressive brown eyes and a perfectly shaped nose. His dashingly pointed mustache was elegantly trimmed. A natural aristocrat, he had the suave bearing of a French diplomat. He left behind a wife, Flora, whose beauty had been compared to that of a Rubens Venus, and a new baby.

When Robert called on Katzau on Thursday morning at ten, a day after his arrival, Katzau had the feeling, on the evidence of only a few minutes' conversation and a short but intense inspection of the emerald broach Robert had shown him, that Robert might well have the potential of one day becoming one of Europe's great jewellers, even though, compared to him, he was as yet grotesquely inexperienced in the ways of the world. But it struck him as entirely possible that Robert had the requisite style, social insight, ambition, good looks and, above all, the absolutely essential ability to distinguish, not only in professional matters, what was genuine from what was fake, at a time when the world of taste took delight in anything that was unreal, a time when the distinction between the authentic and the inauthentic was becoming increasingly blurred.

For Katzau, involving Robert in The Case of the Missing Rubies was an excellent way to test his visitor's calibre. For some years he had been looking forward to combining forces, during the summer season, with a jeweller who, like himself, possessed pride, dignity and imagination, a man who, while showing proper deference to people of power and wealth, or pretended power and pretended wealth, did so without raising any doubt in his own mind that he was, in all matters that really counted, that is, all matters touching the life of the mind, the equal of anybody. If Robert passed the test, he might be the man.

In the Duchess's salon he would meet large numbers of titled and untitled guests whom he might quickly win as future customers in his stores in Frankfurt and Baden-Baden. He would be no threat to Katzau, who did not deal in precious jewels. On the contrary, Robert might become his partner. Katzau had good relations with his present neighbour, the jeweller Theodor Klammerer, the bookish owner of Boutique Number Three, a nice man and an amateur philosopher. "But," Katzau had told a friend only last week, "as a jeweller, Theo is not really serious. Imagine, he sells trinkets with semi-precious stones, and even watches. Soon he will descend to my level!" Since there was no water supply in the boutiques, Katzau and Klammerer could not help encountering each other whenever they used the facilities of the Conversationshaus, which they always seemed to do at around the same time. Moreover, they often shared the buckets of water they carried over.

Katzau told Robert he intended to enlist him to help him solve the mystery of the stolen earrings. Naturally, Robert was delighted. The beginning of his trip could not have been more promising. After all, it was not Katzau but the Duchess of Hamilton, who held the key to Robert's future in her hand. A recommendation from Katzau was good, but was obviously not the same as a recommendation from Marie, the adopted granddaughter of Napoleon, the widow of the eleventh Duke of Hamilton, the daughter of the Grand Duke Carl of Baden, the second cousin of Friedrich I—the current Grand Duke, married to Luise, the daughter of Kaiser Wilhelm I of Germany (who, of course, was also King of Prussia) and Kaiserin Augusta, the granddaughter of Goethe's Duke Karl August von Sachsen-Weimar—the niece of Grand Duchess Wilhelmine of Hessen and King Gustav Wasa of Sweden, and, most impressive of all, the niece of the late Tsar Alexander I.

"How do I start?" he asked.

"You talk to the *Haushofmeister*, an Englishman called Edmund Jenkins who knows all there is to know about the House of Hamilton. Then, Herr Koch, let your instincts be your guide. Go everywhere and keep your eyes and ears open. Keep in touch with me. Of course you have to move fast."

"What's the Duchess like?"

"An amiable old lady, but she does not quite have her mother Stephanie's panache. About sixty-six. Quite Catholic. Patroness of the monastery in Lichtental. Active art collector. Very proper and conservative. Has inherited her mother's obsession with Napoleon. The Bonapartes are at the top of her pyramid. When Napoleon's nephew, Louis Napoleon, the Emperor Napoleon III, married Eugénie, Countess Montijo, Stephanie was appalled. Clearly a *mésalliance*, she thought. Her daughter, Marie, would have said the same. A Bonaparte emperor simply does not marry an impoverished Spanish countess whose vulgar mother, as everybody knew, had put her up for sale to the highest bidder. One wonders what our duchess would say if she ever finds out that Louis Napoleon, while in exile in England, carried on a shameless affair with the blond daughter of his uncle Napoleon's jailer in St. Helena, Sir Hudson Low."

"I won't tell her," Robert promised.

"Good."

"What about her son William, the twelfth duke?" Robert asked, "the Prince of Wales's friend?"

"She is usually displeased with him. She likes Charles, the younger son, better. She thinks William takes after his father, with whom she had a notoriously difficult marriage. She lost the poor man, who was rich as Croesus, twenty years ago, when he suffered a fatal accident late at night in the Maison Dorée in Paris, perhaps as a result of a stroke, more likely because he fell downstairs after a drunken dinner party. The Duchess and the two sons rushed to Paris. He was still alive when they came. He died soon after. The Emperor Napoleon III generously made a warship available and had the body taken to Scotland. The two sons accompanied the casket to the ancestral castle of Brodick, on the island of Arran, in the Firth of Clyde near Glasgow, where the eleventh duke joined at least some of the ten previous dukes.

None of this, I'm afraid, is very relevant to The Case of the Missing Rubies."

"True," Robert said. "I will do what you suggest. I will go and see the *Haushofmeister*."

"You will find him most helpful." Katzau hesitated before going on. "He is really a remarkably well informed and resourceful *Schammes*."

Robert smiled.

Each man had sensed from the beginning that the other was Jewish. But each took pride in having left the ghetto behind while still being a solid member of their respective Jewish communities. Each only used familiar Hebrew or Yiddish words like *Schammes*, which meant the gentile servant at the synagogue, when there was a reason. They saw no need to advertise their affiliation to a world that only reluctantly, and by no means universally, welcomed the emancipation of Jews. Katzau's grandfather, a rabbi in Budapest, had already been enlightened enough to be a close friend of the eighteenth-century Austrian jurist Joseph von Sonnenfels, a converted Jew who opposed the death penalty and edited the magazine *The Man without Prejudice*. More recently, Koch's father, a country doctor near Jena, had given up Jewish rituals.

On this occasion, Katzau used the word *Schammes* without any special emphasis to signal to Robert that there was no need to waste time on matters that were obvious. Robert understood the signal perfectly.

"Herr Katzau," Robert weighed each word carefully, "leaving aside the immediate and very urgent matter of the missing rubies, do you think it would help my chances with the Duchess if I made it known in Baden-Baden that my father was most probably a genuine, natural son of Napoleon? That, therefore, the Duchess and I are perhaps, in a way, first cousins?"

Katzau raised his eyebrows.

"Herr Koch, what precisely are you saying?"

"I am precisely saying that it was Napoleon's custom to celebrate his military victories by spending the night in the arms of the most beautiful woman in the neighbourhood. The lady chosen for the purpose during the night of October 14, 1806, the night after he destroyed the Prussian army at the Battle of Jena, was Red Esther, also known as Long Esther, my grandmother. Apparently her husband Shmuel did not mind. Or was not consulted."

"Let me correct you, Herr Koch," Katzau observed with *gravitas*. "You are wildly exaggerating. They most certainly did not spend the night together. Three minutes maximum. In any case, what is the evidence?"

"In 1823, my father went to Leipzig to study medicine. Where would a poor country Jew, the son of a peddler, get the money to study medicine in Leipzig if not from the Bonaparte family in Paris, which scrupulously discharged its obligations in this and many other similar cases? Napoleon won many battles."

"I could think of a number of answers to your question."

"Please do not trouble yourself, Herr Katzau," Robert said, with seemingly genuine fervour. "We Kochs will not be talked out of our belief. No logical argument can shake us. Napoleon opened the ghettos in all the countries he conquered. He brought the ideals of the French Revolution with him. He put an end to the Middle Ages. He was our liberator, the father of our liberties."

"Not only of your liberties," Katzau observed dryly. "I am glad you approve of your grandmother's self-sacrifice. That demonstrates a healthy sense of values."

"Thank you."

"I have always wondered," Louis Katzau said, stroking his whiskers as he often did when he was trying to provoke, "what is the point of being emperor and winning all those battles if you cannot assert your power and disregard lesser people's laws and conventions? After all, Napoleon was not bound by Count Almaviva's foolish, unnecessary and premature surrender of his prerogatives."

Robert was, of course, familiar with *The Marriage of Figaro*, which revolved around the attempt by Count Almaviva to exercise his ancient feudal right to spend the first night of Figaro's marriage with Figaro's bride, Susanna.

"Napoleon was not Red Esther's feudal lord," Robert retorted, "but, as conqueror of Germany, her liberator. She became my grandmother out of gratitude! You envy us German Jews because Napoleon did not liberate you."

•   •   •

In 1843, twenty-five years after the death of the Grand Duke Carl at the age of thirty-two, Stephanie gave up her right to reside in a suite in the Neue Schloss in exchange for the sole ownership of her husband's family's monumental town house, with its imposing facade of four classical columns. It had been built by Friedrich Weinbrenner, the architect who had also designed the Conversationshaus. She was delighted to be able to move from the top of the hill overlooking the *Altstadt,* the old town, where she had to share premises with her in-laws, to the centre of town where she would be on her own. When she died in 1860 and her daughter Marie inherited it, it became the Palais Hamilton.

It took Robert no more than ten minutes to walk to it from Katzau's boutique, across the narrow bridge over the modest Oos River and the Lichtentaler Allee, Baden-Baden's famous street of fashion.

Haushofmeister Edmund Jenkins, a tall, bearded man in his early sixties, wearing gold-rimmed spectacles, spoke German with a slight cockney accent. He had command over a staff of thirty-one, made up, above all, of the Scot MacAustin, her *Leibkutscher* (personal coachman), a local celebrity in charge of the best stable in Baden-Baden, and three ladies-in-waiting, two *Hofökonomieräte* (financial managers), three chambermaids, one *Beschliesserin* (responsible primarily for locking things up), one *Silberdiener* (in charge of the silver), two cooks, three wardrobe mistresses, one hairdresser and one *Stalloffiziant* (stable manager). The rest were lackeys who performed diverse duties. Naturally, they all had to work overtime while the Prince of Wales and his retinue were their employer's guest.

At four in the afternoon of Thursday, August 23, the *Haushofmeister* received Robert in his office on the second floor.

"I cannot tell you how grateful I am to Herr Katzau for taking an interest in this matter," he said, referring, of course, to Josephine's rubies. Robert was surprised at how relaxed Jenkins was, under the circumstances. "And I am obliged to you, too, Herr Koch, for acting as his...?"

"Confidential intermediary," Robert replied. He did not reveal that he had met Louis Katzau for the first time only this morning.

"Very good. So I will speak to you as openly as I have always spoken to him. As you know, Herr Katzau is a man of unusual discretion, entirely reliable, with very wide connections. I value his judgement enormously. Naturally, while His Royal Highness is under our roof, I myself cannot devote the necessary time to the matter. You see, it is of unusual difficulty because it is so bizarre."

"Bizarre?"

"Yes, Herr Koch. Bizarre. The earrings themselves are far less valuable than the tiaras and diamond necklaces and many other pieces the thief left untouched. Their value is primarily a function of their origin—that they were Josephine's. I assume therefore that the motive for stealing them was personal and political. I think it would be a waste of time to spend a great of energy looking for them, say, in pawnshops. At this stage, in any case. The thing for us to do is to discover the motive. The rest will follow."

"I assume no member of your staff would have such a motive."

"My job is to trust none of them. I have no doubt that with the right combination of money and flattery any of them can be bought. Of course, in the little time I have had at my disposal so far I have cross-examined only those responsible for access and security. They say all the right things. I vouch for none of them. Even if I did, the fact remains—the earrings have disappeared. Her Highness is in a state of acute agitation. *Res ipsa loquitur.* The thing speaks for itself."

"No doubt, since, as you say, the thief obviously was not attracted by the earrings' market value," Robert mused, "Her Highness would be just as upset if I discovered that they were fakes."

In his middle twenties, before turning to designing and selling jewellery set in precious stones and pearls, Robert had learned a painful lesson. After spending two years in a lowly position at the *Vereinsbank* learning, among other things, how to multiply three-digit figures in his head, he invested his wife's dowry in an enterprise selling imitation pieces just before they became fashionable. He lost every pfennig of the dowry. So, naturally, this was the first question that came to his mind. But it surprised the *Haushofmeister*.

"Surely, Herr Koch, you don't mean the earrings she wore at her coronation?"

"No, of course not. But that was nearly eighty years ago. Anything could have happened in the eighty years between then and now. Especially recently! You see, Herr Jenkins, nowadays nothing is easier than to manufacture copies that only an expert can distinguish from the original. Unreal things are all the rage. A quick study of a reproduction of the coronation picture in the Louvre would enable me to create an excellent likeness of Josephine's earrings in two hours."

"But why should you?" The *Haushofmeister* shook his head. "Or why should anybody do so and place the copies in the Duchess's jewellery case while keeping, or selling, the originals? Or are you indirectly suggesting, Herr Koch, that I should follow up your trend of thought and ask you to produce such a copy and hand it to Her Highness pretending that we had found the original?"

"Oh no, nothing was further from my thoughts." Robert made a mental note of the workings of Herr Jenkins's mind. "Let me try something else. Has anybody ever questioned Her Highness's right to possess the earrings in the first place?"

"That is certainly an intriguing line of reasoning, Herr Koch. Her Highness has always said she inherited them from her mother. But I happen to know there was nothing about them in the Grand Duchess's will. And Her Highness has never been specific about the time and manner she received them. Perhaps she has forgotten. So it is entirely possible that among the—by now hundreds—of Bonaparte and Beauharnais descendants there are some who may claim to have a prior right to them. Though I have never heard of anybody pressing such a claim."

"Another question occurs to me." Robert's mind was racing. "Would the earrings ever have been part of the French crown jewels?"

"Another excellent question, Herr Koch. I happen to know a good deal about the matter. The problem is which crown jewels. The Bourbon crown jewels? The Bonaparte crown jewels? By 1803, a year *before* the coronation in Notre Dame, at which Josephine wore them, Napoleon had already recovered all he could of the Bourbon crown jewels. From then on they were Bonaparte crown jewels. Josephine could wear them whenever she chose. Soon new ones were added. By 1807 she had acquired a laurel-wreath crown, a new tiara, various combs and bracelets, and, in particular, one necklace remarkable for the immense size of the jewels. After the divorce in 1809 and Napoleon's marriage to Marie-Louise, Josephine kept these jewels and in 1811 even acquired an immense ruby and diamond necklace. One wonders how it was paid for. By the way, the year before, in 1810, the year he married Marie-Louise, Napoleon bought a magnificent set of rubies and diamonds for his new wife. These I know became part of the French crown jewels after the restoration of the Bourbon monarchy in 1815. I have my own theory about what happened to the bulk of Josephine's jewellery. This, I think, may turn out to be extremely relevant to our case."

"A theory, Herr Jenkins?"

"Yes, a theory. It has to do with Tsar Alexander I. He had called Europe to arms after Napoleon had burned Moscow in 1812. But after that, as you know, in an immense patriotic effort, greatly assisted by the horrors of the Russian winter, he chased Napoleon out of Russia with the starving remnants of his army. A grand alliance, under his leadership, finally crushed Napoleon in Leipzig in October 1813. Napoleon abdicated and was sent to Elba. The Tsar entered Paris in triumph, in March 1814. He took the position that he had never made war on the French people, only on Napoleon. Like his main allies, the King of Prussia and the Kaiser of Austria, he was resolved to protect Josephine, even though she had never faltered in her loyalty to Napoleon and was appalled that her successor, the Kaiser of Austria's daughter Marie-Louise, did not follow him to Elba. The Tsar was a chivalrous romantic, very good looking, with mystical inclinations, married to Grand Duke Carl's sister Luise-Elizabeth, although they were estranged. He expressed the wish to call on Josephine at Malmaison. His aide, Prince Leopold of Sachsen-Coburg wrote a letter to Hortense, Josephine's daughter, asking her to arrange a meeting. I am sorry, Herr Koch, I am taking such a long time to set the scene."

"I think, Herr Jenkins, I know what is coming."

"You do?"

"The Tsar fell in love with Josephine."

The *Haushofmeister* was only mildly amused.

"Not quite, Herr Koch. But he was charmed, no doubt about it, very much so. She charmed everybody. Of course, it was widely known that she was hopelessly extravagant and that after her divorce she had run into heavy debt. The outcome of her conversation with the Tsar is public knowledge. It was the guarantee of a fixed income for the rest of her life, some said as high as a million francs a year."

Only this morning Robert had heard a great deal about Josephine's willingness to oblige men who liked her. But he refrained from expressing any theories of his own as to what precisely she may have given the Tsar in return.

"How extraordinarily generous," he said.

"Indeed, Herr Koch. It was tragic that she caught a chill very soon after this visit and died of the complications. Grand Duke Carl and his wife, Stephanie, were at the funeral. In short, Josephine was not given the time to enjoy the money. She was only fifty-one. It is my view that the *quid pro quo* for the guarantee of an annual stipend was her jewellery, I mean her share of the Bonaparte crown jewels, including the ruby earrings she wore at her coronation. How they came into the possession of Her Highness the Grand Duchess Stephanie is anybody's guess. But the Russians may very well still consider them their property."

"I understand there is no shortage of Russians in Baden-Baden," Robert observed dryly.

"Indeed, not since they occupied Baden after the Battle of Leipzig when, on his way to Paris, Tsar Alexander took the salute of the Grand Duke's troops in nearby Karlsruhe, has there been a shortage of Russians in Baden-Baden. It was his wife's first return home after twenty years. Of course, Herr Katzau is thoroughly familiar with all these facts."

"But not with your theory, Herr Jenkins." Robert rose and bowed to the *Haushofmeister*. "I have no doubt he will be most interested in it, and immensely grateful to you, when I relate it to him."

Chapter 3

A courier from the Palais Hamilton delivered a message to Louis Katzau on Thursday afternoon while the *Haushofmeister* was talking to Robert. It stated that it was His Royal Highness the Prince of Wales's intention to call on Herr Katzau tomorrow morning at ten-thirty. Was that convenient? Katzau scribbled a reply declaring he would be deeply honoured.

He had better think of a good Jewish joke to tell the prince. It was deeply flattering to him that he was the only Jew other than the Rothschilds who was granted the privilege of doing so. So the Prince had told him the last time he was here.

That was not the only thing he had to prepare. The Prince might have some constructive ideas on the search for Josephine's lost rubies. This was the kind of thing that would undoubtedly amuse him. It was safe to assume that at the Palais Hamilton it was considered too painfully embarrassing to be the subject of light conversation.

The *Haushofmeister*'s theory about the Russians, which Robert had already relayed to Katzau, seemed plausible enough. The Prince's perspective would certainly be a little different. His first idea might very well be that as Napoleon Bonaparte—"Boney"—had been England's arch-enemy, nothing would please a patriotic Englishman more than to play games with a sacred French relic. What was more French than Josephine's earrings? Although he, Edward, was profoundly, unshakably pro-French, he was bound to see this in the perspective of the ancient

English-French antagonism that he was working so hard to counteract. It was not least thanks to him, Katzau knew, that ex-Empress Eugénie, Napoleon III's widow, had found refuge from the Third Republic in Chislehurst, Kent.

Everyone was aware of the low opinion Queen Victoria, the Prince's awesome mother, held of him, caused in part by the knowledge that there was nothing she could legally do to prevent him from one day succeeding her. The next best thing was to neutralize him, to prevent him from playing a useful role in Her Majesty's government. By now he was forty-three. He spent a good deal of time in Paris, in reputable and disreputable company. He had liked Napoleon III, about whom his mother had, to put it mildly, serious reservations while he was in power; she was kind and compassionate towards the Emperor, however, following his release from captivity in Kassel, when he lived out his days in exile in England. One of the Prince's closest friends in Paris was the vivacious and beautiful Duchess Anna de Mouchy, the granddaughter of Caroline, Napoleon's sister and Queen of Naples, and of her husband Marshall Joachim Murat, an innkeeper's son. The Prince occasionally also frequented the salons of the pre-revolutionary aristocracy, but was more often a guest in the sumptuous houses of members of the fallen imperial regime, usually prominent in banking and commerce. He had nothing to do with representatives of the Third Republic.

Now, Katzau wondered, what in specific terms would be the Prince's theory? Maybe that some drunken Oxford undergraduate might consider Josephine's earrings legitimate trophies, like, say, Napoleon's hat, or some regimental colours seized at Waterloo, and that the earrings' rightful place was near Antonio Canova's gigantic marble statue of the heroic, classical, nude Napoleon in the Duke of Wellington's Apsley House on Hyde Park Corner in London.

Katzau had another thought. After all, Josephine was, by adoption, the Duchess of Hamilton's grandmother. Edward, too, had a grandmother: Queen Victoria's mother, the Duchess of Kent, Mary Louisa Victoria, the daughter of Franz I, Duke of Sachsen-Coburg-Saalfeld, the sister of King Leopold I of

Belgium. The Duke of Kent had been her second husband. The first one was Emich Charles, the Second Prince of Leiningen, a rather useless elderly gentleman whose domains on the Mosel had been seized by the French in the revolutionary wars and who had been given the impoverished principality, that is, the village of Amorbach and the lands around it in Lower Franconia, in compensation. He died in 1814, when his wife was twenty-eight, leaving her in uncomfortably straitened circumstances. They had two children. The younger one, Queen Victoria's half-sister, became the Duchess Feodora of Hohenlohe-Langenburg and lived right here in Baden-Baden, conducting a lively salon frequented by artists, musicians and writers. Victoria was fond of her and had visited her several times. Once, when she was here, together with the Prince of Wales, Prime Minister Benjamin Disraeli suddenly turned up, to discuss with her his plan to buy up the shares of the Suez Canal. They did so while Edward was playing tennis.

Duchess Feodora died in 1872, at the age of sixty-five. Katzau had known her well.

He slept badly that Thursday night. As he tossed and turned, a scene came to his mind. He remembered the Queen's last visit to Baden-Baden., Travelling under the name of Countess Balmoral, she had come at Easter 1880—three and a half years ago—to celebrate the twenty-third birthday of her youngest daughter, Beatrice. Victoria paid her respects at her half-sister's grave. And she stayed at her late half-sister's house, Kapuzinerstrasse 14, not far from the station, a Swiss chalet. In the afternoon the *Kurorchester* serenaded her. In the evening, there was a birthday dinner. Among those present was her late half-sister's daughter, Adelaide, who, when she was nineteen, had been on Emperor Napoleon III's list of possible empresses. (Eventually, he chose Eugénie.) The idea had occurred to him that it might not be a bad idea at all, and perhaps even quite amusing, to be married to the half-niece of Queen Victoria. And Adelaide, too, found the idea rather intriguing. But her parents were appalled by the prospect of having a vulgar opportunist and congenital ladies' man as a son-in-law, even if he was the

Emperor of France. Therefore, Adelaide obediently wrote a letter to him, no doubt dictated by her father, saying she had decided she did not feel worthy of the exalted position the Emperor had so graciously offered her.

Also present at the birthday dinner was Adelaide's brother, Prince Hermann von Hohenlohe-Langenburg, and, needless to say, the Duchess of Hamilton, accompanied by her daughter, Mary, who at the time was still married to Albert I of Monaco.

Katzau, as he lay in his bed trying to sleep, reconstructed the scene. He had a lively imagination. The Duchess, of course, wore Josephine's earrings. She said *en passant* they had been her grandmother Josephine's. The birthday child developed a frantic, overwhelming, absolutely irrational desire to be given them as a birthday present. She said so to her mother, who doted on her. After the dinner was over, some courtier of other, no doubt acting for Queen Victoria, asked the Duchess to sell them to her.

The Duchess indignantly refused. The head of the most powerful empire the world had ever known, at the height of her power, was not used to refusals.

To take revenge, three years later...?

The next day, as he drank his morning coffee, Katzau thought about the scenario that had kept him awake all night. In case somebody found this theory a little-far-fetched, he developed another one. On May 1st, 1880, a few days after the Queen's and Princess Beatrice's empty-handed departure, Victoria's half-nephew Prince Hermann zu Hohenlohe-Langenburg sold his late mother's house to the Queen's agents, as Katzau happened to know, for 130,000 marks. Evidently, the thought that Prince Hermann might one day sell her half-sister's house to somebody undesirable was intolerable to Queen Victoria. Suppose her agents had at the same time once again approached the Duchess of Hamilton and asked for Josephine's rubies—and been refused? Would they not naturally been given instructions, sooner or later, to take matters into their hands?

•   •   •

Edward, swinging his gold-tipped cane, his greying beard freshly trimmed, plump, dressed for the races and exuding a pleasant aroma of eau de cologne, arrived at the boutique punctually at ten-thirty on Friday morning. His adjutant, Tyrwith Wilson, was with him. They had crossed the bridge over the Oos River and traversed the Lichtentaler Allee. As they entered, the Prince gave a friendly nod to the dozen people who had recognized him and followed him. After Louis Katzau welcomed him, the Prince quickly dispatched his adjutant across the Promenade to the café in the Conversationshaus to have a cognac, or two, and ordered him back in precisely forty-five minutes. Katzau guided his eminent guest to the little guest room at the back of the boutique.

"I assume Your Highness was unable to attend the races yesterday?" Katzau opened the conversation. They spoke German. Katzau's English was indistinguishable from Hungarian. The Prince's German, in contrast, was flawless, to be expected from a man whose blood was one hundred percent German. "I understand," Katzau said, "some of the races were very exciting."

"I know, Herr Katzau. I'm going later today. But my horse The Scot is not running until the steeplechase next week."

The Prince took out a copy of the racing program, with the list of the one hundred and eighty-nine horses that had been entered for the season. He recognized many of the names.

"I see the Duke of Hamilton's City Arab is the favourite," he said while Katzau's mind was on other things. "I suppose that's no surprise. He told me he was bringing six horses over from Newmarket. Not bad. Ah, and here are a few horses from Chantilly and Bar-Le-Duc. Probably the first time since the war. Good thing the wounds are healing. Sport should always lead the way. I think I'll put a few marks on La Meuse."

"I understand," Katzau's tone was jovial but respectful, "that tonight they're going to give Your Highness a dinner at the International Club. They've put up a festive tent, and even installed some electric illumination, in Your Highness's honour. For the first time."

"That's very good of them."

The Prince was polite rather than enthusiastic. The Club on the Lichtentaler Allee 28 was a beautiful residential three-story building that had been inhabited earlier in the century by Queen Friederike of Sweden and for some years owned, if not inhabited, by Frankfurt's Amschel Mayer Rothschild, the founding father of the bank.

"There will be a hundred guests," Katzau said, "and a gypsy band will play 'God save the Queen'."

"Splendid."

Katzau picked up a golden cigar box from a side table. He offered a cigar to the Prince and took one himself.

"Two years ago," Edward said while Katzau lit his cigar, "my sister, the Crown Princess of Germany, gave me a dinner in Berlin. I counted the guests. There were fifty-five—all of them related to me. This dinner probably won't be very different."

They both laughed.

"Your Highness should be proud of his *Mischpoche*!" Katzau observed.

"My what?"

"*Mischpoche* is the Jewish word for family."

"I must remember that!" The Prince was delighted. "I think I will use it in future. *Mischpoche*. If the right occasion comes along."

"For example," Katzau suggested, "when Your Highness has dinner with one of the Rothschilds. They might very well enjoy a joke about their *Mischpoche*."

"Do you have a suitable joke on hand?"

Katzau inhaled his cigar.

"The Rothschild matriarch in the Frankfurt ghetto was nicknamed Gutele. One day there were rumours of an impending war. A neighbour was worried about her son, who had just reached military age. She asked Gutele whether she thought there was going to be a war. 'War?' Gutele said. 'What nonsense! My boys won't let them!'"

"Perfect!" The Prince laughed boisterously. "Very good,

very good, indeed. I wish I had a similar joke about the Sachsen-Coburgs. In my experience Jews are proud of their parents' and grandparents' poverty, and can't hear enough of it. But the Sachsen-Coburgs? They don't make jokes about anything. They certainly don't make jokes about Napoleon seizing their territory and reducing them to starvation and beggary. For years, I've discovered, there was hardly a cow left in their little country. And there wasn't enough food to feed their geese. And within one generation this ancient impoverished family—my father's family!—had gained a solid foothold on half the thrones of Europe. Fifty-five of them were sitting at that dinner table in Berlin. One has to take off one's hat to my great uncle Leopold who, at fifteen, was thrown on his own resources and in a few short years time managed to marry the heiress of England. How did that happen, you might ask. Well, I'll tell you how it happened. He was in the suite of Tsar Alexander in June 1814, when the Allies were in London to celebrate their victory over Napoleon. Leopold was eighteen years old and exceptionally handsome and ambitious. He caught the attention of Charlotte, who was to inherit the British Crown. Unfortunately, she died before he could become a prince consort. But he did not give up. Soon after Charlotte's death, he urged his sister to accept an offer of marriage from the Duke of Kent. This sister was to become my grandmother. She had lost her first husband, leaving her with two small children, very poor. A very plucky lady, indeed. It can't have been much fun for her to marry my grumpy grandfather who was twenty-three years older than she was and had to be forced into the marriage. It can't have been much of a consolation to her that he was the brother of George IV, who had no descendants and that any child produced by that marriage would inherit the Crown of England. No wonder she gave my mother, and, for that matter, Lord Melbourne, such a hard time. But did they make jokes about their troubles? Not on your life!"

Katzau looked at the cuckoo clock over the door. In a few minutes the adjutant would come and take the Prince away.

There was still time to tell him about the missing earrings. He did so.

The Prince lapsed into a reverie.

"Ah, Josephine—every Frenchmen's heart beats faster when he hears the name. I must tell you something, Herr Katzau. It has nothing directly to do with Josephine, but it gives you an idea of what I feel about Napoleon. When I was fourteen, in 1855, I was in Paris with my mother and father when the Emperor took us to view his uncle's coffin. It was covered with a violet velvet pall covered with hundreds of golden bees, the Bonapartes' emblem, and had been placed in temporary quarters in the *Invalides,* before the crypt was completed. I will never forget it. At the foot of the coffin there were a number of sacred relics—the hat Napoleon had worn at Eylau, the sword he had used at Austerlitz and the plaque of the *Légion d'Honneur.* A number of veterans of the First Empire, holding flaming torches, stood guard. What a moment! Even my mother was so deeply moved that she put her hand on my shoulder and said 'Bertie, kneel down before the tomb of the Great Napoleon.' Dutifully, I knelt down."

The Prince of Wales paused.

"Another thing I remember from the same trip," he went on. "Later that day, when the Emperor and Empress drove us around Paris in the imperial carriage, the crowd shouted '*Vive la Reine d'Angleterre! Vive l'Empereur! Vive le Prince Albert!*" It has a nice ring to it, doesn't it? *Vive le Prince Albert!'* That was nearly thirty years ago."

Katzau wondered how he could gently nudge the Prince to concentrate on the urgent problem at hand.

"I assume Your Highness has never visited Josephine's grave in Malmaison?"

"No, I'm afraid not. Well, now. So you say those earrings have been pinched. How extraordinary. Does everybody know about it?"

"No, Your Highness. The matter is being investigated with the utmost discretion. They"—Katzau nodded in the direction of the Palais Hamilton—"they know me and think I might be able to come up with some ideas. They would be very angry with me if they knew I had told Your Highness."

"Don't worry," the Prince laughed. "I won't snitch on you."

"The *Haushofmeister* and I believe the motive must be political because none of the more valuable jewellery was touched."

"I see." At last, the Prince decided to concentrate. "I see it quite clearly. It's perfectly obvious to me who did it. Is it not true that my hostess, the Dowager Duchess of Hamilton, visited her relative, the Ex-Emperor Napoleon III, after his defeat, sick and broken, in his captivity in Kassel?"

"Yes, Your Highness."

"Today's Prussians have no sense of chivalry. Maybe they behaved better when they were our allies in the days of Frederick the Great. I would certainly hope so. Bismarck's Prussians will never forgive the Duchess for this gesture of humanity towards their prisoner when he was a humiliated man, clearly close to death, a man who knew in his heart of hearts that he himself was the primary cause of his own disaster. Even if—and this is now quite clear—Bismarck deliberately provoked the war, for his own reasons. I can easily imagine some cocky subaltern in Berlin bribing the *Haushofmeister* or any of the Duchess's servants to punish her for being nice to a Frenchman. I don't often quote Republicans but I think Gambetta was quite right when he proclaimed after 1871 *Le Prussianisme—voilà l'ennemi!*"

"I never thought of that, Your Highness," Katzau said. "That's a most plausible theory." Edmund Jenkins thought it was the Russians. Edward thought it was the Prussians. Why not? As to the idea of bribing the *Haushofmeister*, Katzau thought, on the basis of what Robert had told him, that was by no means implausible. A man who made a point of not trusting any member of his own staff was not trustworthy himself.

"Do you know what the German Crown Prince said to my mother when he visited her soon after the end of the war?" asked Edward.

Katzau gave the matter a quick thought.

"You mean," he asked, "when he made a dutiful visit to his mother-in-law?"

"Yes, that is what I mean," the Prince nodded. "I've always known you were exceptionally well informed, Herr Katzau. Yes, they get on splendidly. I also get on very well with my brother-in-law. As successor to the throne he is exactly my German counterpart. Fritz is part of our—now what was the word?"

"Mischpoche."

"Ah yes, *Mischpoche*. He has no use at all for Bismarck. But he stood behind him during the war. As you know, he commanded the Third Army Corps. Well, he said to my mother that the German Chancellor was very clever and energetic but 'bad, unprincipled and all powerful' and he would not be at all surprised if one day he were to make war on England. The Franco-Prussian war, he said, had been just as much Bismarck's doing as Napoleon's."

"One would hope," Katzau's voice was low, "that Bismarck never found out what the Crown Prince had said to the Queen.."

"Indeed. I shudder to think what would have happened. My sister thinks Bismarck corrupts all his subordinates. Yes, 'corrupts' is the word she uses. It would take years to repair the damage after he's gone. And he has no intention of going. Unless you wanted to be his abject slave, political life in Berlin was intolerable, she says, and his followers and admirers are fifty times worse than he is himself. So it wouldn't take much doing for any of them to corrupt our dear Duchess's servants and pinch the earrings."

At this moment, precisely on time, Adjutant Tyrwith Wilson returned. It was evident that he had had not one, not two, but at least three cognacs.

"Buy something for Mrs. Wilson," the Prince commanded. "But don't expect me to pay for it. And, whatever you choose, do not make it a bust of Bismarck!"

Chapter 4

For those who did not go to the races, Saturday, August 25, 1883, was the day to recover from the *Reunionsball*, which had followed the festive dinner at the International Club and prepare, or have their servants prepare, their costumes and masks for the grand *Kostümfest* in the evening. For many, the prospect of anonymity was tantalizing. The first performance of Johann Strauss's *Fledermaus*, with its magnificent ballroom scene in the second act, had taken place in Vienna less than a decade earlier and must have served as inspiration for hundreds of similar events, wherever well-endowed hosts, or public institutions like the municipality of Baden-Baden, could afford to supply their guests with appropriate flows of Champagne. True, Baden-Baden may only have ten thousand permanent inhabitants, but more than sixty thousand people visited Europe's summer capital annually. Masked balls presented golden opportunities to gifted amateurs and professional beauties, even if the great days of the *grandes horizontales* had come to an end with the Prussian victory over the *belle époque*. But there were still plenty of *petites horizontales*, professional and amateur in operation. No doubt many people who hoped for amorous adventures preferred to wait for the carnival season in those parts of Europe, mainly in the south, where during that time traditionally—for reasons that had to do with Lent—*everything* was permitted. There, so it was widely assumed, if masked encounters had unpleasant consequences of a legal nature in the area of family relations, some judges (who may well have participated in the festivities, like the administrators of justice in the *Fledermaus*) traditionally took a lenient view.

Robert was getting impatient. He had arrived in Baden-Baden on Wednesday. Now it was Saturday. He had had to close his store in Frankfurt while he was away. True, he had not expected to make friends with a man as potentially useful as Louis Katzau, but when would he know for sure that he wasn't wasting his time? Any day now Uncle Gustav would want his money back. Should Robert give himself a deadline—say—until next Wednesday? At the moment, a quick solution to the Duchess of Hamilton's puzzle seemed unattainable. Discovering a plausible motive was only the first step. The rest was bound to take a long, long time, and, in any case, there was no guarantee that he would play a decisive role in its conclusion and could become a major beneficiary.

It was unwise to rely on Louis Katzau alone. Robert felt he should talk to some of the local jewellers and assess what kind of obstacles they would put in his way to block a new competitor, should he decide to risk coming here and open a store next summer.

He chose to see Ludwig Weiler, Gernsbacher Strasse 1. Weiler would give him a general impression. He hoped he would be able to engage him in conversation without having to tell too many lies. According to Weiler's advertisements in the Richard Pohl's *Badeblatt*, he was not the kind of jeweller he aspired to be and was unlikely to consider him a major threat.

!!!!DIAMONDS!!!!
At wholesale prices!
I buy them uncut and cut them myself!
Ring with one diamond — beginning at 25 marks
Earrings with diamonds — beginning at 35 marks

It was ten o'clock in the morning. Robert went into the shop. Ludwig Weiler was an attractively ugly old man with a hunchback and steel-rimmed glasses. His face looked a little like Voltaire's and it soon became clear he also had some of Voltaire's spirit. From time to time, a little drop of saliva formed at the corner of his mouth, which he wiped away with a red handkerchief. Nothing could have prepared Robert for the amazing conversation he was about to have.

A happy young couple was inspecting engagement rings, bought one and left. Opposite the entrance door there was a glass case containing old clocks and trays with imitation brooches, bracelets, necklaces, decorated ribbons, pendants, watch chains, hat clasps and—Robert noted with some interest—*Empire* earrings.

"Are you a collector?" Ludwig Weiler asked.

"Not exactly," Robert replied. "But I can see that some of these are excellent pieces. They look almost genuine."

"How do you know they aren't?" There was a playful glint in Weiler's smile.

"Because," Robert laughed, "you wouldn't be here, Herr Weiler. You would be in one of those boutiques in the Kolonnade." He looked at the earrings in the tray more closely, without as yet touching them.

"Well," he said, "it may very well be that some are genuine."

"You can tell the difference, Herr...?"

"Koch. Robert Koch."

"Robert Koch?" Ludwig Weiler asked. "Not the bacteriologist?"

"I'm afraid not," Robert replied. He had been asked that question before. A year ago, in Berlin, the bacteriologist who bore his name had isolated the bacillus *tuberculosis*. He was now on an official mission to Egypt and India to study cholera.

"I have the greatest admiration for Dr. Koch," Ludwig Weiler said. "Since you can tell the difference," he said, "between a genuine brooch and an imitation brooch you must be a jeweller. Am I right?"

"Right, Herr Weiler. I have recently set up a little store in Frankfurt."

"I must tell you what I tell all young jewellers like yourself who look as though they might very well have talent for the profession. For ladies who think they are at the top of the pyramid, a display of expensive jewellery is not a luxury but a necessity. You must always understand that you will serve means of survival to your customers."

"I will try."

Robert smiled while picking up one pair of earrings. "Do you think I could have a closer look at these?"

To judge by the reproduction of Jacques-Louis David's painting Katzau had shown him, they resembled precisely—or could very well be—Josephine's. He placed them in the palm of his hand and examined them carefully while his heart was suddenly beginning to pound.

"You think, Herr Koch," Ludwig Weiler's glasses fell to the tip of his nose, "these are Josephine's necessities that have been missing?"

"So you, too, have heard." Robert's voice was low.

"There are no secrets in Baden-Baden," Ludwig Weiler observed. "Not for long, anyway. But I can tell you one thing. These are not the earrings you are looking for. I will tell you later where they are."

Who would have thought that an ordinary conversation with an ordinary jeweller whom he had never met before would so quickly turn into such an unexpected, momentous revelation? If Weiler was telling the truth and knew where the stolen earrings were, the question arose how he, rather than Weiler, could eventually manage to appear to have had a hand in the solution and thus ingratiate himself with the Duchess.

"I won't ask you now, Herr Koch, why you are interested in these earrings," Weiler continued. "All I will say is that it is absolutely certain that, once the truth is revealed, the Kaspar Hauser problem"—he said this as though there was nothing astounding about the bizarre connection, as though it was the most natural in the world—"will be cleared up once and for all. Those falsely accused of baby-snatching and murder half a century ago will at last be exonerated."

•   •   •

In 1828, the sixteen-year-old Kaspar Hauser was brought before the authorities in Nürnberg—bewildered, incoherent, stumbling, barely able to walk. Apparently he had grown up in a dungeon, looked after by some unknown caretakers. He could speak only a few almost unintelligible sentences in a south German dialect and could hear but not understand. He had an aversion to all food and drink except bread and water. The authorities made arrangements for him to be taught reading, writing and the Christian religion.

The story had all the elements of a fairytale, with strong metaphysical overtones. It raised fundamental questions about original sin, nature and nurture. Edgar Allan Poe and Herman Melville were fascinated by it. Soon hundreds of brochures and articles speculating about Kaspar Hauser's origins appeared. Was he just an unwanted child? There was never a shortage of unwanted children to be disposed of, one way or another. He was not the first *enfant sauvage* to emerge on the scene since Rousseau had discovered the corrupting influence of civilization and the pristine virtues of Natural Man. This was the time of the Romantic Movement. Kaspar Hauser became "The Child of Europe," a celebrity, a *Tiermensch*, a human animal.

He was treated with kindness and humanity by some and brutality by others who considered him a fraud. The idea of fraud was by no means far-fetched since there were many contradictions in his story, once he was able to tell whatever he remembered of it and could express. Accounts of his mental and physical development were of absorbing interest to the general public and to scholars. He even wrote a short autobiography and was able to describe his dreams in some detail.

A strange English lord, Philip Henry, the fourth Earl of Stanhope, the nephew of William Pitt, arrived in Nürnberg, took Hauser under his protection and sent him for his safety to the small town of Ansbach, where he became clerk in the office of Anselm von Feuerbach, the President of the Court of Appeal, a famous criminologist who was credited with having abolished torture in Bavaria. Stanhope later turned against Hauser. Feuerbach became a crucial element in the Kaspar Hauser story. He wrote a book about him, *Kaspar Hauser, a Case of a Crime against the Soul of a Human Being*. The book, published in 1832, made Kaspar Hauser even more famous all over Europe.

There were two attempt on Hauser's life, in 1829 and 1831. Finally, on December 14, 1833, Kaspar Hauser was stabbed in the *Hofgarten* in Ansbach and died three days later. He was twenty-one. The violent ending of the story had resonances of the Crucifixion.

One thing was still missing, to make it perfect for the Romantic age, an indication that Kaspar Hauser had been a royal prince. Soon, the learned jurist provided such an indication, first privately. In a secret memorandum to Queen Caroline of Bavaria, the second wife and widow of King Maximilian IV of Bavaria, the sister of Grand Duke Carl of Baden and therefore the sister-in-law of Stephanie. The memorandum was written in 1832, that is, before Kaspar Hauser's murder. In it, Feuerbach stated that, on the basis of his findings, Kaspar Hauser was the legitimate child of a princely family that had removed it to make way for another. As to the identity of the family—"the pen almost refuses to write this down"—the answer was the House of Baden, Queen Caroline's own family.

•   •   •

Back to the moment when Ludwig Weiler mentioned Kaspar Hauser.

Robert raised his eyebrows.

"Are you wondering, Herr Koch, in what way the theft of a pair of earrings in the Palais Hamilton could possibly clear up the Kaspar Hauser mystery, a mystery that has stumped the world for fifty years?"

"Frankly, Herr Weiler, yes."

"How well acquainted are you with the family tree of the House of Baden?"

"Reasonably well. We jewellers have to know such things."

"Quite right. So I don't have to waste valuable time by reminding you that the old Grand Duke, Carl Friedrich, who had ruled of Baden for seventy-three years, beginning in 1728 when he was ten, had two wives, one after the other. His successor was Carl, a descendant of Wife Number One. Wife Number Two had a very good reason to take steps to secure the succession to her own descendants. According to the Baden law governing the succession, if Carl died without male descendants those of Wife Number Two would inherit the throne. So the moment Stephanie gave birth to a son, the descendants of Wife Number Two had every reason to pay somebody to swoop down and snatch him, substitute a dying baby, and tell poor Stephanie that unfortunately her baby was dying and it was even too late to have it baptized. According to Feuerbach, the mother of the baby that had been snatched, the mother of Kaspar Hauser, was Carl's wife, our Stephanie."

It took Robert a moment to let that sink in.

"And did she know," Robert's throat was dry, "what had happened to her baby?"

"Most of us think she did, but officially she denied it. In a letter to her close relative Napoleon III she called the story *une fable insensée,* a senseless fable."

"And her daughter, the Duchess of Hamilton," Robert asked, "does she believe she is Kaspar Hauser's sister?"

"I think she does," Weiler responded. "I understand this is a matter that cannot be discussed with her."

Robert mulled this over.

"And in the five years that Kaspar Hauser was a free man, did either mother or daughter ever try to make contact with him?"

"Nobody knows. According to one legend Stephanie once went to Ansbach with a maid to have a look at him through a fence while he was strolling in a garden. But she did not to talk to him."

"I suppose our Duchess was too young."

"Not really," Weiler made a quick calculation. "She was sixteen when her brother died."

Robert played with his mustache in silence. He was thinking of his own new baby, a girl.

"I cannot understand," he said at last, "how Stephanie could have continued associating with her husband's family knowing what they had done."

"I have a simple answer to that question, Herr Koch, as you will find out in a minute. So far everybody has been wrong about most of this. Feuerbach asked himself the inevitable lawyer's question 'cui bono?'—who would benefit from the baby-snatching? The answer was, clearly, the descendants of Wife Number Two, whose grandson Friedrich is now our beloved Grand Duke. The evidence simply had to fit the answer. Soon everybody believed the House of Baden was guilty of baby-snatching and later of murder. Soon even the inhabitants of the House of Baden themselves believed it. Many still do. And not everyone of them finds it possible to rationalize the horror. One, the older brother of our present Grand Duke Friedrich I, who is more robust, would have become Grand Duke Ludwig II if he could have lived with the inherited guilt. But he took refuge in insanity, which naturally disqualified him from ascending the throne. You see, the crime made so much sense and Feuerbach was such an eminent authority. Most ordinary citizens, and not only Republicans, believed it because they suspected that the high nobility was capable of doing anything, of committing any crime, to retain their rights and privileges."

In the Germany of 1883, jewellers who intended to sell necessities to the titled and untitled were rarely Republicans. However, Robert was surprised at himself that he did not feel any urge to protest an observation that, under different circumstances, he would have found outrageous.

"How long have you been in Baden-Baden, Herr Koch?"

"Since Wednesday."

"This is hardly long enough for you to have observed that everybody in Baden-Baden is taking part in a colossal masquerade, pretending to have forgotten the revolutions of 1789, 1830, 1848 and the Paris Commune, only thirteen years ago. They know in their hearts of hearts that it is only a matter of time before the crowns on the heads of the princes who still exercise power will tumble into the gutter, just as Napoleon III's did not so very long ago, and that in the meantime the only thing to do is to drink Champagne, go to masked balls and have a splendid time."

"Let us not complain, Herr Weiler, about something that is good for our profession."

"I am not complaining. I'm stating a fact. But you haven't come to see me to hear such things. The fact is that people do not have any faith any more in the superior morality of people with titles. *Au contraire.* That is why everybody accepted Feuerbach's conclusions, although they were largely wrong. I now know that just one member of the House of Baden is guilty, and not very guilty at that, since there were mitigating circumstances. He is a descendant of Wife Number One and not of Wife Number Two. And his motive had nothing to do with the succession. The earring will prove it."

Weiler waited patiently while Robert worked this out.

"You mean Carl?"

"Yes, I mean Carl."

.   .   .

Carl and Stephanie were married 1806. Stephanie was seventeen. From 1806 until 1811 they did not have a "common household." But on June 5, 1811, their first daughter, Luise, was born. Who knows when and where she was conceived? Five days later Carl's grandfather, the old Grand Duke, died and Carl succeeded him. At the end of the year, Carl and Stephanie at last formed a common household, with the consequence that Stephanie's second child, Kaspar Hauser, was born on September 29, 1812. He may have been conceived in the connubial bed at the end of 1811. But it was Weiler's contention that the child was not conventionally conceived and was not legitimate and that Carl was not the father.

Napoleon and Josephine were divorced in 1809. He married Marie-Louise on March 21, 1810. Carl and Stephanie attended the wedding. A year later, on March 20, 1811, Marie-Louise gave birth to Napoleon II, the King of Rome. At the end of 1811, Stephanie was in Paris—alone, after her first child, Luise, was born. By then she was already Grand Duchess. That is when the event occurred to which Louis Katzau had referred (while claiming that he did not believe it for a minute) when he spoke to the two Hamburg ladies on Wednesday. Napoleon and his adopted daughter, Stephanie, Katzau said, had "sexual congress" for the second time, at a time when Napoleon was trying to persuade the Kaiser of Austria and the King of Prussia, both of whom he had recently defeated, to send troops to help him in his forthcoming military campaign against his former friend Tsar Alexander I, the husband of Stephanie's sister-in-law Luise-Elisabeth.

This diplomatic work was time-consuming and strenuous. No wonder Napoleon welcomed a few minutes' amorous relief.

•   •   •

"You say," Robert recapitulated what Weiler had just said, "that only Carl was guilty of baby-snatching and murder. The other members of the House of Baden were wrongly accused. And that there were mitigating circumstances."

"That is what I am saying, Herr Koch. Once Stephanie was pregnant and Carl knew he could not be the father of his wife's second child, he demanded to know who the father was. No one will ever know why Stephanie did not lie and invent some name. Instead, she said 'Napoleon'."

Robert's mouth opened slightly.

"Why are you so surprised?

"I...I...I..."

The reason why Robert was temporarily tongue-tied was because, if Weiler was right, he, Robert, could very well be Kaspar Hauser's nephew once removed. That took a little time to sink in.

"Are you so astonished," Weiler asked, "because one is not supposed to do that kind of thing with one's adopted daughter?"

"I...I suppose so," Robert stuttered.

"Remember, they were not related. Even Josephine was not related to Stephanie. Her first husband was, distantly. In any case, Josephine was no longer a factor. She had been jealous when the fourteen-year-old Stephanie flirted with her husband, when she first invited her to come to the Tuileries, but that was a long time ago.

"Herr Weiler," Robert hesitated before he articulated the question, "do you think Stephanie, now a mother and wife, went to Paris in 1811 specifically to do again what she had done once when she was merely fourteen, to offer herself to Napoleon and find out what it felt like now?"

"No, Herr Koch," Weiler wiped his mouth with his red handkerchief, "I consider that impossible. True, she adored him. True, she was profoundly unhappy in Baden and husband's family was frigid to her, deeply resenting that she had been forced on them. Still, she was just beginning to tolerate her husband. Stephanie was a brave, determined, sensible woman. I can't imagine that she would have been so foolhardy as to gamble with her future, to go to Paris in order to tempt Napoleon to seduce her for the second time and risk conceiving his child."

"Why then did she go to Paris—without her husband?"

"I have no idea. Whatever the reason, she found herself late at night in the Tuileries. The date was December 27, 1811. Marie-Louise was somewhere else. The two of them were alone. Suddenly, out of the blue, with his usual speed and violence, he imposed himself on her. He overwhelmed her. He did not quite rape her. But nearly. That is how he scored all his victories—by surprise, speed and violence. Before she understood what had happened, she had conceived his child."

"Are you just guessing?"

"No, Herr Koch. One of Marie-Louise's ladies-in-waiting, the *Gräfin* Theresa von Huberstein, was listening at the door. She never told Marie-Louise about it, but she mentioned it in her memoirs. I need hardly add that Stephanie was not the only lady with whom Napoleon had a few short minutes of pleasure while never quite taking his mind off his duties of state."

Robert scratched the back of his head. He was thinking of his grandmother, Red Esther, and her marriage to her husband Shmuel.

He came back to the point.

"May I return to your question—why did she tell Carl the truth? Why didn't she lie and invent some name?"

"I have thought about this for a long time. I think I have the answer. I believe that as soon as Stephanie understood what had happened, she felt the deepest shame and remorse. She could not imagine that she could ever integrate a child of Napoleon's into the family, even if she would tell her husband that the father was somebody else. So she told Carl the truth in the hope that he would somehow dispose of the child and that the subject would never be mentioned again. After all, such things also happened to ordinary people all the time, and the church orphanages were full of children waiting for homes. A few years later, after having conceived three more children with Carl, when he became mortally ill of what appears to have been a venereal infection, she looked after him with the greatest tenderness. She bore him no grudge. He died in 1818, only one year after Marie, our Duchess, was born."

Both men were silent, each pursuing his own thoughts.

"Oh," Weiler exclaimed, "I nearly forgot!"

"Of course," Robert responded. "The earrings! What about the earrings?"

"They provide the proof," Weiler said. "*Gräfin* von Huberstein included in her memoirs a crucial document, after the paragraph on Napoleon's amorous encounter with Stephanie. It was a bill for seven thousand francs from the jeweller who had provided much of the jewellery Josephine wore at her coronation *for a pair of earrings identical with Josephine's*, delivered, by order of His Majesty, into the hands of the Grand Duchess Stephanie of Baden. But there was one important difference. They were to be rubies. Josephine's, as Napoleon remembered, and as anybody can see today from Jacques-Louis David's paint-ing in the Louvre, were emeralds. The date of Napoleon's gift to Stephanie was December 28, 1811, the day after their encoun-ter. The earrings the Duchess of Hamilton inherited from her mother were rubies, not emeralds."

"Yes," Robert said, after a moment's reflection. "I suppose that is a pretty good indication."

"As good as we are likely to get."

"I suppose the gift," Robert mused, "was typical of Napo-leon. No words. A reminder of Josephine, the only woman he ever loved. But why steal the earrings now?"

"I prefer the word 'borrow'. I understand the Grand Duke of Baden has asked the Duchess to lend the earrings to his law-yers for inspection. They are preparing a lengthy, detailed state-ment on the events of 1811, in order to exonerate the family. They want to scrutinize the earrings, compare them with oth-ers and identify them beyond a shadow of a doubt. Their pur-pose is to put the blame where it belongs, on Grand Duke Carl, the Duchess's father. To nobody's surprise, she has categori-cally refused."

"So the Grand Duke instructed his people..."

"No need to finish the sentence," Ludwig Weiler smiled. "You asked 'where are the earrings now?' The answer is, 'In Karlsruhe.' Under lock and key in Grand Duke Friedrich's pos-session."

Chapter 5

Sunday, August 26, 1883, was the day on which the festivities celebrating the twenty-fifth anniversary of the Iffezheim races reached their climax. The Prince of Wales participated in a special tennis tournament in the morning, on the courts of the first German tennis club, which had been founded two years earlier by the Reverend Thomas A. White. In the afternoon he took part, in the meticulously planned *Blumen-Corso*, the flower parade along the Promenade and the Lichtentaler Allee, in the company of his hostess, the Duchess of Hamilton. (The rules and regulations, filling a whole page, had been published in Richard Pohl's *Badeblatt* beforehand, and resembled the detailed plans for a major military operation.) The beflagged coaches and carriages taking part belonged to the usual princely families, financial princes included. Their owners were politely requested to decorate their *equipages* with flowers in baskets. The *Corso-Commissär*, William, the twelfth Duke of Hamilton, was to proceed on horseback and wear a yellow riding costume and, by virtue of his high office, a red-yellow armband. Ladies were encouraged to be dressed in costumes *à la Louis XV*, but this was not obligatory. In case of cool weather, participants were permitted to cover their legs in furs and blankets. In case of rain, the event was postponed to September 2.

After the *Blumen-Corso*, the Prince and the Duchess attended a concert by a much praised military band. At night there was the *Nachtfest* on the *Promenadenplatz*, right in front of the

Kolonnade. However exhausted, they would not have been forgiven had they chosen to skip it.

Long before all this unfolded, at eleven in the morning, Louis Katzau, this time with a pink carnation in the buttonhole of his formal black *Gehrock*, met Robert in the café in the Conversationshaus. The boutique, obediently decorated with flowers, was closed. The café was already crowded. They ordered a bottle of Katzau's favourite local white wine, *Merdinger Bühl Auslese*.

Robert, more modestly attired than Katzau in a grey suit but wearing a diamond pin in his black silk tie, gave him his report on Ludwig Weiler. Katzau waited patiently until he had finished but then exploded in a theatrically Hungarian spasm.

"Why didn't you consult me before going to see that chronic, pathological liar? That man is not capable of speaking a word of truth. Everyone in Baden-Baden knows it."

"But why would he make up that story?" Robert asked a little too defensively for his liking. "It seemed to make a lot of sense."

"To make himself interesting, of course," Katzau replied with heat. "Why else? That's a very good reason for telling lies. But you don't need a reason. If you have a lively imagination, why not use it to dazzle an innocent visitor from far-away Frankfurt? Singers sing, painters paint, liars lie. After fifty years, after endless speculation about Kaspar Hauser, the Hunchback of the Gernsbacher Strasse at last comes out with the truth? No, Herr Koch, don't you believe it."

Katzau suddenly lapsed into deep thought and stroked his Franz Joseph whiskers.

"Do you know how I can prove he's a liar? Because the earrings in the David picture in the Louvre are not emeralds! They're rubies. Josephine is wearing a dark red coronation gown. Do you think she would wear *green* earrings? After all, she is French and has some taste! Unlike that German philistine Ludwig Weiler."

At this moment, a young man in a well-worn brown coat

rushed into the café, out of breath, frantically looking for somebody.

"That man is looking for me," Katzau announced.

He had never seen this young emissary of the Duchess's *Haushofmeister* Edmund Jenkins before, but he was right.

"I have this from Herr Jenkins," the man said, after having first made sure that Katzau was Katzau. He handed him an envelope. "While His Royal Highness is here," he explained, "Herr Jenkins has to check all the letters and messages that come in. He wants you to read this and let him know what you think of it."

It took Katzau nearly ten minutes to read the whole letter, at the end of which he used an expressive Hungarian epithet that Robert was not meant to understand. The letter was written with great care, in a calligraphic hand, clearly written by a man used to writing.

Your Highness,

You probably do not remember me. For three months late in 1865 I was a lackey in your employment in the Palais Hamilton. I left not because I was dismissed but because I decided that at twenty I was not too old to do what at first I had not wanted to do—first, become an apprentice in my father's carpentry workshop in Oos, then to do more important things. I will explain later.

I remember you well. I have always had the greatest respect for you. The last thing I want to do is cause you pain. I have no right to criticize you for being who you are, and for acting in accordance with your position. You mean well, you work hard, you are a generous benefactor of the Lichtental monastery, you serve many other good causes and you perform your function in life as conscientiously as you can.

The earrings that have disappeared from your jewel box are now in my possession. I remembered your wearing them on one memorable occasion with pride, and identifying them as having belonged to the Empress Josephine. In a moment I shall describe this occasion, which occurred in October 1865. I also remembered where you kept them. A week ago, I had no difficulty persuading one of your servants to remove them and hand them to me. I appeal to you not to initiate a formal or informal investigation, to have that person dismissed. She is not a thief. She understood why she was helping me and realized that I will return the earrings to you as soon as possible.

At the end of this letter I will tell you what favour I would like you to do for me in exchange. But it is important that I tell you first why I am acting in this way. I do not expect you to approve—but I want you to understand. Since I know you to be a good person, I think you will. However, my explanation will take a little time.

You are not really interested in political ideas, although in your salon, as I remember well, there was always a great deal of political talk. Everything I heard you say suggests that you would oppose anything that might change the existing order. No doubt you regretted the demise of your imperial relative's French regime, especially in the way it happened, but you are, of course, a German patriot. Occasionally you skillfully followed in your revered mother's footsteps and used your position to bring eminent French, Prussian and Austrian and other personalities together to discuss their disputes. But you never received in your salon any republicans or socialists, unless they were artists, whose political views were of no interest to anybody. You never demonstrated any sympathy with republicans or socialists.

There is a deep gulf between us, not only—obviously—in social position but also in the way we think. I doubt whether you go as far as our chancellor, Prince Otto von Bismarck, who has decided to treat people like my father and me as dangerous outlaws, but your views are probably not very far from his. I find this deplorable. Still, I am writing this letter to try to make you appreciate that the reason why I borrowed your grandmother's earrings is honourable.

As you follow in your family's tradition, so do I follow in mine. My father participated in the revolutionary war of 1849, when I was four years old, too young to have known the circumstances in many parts of Europe that caused the uprising and, in Baden particularly, the devastating poverty of most of the rural population, the medieval living conditions and the terrible repression that followed the restoration of the ancien régime that had caused the French Revolution and launched Napoleon. That is why the whole of the country rose up and why most of the army supported the revolution and sided with the insurgents, thereby committing high treason no doubt in your eyes, and in your mother's eyes, and, above all, in Grand Duke Leopold's eyes. I need hardly remind you that you all fled to Bad Ems, the others to Alsace and to Mainz. Soon, as you remember, the Grand Duke appealed to the Prussians for help. They quickly responded, with great enthusiasm, speed and efficiency and, under the command of your friend Wilhelm, now the Kaiser, then The Crown Prince, mercilessly crushed the revolution, and you all returned to your palaces. It cannot have been easy for you to pretend all these years that nothing unpleasant of this sort had ever happened.

The crushing of the revolution was easy for the Prussians and their allies. Resistance was not. My father still talks about it. It did not matter that almost every patriot supported the revolution. The Prussians outnumbered us four to one, he says. We had thirteen thousand untrained, demoralized men, they had sixty thousand drilled professionals. They took hundreds of prisoners. On one occasion, the Prussian general von Peucker conducted an exercise on the Leopoldsplatz, right in front of what later became Your Highness's Palais, and had his prisoners parade in front him. There had been rumours that the Prussians had had their noses and ears cut off. Now, onlookers were relieved to see that this was not true.

Fortunately, my father was able to flee to Switzerland, together with Friedrich Engels who was twenty-eight at the time and became his friend. He is still proud of that. You probably have not heard of Engels. He was the partner of Karl Marx, who died in London last March. The two of them had issued their Communist Manifesto together, the year before Engels's flight to Switzerland. He had never believed the insurgents in Baden had a chance. But he joined them as a volunteer because he wanted to fight the Prussians. Rarely had military operations been carried out in such a slovenly, stolid manner, he said, as the insurgents'. But quite apart from that, in his view, they did not pursue a sufficiently resolute revolutionary policy. He learned a great deal from the experience, above all that defensiveness was the death of every armed uprising.

Your Highness, I assure you I have never participated in any armed uprising against the forces that Fate has decreed you represent.

But my decision to borrow Josephine's earrings was certainly done in the spirit of Friedrich Engels and Karl Marx.

As a result of the failure of the revolution in 1849, eighty thousand people, more than a twentieth of the total population of Baden emigrated, mostly to America—from all of Germany, a quarter of a million. Clearly, only a few of those who left their homes were men like Friedrich Engels, Karl Marx and my father, radicals who thought there was something profoundly wrong with the society at home, who tried to understand the reasons and wished to change the social order. Most of those who left had simply given up any hope for a decent life and saw a brighter future for themselves and their children elsewhere.

In 1865, when I was twenty and entered Your Highness's service as a lackey, I did not yet share my father's views. Secretly, I suspected he might well be right, but I did not want to admit this to him because in my school years we had many disagreements. I was determined to go my own way, observe the world, think my own thoughts and come to my own conclusions.

I made a decisive observation while I was in your employment, nearly eighteen years ago. Your Highness was unknowingly very much part of it. As you now read this you may smile, you may shake your head in disbelief or puzzlement. At the time, there was no reason for you to give a moment's attention to the thoughts of your servants as they followed the Haushofmeister's instructions and tended to the needs of your guests, one of whom, on that particular occasion, was the Empress Eugénie of France herself, accompanied by a staff of five persons, including Admiral Jurien de la Gravière, who had recently been demoted from his Mexican command. The Empress had been taking the cure in Bad Schwalbach incognito under the name of Comtesse de Pierrefonds—the cure for serious difficulties in her marriage to Louis Napoleon who was seeking solace from his ever worsening troubles, and no doubt from premonitions of disasters to come, in the arms of at least one mistress.

What was it, you ask, that I observed that had such a decisive impact on me? The answer is, nothing that I observed outside myself while I was chasing away curious spectators on the Leopoldsplatz, opening doors for the Empress, offering her a glass of wine on a silver tray or reminding her that she left her umbrella in the équipage. No, what shook me was what I observed inside my-self on one particular occasion—the banquet at the Neue Schloss that Grand Duke Friedrich I gave in honour of your guest, the Empress Eugénie. That is when I had a crucial insight. It was a banquet attended by the Grand Duke's father-in-law, King Wilhelm of Prussia, now our Kaiser, and your special friend Queen Augusta. There he was, King Wilhelm himself, the man, then already in his sixties, who, as Crown Prince sixteen years earlier, had crushed my father's revolution. Did I feel any urge to strangle him? No. It would have been useless in any case. I knew that he was not in charge. The power was being exercised in his name by the giant who was also present at that banquet, who by sheer power of personality, superior intelligence and unshakeable will power, dominated the table, and was about the dominate the world, Otto von Bismarck, Prussian Ministerpräsident since 1861.

I was standing behind the Empress's chair and wished my French was better. You may remember, Your Highness, that in honour of the current Empress of France, you were wearing the earrings you had inherited from that other Bonaparte empress, your grandmother the Empress Josephine. You drew everyone's attention to them. Queen Augusta remarked, as she looked at them closely, how shockingly badly Napoleon had behaved towards Josephine, and with how much dignity she had borne her misfortune. Bismarck's comment was amiable and sentimental, unexpected in a man who hates the human race and treats all his opponents with cynical brutality. "Josephine," he said, "was every lovesick German schoolboy's ideal Frenchwoman." He meant it, too. Unlike most of his followers, and most of the newspapers nowadays, he never hated the French, and he does not do so now. He only hates those who stand in his way, whoever they are.

I followed most of what was being said perfectly well, the witty aphorisms of Bismarck whose manners were impeccable, the charming replies of the Empress, the gallantries of the sprightly King Wilhelm and the polished, worldly-wise comments of Queen Augusta who proved herself worthy of being the granddaughter of Duke Karl August of Sachsen-Weimar, Goethe's patron and friend.

You may think my tone sounds a little strange, coming from

the son of a revolutionary. You are quite right. As I say, I also found my responses strange. I could not understand them at all. I just gazed at Bismarck—hypnotized, helpless. I did not want to take revenge on kindly old King Wilhelm for what he had done in 1849.

I must say, although I was only twenty, I saw things clearly and have since been proven right. That Bismarck wanted a united Germany was a sentiment he had in common with everybody else, including Empress Eugénie and her husband who—what tragic irony!— five years later became his prisoner, as I need hardly remind you. As a true heir of his uncle, your imperial relative supported nationalist revolutions against feudal oppressors everywhere, in Germany, Italy and Poland, and Bismarck despised him for it. He had no use for any nationalistic humbug, German or anybody else's. But Louis Napoleon's support for the principle of nationality was usually half-hearted and ineffectual, anyway.

Forgive me, please, Your Highness, but to explain my action I must say a few things you may not wish to hear. The Germany Bismarck was creating few of us wanted. He was creating it, not the people of Germany. Nor were we convinced that the only way to create it was by waging three wars. Certainly, the Kaiser did not approve of Bismarck's methods, although he lacked the strength to dismiss him. Your friend Queen Augusta may have told you that he burst into tears, on January 17, 1871, the day before he was proclaimed Kaiser at Versailles, after France's humiliating defeat. He believed, quite rightly, that he was saying good-bye to the old Prussia of which he had been king since 1861. Since, unlike Bismarck, Wilhelm is a modest man, he may also have sensed that it was profoundly wrong, and dangerous, to announce the unification of Germany not at home in Germany, but on French territory before peace was concluded and while still laying siege to Paris.

Today Germany is a militarist, undemocratic nation, dominated by Prussia that rules over far more people than all the other Länder combined. It is a Germany run by a federation of monarchies, a Germany in which not any political party but Bismarck's generals, bankers and industrialists exercise the controlling influence. He hates all political parties, not only our party, which he tried to weaken by taking the wind of our sails and having the government itself take the initiative to introduce social insurance against accident, sickness and old age.

Bismarck does not understand that his kind of Germany is archaic and cannot last. Friedrich Engels and Karl Marx welcomed Bismarck's creation only because they know, as I do, that his system is bound to lead to a Communist revolution.

This brings me to the point. Bismarck's Sozialistengesetz, the law against socialists, has declared us Reichsfeinde—enemies of the Reich. The law was passed five years ago, following an attempt in Berlin on June 2, 1878, by a certain Dr. Karl Nobiling, whose motives were never established, to assassinate the eighty-one-year-old Kaiser by shooting him from a window on Unter den Linden as he drove by. The Kaiser was badly hurt, as you know, but recovered. Your Highness may remember that Dr. Nobiling had no known relationship to socialism and killed himself immediately after doing the deed. Nothing could have suited Bismarck better. Since then we have been forced to go underground. Thanks to our constitution, and thanks to Germany being, after all, a Rechtsstaat, a state governed by fundamental laws, our party is still legal and the legislation banning it cannot last for ever. But for the moment the Sozialistengesetz has done our press and our party organization great harm.

Therefore, I am asking Your Highness to do me the favour of sending a cheque for one hundred thousand marks, to finance a newspaper in Zürich for distribution in Germany, made out to Louis Katzau, to his address, Boutique Number Five, Kolonnade.

The moment Herr Katzau receives the cheque, I will return Josephine's earrings to Your Highness.

May I humbly conclude with expressions of the deepest respect.

•   •   •

Katzau saved his explosion *"Az Istenit!"* until Robert had finished reading the letter, and then added, for good measure, first *"Teremburajat!"* and then *"Ördög ès polol!"* It was not clear to Robert whether he meant to say "Oh, my God, what am I going to do now?" or "The gall of the man!" Or neither.

Robert wanted to say, "Well, I guess that solves the case. I'd better think of something else to catch the Duchess's eye," but there was something in Katzau's manner that made him hesitate.

"Do you know who wrote this?" he asked.

"I do not," Katzau spouted. "That letter makes absolutely no sense, who ever wrote it. He must know very well *this*"—he waved the letter in the air—"is not the way to get any money out of the Duchess. Does he imagine she would not have some-one go to Oos and visit the two or three carpenters in the neighbourhood and track him down? And then have him locked up! He must know extortion is covered by the Criminal Code."

"So why did he write it?"

"My dear Herr Koch," Katzau replied, "I've given up a long time ago trying to understand the Marxist mind. Not that they are easy to find in Baden-Baden. I don't suppose you have had many opportunities to study them in Frankfurt?"

"I am afraid not," Robert smiled. "Not in my circles."

"I suppose this *ganif*"—a Yiddish word for crook—"is simply a disgruntled servant of the Duchess who was fired, probably for good reason, went to Heidelberg to study Hegel and got into bad company."

"What are you going to do?"

"Easy. I will send a courier to the *Haushofmeister* and suggest he tear up the letter and forget all about it."

Chapter 6

Monday, August 27, 1883, was the second *Renntag*, the climax of the season. The galleries were overcrowded so that sizable sections of High Society, mainly members of the International Club, had the greatest difficulty finding accommodation in the paddock worthy of them. Four hundred and seventy five coaches were counted, among them eight *Vierspänner* (carriages-in-four), two hundred and fifty-eight *Lohnkutscher* (rented carriages), ten omnibuses and one hundred and forty-eight *Bauernwagen* (farmers' carts). Punctually at two o'clock Grand Duke Friedrich appeared, in the company of the Duchess of Hamilton. The Grand Duke was to present the highest prize—forty thousand marks and a gold cup, the *Jubiläumspreis von Baden*. Edward, Prince of Wales, arrived separately with his friends, in gala uniform. There was talk about his horse The Scot, which was scheduled to run next week. In the evening the Grand Duke was to give a *Festessen*, a banquet, in the Neue Schloss.

Robert had given himself a deadline—Wednesday. If by then he had not been able to improve his chances to strike gold out of Josephine's earrings, he would return to Frankfurt and postpone the Baden-Baden experiment until further notice.

In the morning he dropped in on Louis Katzau who, however, was busy selling a set of Meissen shepherdesses to an elderly couple from Warsaw. Robert did not wish to disturb them. Outside, on the Promenade, a brigade of chattering municipal employees were gathering the wilting debris from yesterday's *Blumen-Corso*. The centre of activity was in Iffezheim, not here. How could he use his time profitably? Robert strolled across to the practically empty Conversationshaus, casually inspecting the four halls commissioned by Édouard Bénazet thirty years ago to be the site of the most beautiful casino in the whole wide world, calamitously closed by the newly united Germany not for puritanical reasons but to contain French influence—the Salle Louis XIII in white and gold, with the huge flower arrangement at the centre flanked by two fountains, the Salle Louis XIV, with the walls and furniture covered by red damask, the ceiling with paintings in the style of Versailles and the floor with a priceless Aubusson carpet, the small Salle Pompadour in the style of Louis XV, and finally the Renaissance Salle Louis XIII, used for concerts and dances. There, the walls were decorated by Italian frescoes and the chandeliers placed on top of columns of classical caryatids.

"Not bad," he muttered to himself as he walked across to the enormous, although also almost deserted, Trinkhalle, the ninety-metre long pump room with its sixteen columns built in the style of fifteenth-century Florence and designed to dispense thermal waters to cure any ailment of your choice, including obesity. Already in 1830, ten years before it was built, fifteen thousand visitors a year had arrived in Baden-Baden, presumably none without at least one ailment. The figures of how many had frequented *Aquae Aureliae*, where the Romans had harnessed the mineral hot springs in 117 A.D., were not available. Today, you were not limited to mineral waters. You could also drink milk from cows, goats and mares. But Robert preferred a cup of lukewarm carbonated water spiced (so it said, above the tap) with chlorides, arsenic, sulphides, silicates, calcium, iron, lithium, phosphates and potassium—he hoped in sufficiently large doses to bring him luck quickly.

It had the immediate effect of loosening his tongue, as he was surprised to note with pleasure when he suddenly found himself shamelessly addressing a handsome young lady from

Stuttgart, aged about twenty-two. She wore a low-cut green blouse and a tight-fitting long black skirt.

"Let me see, *mademoiselle*," he said, pretending to decipher the label over her tap, "what you are consuming. Aha—very promising."

"Promising what?"

She had remarkable dimples.

Careful, Robert, he said to himself. Remember Baden-Baden's reputation. Not all therapies are beneficial.

"Promising eternal youth," he replied, a little too pleased with himself for his quick wit. "Why aren't you in Iffezheim?" he asked.

"Because that is where my aunt is. I needed time off. We are staying at the Englische Hof. My name is Ilse. Ilse Zimmermann."

A few moments of innocuous flirtation with this spirited guest of the expensive Englische Hof would by no means be incompatible with the terms of his engagement in Baden-Baden.

"My name is Robert Koch," he said, "and I am not a bacteriologist."

"What's that?" Fräulein Zimmermann asked.

Robert explained.

"Well, what are you then?" she asked.

"I'm a detective."

His tone made it clear that this was neither true nor false.

"Oh, how exciting," she laughed. "How come you don't have an English accent?"

Robert did not quite follow Fräulein Zimmermann's reasoning.

"My aunt loves detective stories. They are all in English but my English is terrible. So I can't read them. But she talks about them all the time. I did not know we had detectives in Germany. Are you looking for a murderer? Right here in the Trinkhalle?"

"I am afraid not."

"May I ask...?"

Why not tell the truth? Robert said to himself. The

Haushofmeister had not bound him to silence. How else create the conditions for a miracle?

He told as much of the truth as was important at the moment, including the reason why he had involved himself in the case, that he hoped to track down the thief in order to be appointed court jeweller of the Duchess of Hamilton.

"The Duchess of Hamilton?" He liked her Stuttgart inflection when pronouncing the word Hamilton. "Somebody was mentioning her only the other day. Now let me think. There is somebody in town who has nothing good to say about her husband."

"Her husband? But he's been dead for years!"

"Or maybe it is her son. Oh yes! I've just thought of who it was. It was the masseur in the Friedrichsbad who talked about him. The masseur is from Scotland. He gave a massage to a nice man I talked to in the hotel. Apparently he performs wonders with his hands. He even connected the Hamiltons with *Maria Stuart*."

Maria Stuart is the name of Schiller's play about Mary, Queen of Scots. Everyone who ever attended a *gymnasium* had to memorize long speeches from the play.

"That's very, very interesting. Let us go there right now."

"To the Friedrichsbad?" she exclaimed. "But it's for men only!" And she quickly added, "For naked men only!"

"Maybe I can smuggle you in." Robert was visualizing the scene, as no doubt she did. "Wouldn't you like that? Disguise yourself as a man."

"That's the nicest invitation I've ever had. No, thank you. I don't think my aunt would allow it. Anyway, I must go back to the hotel. I wish you luck, Herr Detektiv!"

Robert hurriedly walked up the Sophienstrasse towards the Friedrichsbad. The Hamiltons! He had been so preoccupied with Napoleon I and his first wife, and with Napoleon III and his (only) wife, with Kaspar Hauser and Bismarck, that he had never given a moment's thought to the possibility of a motive originating on the Duchess's husband's side.

It had taken five years to build the Friedrichsbad, the most technically advanced and the most sumptuous bath-palace in Europe. Its purpose was to replenish, if that was possible, the treasury of Grand Duke Friedrich, the owner of the casinos. Their closing had emptied the treasury. Inaugurated just six years ago, in 1877, Grand Duke Friedrich I's monument dominated the entrance to the colossal Renaissance building, quite appropriately. Built on the site of the Roman baths, the remnants of the ancient facilities had been excavated, studied, preserved and, to some extent, emulated. On the facade were medallions of the Roman emperors Hadrian and Marcus Aurelius, and of the humanistic scholars and doctors Paracelsus, Johannes Reuchlin, Georgius Agricola and the contemporary chemist Robert Wilhelm Bunsen, who, like the Grand Duke, was still alive. Bunsen was among those who had discovered radioactive qualities in certain minerals in the Baden-Baden waters that had special therapeutic effects. A great deal of research in balneology had, of course, preceded the design of the baths.

Robert had been there on an earlier visit to Baden-Baden a year ago. He particularly remembered the unusual but not disagreeable aroma pervading the whole building, combining chloride with perspiration and peppermint, as well as the elaborate decorations everywhere, many of them elaborations of mythological motifs. Since he was not afflicted by any particular ailment, he had hoped to prevent their onset by making pre-emptive use of the facilities on all three floors, in the recommended sequence, each with a specific purpose. At each point he was aided by competent and polite attendants in white coats, masters of the balneological jargon. He stepped into big pools, small pools, showers of all kinds, steam baths, hydrotherapy chambers with and without inhalators, basins of various depths animated by varying degrees of turbulence, the thermal steam rooms, the jet-spray baths, even the cold water pools, although that was not easy. There was generous provision for rest periods, during which the bathers were wrapped in warm towels. Massages were administered by a regiment of masseurs but were not included in the entrance fee. Last year, he had chosen not to have one. For those with special ailments bathtubs and box-like constructions were available, serviced by specialists. Swimming in the central pool, directly under the huge dome, provided the climactic finale. He had felt he was swimming in a cathedral. This was the only pool designed for nothing but pleasure, physical and spiritual. Robert had wondered at the time whether the balneological textbooks named pleasure as one of the therapies available.

He remembered all this very clearly as he walked up the steps to the Rotunda, the round lobby at the main entrance. He would treat himself to a massage this time. This year, on the occasion of the special anniversary year, Grand Duchess Luise had lent a few pieces from her art collection to be exhibited here—a portrait of her father, Kaiser Wilhelm, by the Munich painter Franz Lenbach, completed in 1873, as well as a silver *Statuette*, placed on a column, of a knight leaning on a sword and carrying a shield with the grand ducal colours painted on porcelain.

A special exhibit of works of art from the Duchess of Hamilton's collection, planned for this space in the Rotunda, was not yet ready for viewing. But a printed notice announced that *ein bescheidener Katalog*, a modest catalogue, would be available on Tuesday.

•   •   •

Herr David MacDonald was clearly the most knowledgeable, quick witted and articulate masseur in Christendom. He was born in Baden-Baden about forty years ago but trained as a masseur in Edinburgh. His father had been one of Stephanie's coachmen and his mother one of her chambermaids. After Stephanie's death in 1860, her daughter Marie kept them on. Herr MacDonald spoke the usual Baden dialect but rolled his r's, as apparently one did in Scotland. Fräulein Zimmermann's hotel acquaintance was right—he did wonders with his soft, strong, snow-white hands. By the time it was over, Robert felt that if inside the very core of his body there was a tiny object—say, a miniature pea—Herr MacDonald could sense it in his fingertips.

A towel around his loins, Robert was first asked to lie on his back on a low massage table in the masseur's cubicle while Herr MacDonald gently but firmly began kneading the back of his neck. The masseur was most interested in the story of the disappearance of Josephine's earrings, which had not reached him yet. But he knew all about the earrings. Years ago, his parents had been amused by the Duchess's glowing pride in owning them. They thought it was reckless of her to tell everybody about her treasures and to make a great fuss about her son William sharing her pleasure in owning them. As for William, he was telling all his friends, Herr MacDonald's parents had reported, that one day he was going to own his great-grandmother Josephine's earrings. This, they said, was asking for trouble.

Herr MacDonald began work on Robert's back while Robert told him the truth about his interest in finding the thief.

"Herr Koch," Herr MacDonald stopped with his hands in mid-air. "There is no shortage of candidates right here in Baden-Baden who would have excellent reasons for stealing the earrings. May I make a proposal? I'll tell you a few things about the Hamilton family. Then you come up with three plausible candidates. If your ideas make sense to me, you don't have to pay for the massage. What do you think?"

Robert was delighted.

Herr MacDonald resumed his work. He was beginning to soften up Robert's back. "Herr Koch, how is your Scottish history?"

"We had *Maria Stuart* at school."

"That's better than nothing. Now, who do you think was regent during Mary Stuart's minority?"

"Hamilton." Nothing ventured, nothing gained.

"Correct. You know it, Herr Koch. But Herr Schiller did not. Little Mary's regent was none other than the Regent of Scotland himself, James Hamilton, Second Earl of Arran, Duke of Châtelherault. As the great-grandson of James II he was heir-presumptive to the throne. And how do you think he became Duke of Châtelherault?"

It is an old Jewish custom to ask a question when you don't know the answer.

"Where is Châtelherault?" Robert asked.

"It's near Poitu in southwestern France, on the river Vienne. A lovely little place. Hamilton got it as a reward from the French for arranging Mary's marriage to the Dauphin. Mary was six. Five years later he made sure that, should Mary die childless, his own claim to the Scottish throne would be upheld. It so happened, as you know, that she did not die childless."

"Too bad."

"Yes, too bad," David MacDonald agreed. "Six years before arranging the marriage to the Dauphin, Hamilton had agreed to her betrothal to some one else, namely to Edward, Prince of Wales. Yes, Edward, Prince of Wales. At that time Mary was only six months old, Edward six years. Needless to say, there were reasons for his, shall we say, indecisiveness, one of which was doubts about his legitimacy. Doubts about one's legitimacy were not an uncommon problem in medieval and Renaissance Europe."

"And later," Robert added.

"True. His indecisiveness was rather spectacular. In 1544, between having agreed, in 1543, to Mary marrying Edward, and five years later Mary marrying the Dauphin of France, he made moves to have his own son, the Third Earl of Arran, marry her, to secure the Hamiltons' succession to the Scottish throne. However, there was a little complication. Henry VIII had already nominated the indecisive Hamilton as future husband of Princess Elizabeth, later the Virgin Queen, in order to lay the groundwork for an Anglo-Scottish alliance."

"Are you telling me all this, Herr MacDonald, merely to indicate that your Baden-Baden candidates stole Josephine's earrings to become King of England or, if that didn't work, to become King of Scotland?"

Herr MacDonald had arrived at the back of Robert's legs.

"Please, Herr Koch, do not rush me. We will now jump two centuries when Lord William Douglas married the heiress of the Hamilton family, since there were no male heirs available, and became head of the Hamilton-Douglas family."

"Which is the name of the current family," Robert remembered.

"Correct. Now let's make another jump. The man who, nearly forty years ago, married our Duchess Marie was Marquis William Alexander Anthony Archibald, who was to become the eleventh Duke of Hamilton and eighth Duke of Brandon. Marie was no longer young. She was twenty-eight. Both her sisters had been married for years. Before that, starting early, there had been a number of suitors for her hand. One of them was—guess who?"

Robert took a wild guess.

"Louis Napoleon," he tried. "The future Napoleon III."

"How did you know? He was just the right age—only nine years older than Marie." By now Herr MacDonald was tapping the inside of his feet. "As a young man," he said, "while he was dreaming his dreams and plotting his plots, he had spent a lot of time in Baden. I suppose, Marie was a normal teenager and flirted with him, and he with her. So he went to Stephanie and asked for her youngest daughter's hand. But she wouldn't hear of it. She did not want a pretender, even a Bonaparte pretender, to a non-existing throne to marry her daughter. She wanted the real thing."

"I suppose there were a number of real candidates," Robert remarked, "lining up for her on the Lichtentaler Allee, were there not?"

"Of course. Real or imaginary. One of them," MacDonald said, "was the Duke of Orléans, the oldest son of King Louis-Philippe. Unfortunately, nothing came of it, nor of a number of similarly ambitious plans. Then something unprecedented happened—a *coup de foudre*. Marie met William and they fell in love. Amazing. Very upsetting. One can imagine Stephanie's consternation. This happened in 1842, right here in Baden-Baden, while Stephanie was not looking. She had to concede that the young man was good looking and a great charmer, clearly a man of the world. But, being a Scot, he was not of her world. To her great chagrin, the engagement she had by then arranged with the safe and sober Prince Karl Egon von Fürstenberg, for whom she had been forced to settle, had to be broken. The principality of Fürstenberg had been dissolved by Napoleon in 1806. Karl Egon consoled himself, two generations later, by becoming one of the founders of the International Club and donor of the Fürstenberg Prize at Iffezheim, and one of the dignitaries who welcomed the Prince of Wales. But Stephanie became reconciled with William when she discovered that he was a member of a family whose claims to the throne of Scotland went back to the mists of antiquity, that he was to inherit substantial estates in southwestern Scotland yielding an income of precisely 157,602 pounds a year—I did not invent this figure, I remember it—once his seventy-five-year-old father died and he became the eleventh Duke of Hamilton, the eighth Duke of Brandon, and acquired a triple marquisate, four earldoms, and seven baronies and became premier peer of Scotland, and, as Duke of Arran, the proprietor of a large portion of that beautiful, magnificent island in the Firth of Clyde, not far from Glasgow. Stephanie did not know that they would have to wait for ten years before this happened, but she was a sensible woman and would never have had any doubts in her mind that all these unheard-of riches were well worth waiting for. Please roll over onto your back."

Robert did so.

"Ten blissfully happy years?" Robert asked, adjusting the towel.

"Far from it." Herr MacDonald began again from the top, first slapping Robert's cheeks. "The years began well enough with a splendid wedding in the *Schlosskirche* in Mannheim on February 23, 1843. First it was solemnized by a Protestant, then by an Anglican minister. For their honeymoon Marie and William travelled to Italy, France and England for six months. On September 14 they arrived on William's ancestral estates. Triumphal arches had been erected on the streets to welcome the bride from faraway Baden, and there were eight hundred guests at the wedding feast."

"I am amazed, Herr MacDonald, that you remember all these details."

"I know all the unimportant things. The important things I have never known." Herr MacDonald began hammering Robert's chest. "I have never known, for example, when the dark clouds first appeared on their marital horizon. Presumably they were still on reasonably good terms when their three children were born. But William was restless. He was a heavy drinker. When he was in Baden-Baden he spent far more time gambling in the Conversationshaus than making conversation at home with his unexciting wife and her unexciting guests, or playing with the children. This was the talk of the town right through the 1850s. By then he spent as much time as he could in Paris, where, thanks to his money and his wife's former suitor and imperial relative, all doors were open. Oh, by the way, he managed to persuade Napoleon III to recognize his right to the title Duke of Châtelherault, which had been conferred in 1548 to his ancestor James Hamilton,. Napoleon had probably never heard of Châtelherault. But he was prepared to do anything for the husband of an old friend. This was an affront to another James Hamilton, the tenth earl and second Marquis of Abercorn, a most eminent man, very much alive today, Governor General of Ireland, the direct descendant of the fourth son of the first Duke of Châtelherault, through the unbroken male line, uninterrupted by anybody marrying a female Hamilton for lack of a male heir. He is making an excellent case today for his own right to the dukedom of Châtelherault and, since he is a man of great accomplishments, and not merely a pleasure-loving absentee land-lord, he despised William, for cultivating his wife's good connections with that seedy, disreputable character in the Tuileries."

"What you are saying, Herr MacDonald, is that the Marquis of Abercorn claims the title."

"He does indeed." Herr MacDonald was testing Robert's stomach muscles. "May I go on? The decade of the eighteen-sixties was the heyday of the *belle époche*, just the right time, before Louis Napoleon's empire finally crumbled, for the eleventh

Duke of Hamilton to enjoy the company of scintillating artists and writers, not to mention women far, far more dazzling than his unexciting, aging Duchess. There are several accounts of William's death in the Maison Dorée in 1863 at the age of fifty-two. He may or may not have fallen downstairs after a drunken feast and broken his neck. He may or may not have had a stroke. Money and jewellery may or may not have disappeared from the lining of his coat. The Empress Eugénie may or may not have found him still alive."

"It must have a great shock for the Duchess," Robert said. "However bad the marriage."

"Oh yes, it was. My mother and father were both there when the news came and she rushed to Paris, with their two sons. I understand the Duchess has had a mild heart condition ever since. By the way, her pretty daughter Mary's first marriage also was troubled, with Prince Albert I of Monaco."

"Oh?"

"She spells Mary the English way—M-A-R-Y. Not very long ago she obtained an annulment from the Papal Consistory in Rome, even though they had a child, on the grounds, I was told, that in her heart she had never agreed to the marriage but had been forced into it by her mother and Napoleon III. I prefer not to comment. Mary is now happily married, as far as I know, to the Hungarian Count Tassilo Festetics of Tolna who serves in the Austrian Imperial Guards. There is also a younger brother, Charles, often called Carlos, about whom I only know—and I can't swear to that—that once, after he had been unusually lucky at the roulette tables, he went in the early morning hours, in a state of advanced inebriation, to the concierge of the Maison Messmer and announced 'I have my hat full of gold and demand to sleep with my aunt, Queen Augusta of Prussia!' This is, of course, a highly dubious story. Although Augusta and her husband Wilhelm I always stayed in the Maison Messmer when they were in Baden-Baden, she wasn't Carlos's aunt at all. His aunt Josephine—please note the name—was married to Karl Anton von Hohenzollern-Sigmaringen. That's as close as he got to the House of Hohenzollern. True, his mother was a first cousin of the Grand Duke who was the son-in-law of Queen Augusta, but that was hardly a closer relationship. But I am straying."

Herr MacDonald began work on Robert's arms, the left arm first. "Let us now consider the older brother, William Alexander, the twelfth Duke of Hamilton, the friend of the Prince of Wales, and a central figure in the present festivities. William is married to the eldest daughter of the seventh Duke of Manchester. He is now thirty-eight years old, three years younger than I am, but has achieved far less than I have—namely, exactly nothing."

"My dear Herr MacDonald," Robert cried, "what is a man in that position supposed to achieve? What did his father ever achieve?"

"Please let me switch to the right arm. Thank you. Men in their position," Herr MacDonald replied with surprising passion, "have many, many obligations. It is no excuse that his father set a bad example. Nor that William was brought up at a time when nothing mattered to people of their kind except the pursuit of pleasure. In 1865, he was twenty years old. And very, very rich. Although the *belle époche* in Paris was no longer as *belle* as it had been ten years earlier, for the young Hamiltons Baden-Baden was pure heaven. One orgy followed another. The women with whom they celebrated their good fortune were the most beautiful and the most expensive in the world. Just listen to the names of the young men, *la jeunesse dorée,* with whom every day and every night the twelfth Duke of Hamilton and his brother consorted—glittering names from the *ancien régime* such as the young Duke of Richelieu, the young Duke of Clermont-Tonnerre, the young Prince of Talleyrand-Périgord, the young Duke of Montmorency, as well as the three Turenne brothers, Guy, Louis and Léon. Then there were heroic names from the days of the first Napoleon, the young Prince Murat and the young Victor Masséna, the third Duke of Rivoli, later Prince of Essling. One of the many revellers from England, apart from the Prince of Wales, was the Duke of Marlborough, who, in bright moonlight, enjoyed sitting at the window stark naked playing the flute."

"Did he play well?" Robert asked.

"He played superbly." Herr MacDonald laughed. "Oh, I nearly forgot William's playmates from the Habsburg empire, led by the Archduke Victor, who had terribly protruding teeth— he was a younger brother of Kaiser Franz Joseph—and his friend Prince Esterhazy, who loved the horses. The Prussian contingent was headed by the three Radziwill brothers, Sigmund, Karl and Leo, the leading Bavarian was the young Prince Albert and Princess Maria Theresia von Thurn and Taxis, and, as for the Russians, let me just rattle off a few of the historic names— Obolenskii, Gagarin, Galatzin, Nesselrode, Trubetskoi, Olsufiev, Menschikov, Orlov-Denisov, Gorchakov, Smirnov, Stolypin, Shcherebatov, Nikolaevich—I could go on..."

"French, English, Prussian, Bavarian, Austrian, Russian," Robert observed sadly, "and not a Scottish name among them."

"That is not so shocking," Herr MacDonald exclaimed as he began slapping Robert's left thigh, hard. "What is shocking is William's conspicuous, outrageous neglect of his responsibilities as a landowner towards his dependents, tenants and retainers. In particular, his high-handed conduct towards his people on the island of Arran. That is outrageous. He treats his estates solely as a hunting park and a preserve for the exclusive use of himself and his friends. During the shooting season nobody else is allowed to visit the island, for fear that they might disturb the game and ruin His Grace's sport. Those who live there are, of course, regarded as a nuisance. This is an insult to the citizens of Glasgow, for whom the island, so close by, is a favourite resort. William's ancestors had made vital contributions to the commercial growth of the city and the port and taken pride in the city's development, and cared for the people. Not many people are sorry for him now that he is in some financial difficulty."

"Oh? That must be a new experience for him."

"It is." Herr MacDonald nodded as he began work on Robert's right thigh. "This is no secret. It all came out into the open two or three years ago when he brought a lawsuit against his estate agent. At that time he owed a million and a half pounds.

Since then he has sold the Beckworth Library he inherited and a number of magnificent paintings. But I understand he's still in serious trouble."

Herr MacDonald paused. "We are nearly finished. Are you ready? Tell me, who stole Josephine's earrings?"

"Please, give me a minute to think."

Robert closed his eyes and went into a trance

"All right," Robert said when he woke up. "The first candidate is the Duchess's *Beschliesserin*, the servant responsible for locking things up, who is a friend of her son William's tenant on the Isle of Arran. William's men had prevented the tenant's lady friend, who lived in Glasgow, from visiting him during the hunting season."

"Excellent. And the second candidate?"

"He's the pastry cook in the Bayrische Hof," Robert replied with impressive assurance. "He used to be William's estate agent. The lawsuit you just mentioned ruined him totally. He's the uncle of one of the Duchess's chambermaids who acted for him."

"Splendid. And the third?"

"That's easy," Robert announced triumphantly. "The third candidate is Mrs. Edmund Jenkins, the wife of the *Haushofmeister* in the Palais Hamilton. Mrs. Jenkins' mother is a third cousin of a valet of the eminent and distinguished James Hamilton, the tenth earl and second Marquis of Abercorn. Surely, if anybody has a valid motive for commissioning a solid strike against William's mother, it is the rightful Duke of Châtelherault."

Robert did not pay for the massage.

Chapter 7

On the morning of Tuesday, August 28, Robert had a pleasant chat after breakfast with Fräulein Gertrud Fröhlich about her happy days with Clara Schumann's eight children in Lichtental, when she was their governess, and was in high spirits as he walked from the Werderstrasse down the hill to the Promenade to visit Louis Katzau. There was absolutely no reason for his being in such a good mood. The glorious weather was no excuse. Judged by any objective standards he should have been in the depths of gloom. He knew, one day before his self-imposed deadline was to expire, that the chances of a breakthrough were remote.

But during the night he had remembered an idea he had immediately after meeting his congenial new friend Louis Katzau, an idea that had been pushed aside by Josephine's jewels and was clearly a direct consequence of Herr MacDonald's stimulating massage. If Josephine's jewels proved to be elusive, as he was beginning to believe, what about asking Louis Katzau whether by next summer some sort of working arrangement might be worked out, perhaps in conjunction with his neighbour in Boutique Number Three, the jeweller Theodor Klammerer, whom he had yet to meet? That way his excursion to Baden-Baden would not have been wasted after all. But it was too soon to broach the subject with Katzau.

Boutique Number Five was crowded. Business was booming. By the time Robert arrived Katzau had already sold a Bohemian crystal candelabra, a Bavarian gold-tipped bamboo cane and a blue-and-white Florentine tile depicting the Madonna and Child, from the school of Luca della Robbia.

Katzau was holding forth. The subject was tonight's electric illumination of the Conversationshaus, the Trinkhalle, the theatre, the big hotels, the Palais Hamilton and the Leopoldsdenkmal, the monument of Grand Duke Leopold who had turned Baden-Baden into a world centre—for the first time. So far only the International Club had been electrically illuminated, in honour of the Prince of Wales a few days earlier. Katzau confided to his customers that the city had made the decision only after it had heard that His Royal Highness Grand Duke Friedrich himself was going to be in town.

A lady in a big white hat sporting precisely fourteen ostrich feathers said that probably the time was not too far off when everybody in Baden-Baden would have a *telephone*. Richard Pohl's *Badeblatt* carried a little news story she had just read, to the effect that the cities of Holland and Belgium were already being connected by telephone. Why was Baden-Baden so late?

Since Katzau did not have the answer, he preferred to discuss tonight's costume ball—the *Cercle-Ball*—another "regular Roman Carnival in August," he called it. What were the ladies and gentlemen present going to wear? The ball's theme was *paysan ou domestique*, deliberately prosaic to render the contrast with the accompanying (unofficial) bacchanalia even more delectable than they would have been had the theme been the more appropriate Court of Louis XIV. There was no need for Katzau to spell out that no doubt masked revellers would find the idea of amorous adventures with unidentifiable fellow-revellers disguised as members of the lower classes pleasantly alluring, nor did he have to remind his audience that ladies (other than professional *cocottes*) frequently dreamed about such exhilarating couplings but rarely executed them. No, he did not mention that. But he did say that everyone had to wear a costume, mere evening dresses for ladies and tail-coats for gentlemen not being sufficient. Masks, however, were not obligatory. One lady said she was going as a Hungarian gypsy, another as a washerwoman, a third as a dairymaid, whereas one gentleman had made arrangements in his hotel to borrow a cook's uniform, another intended to go as a blacksmith and a third—very daringly—planned to attend the ball disguised as a *sans-culottes*, a French revolutionary soldier—from the country, of course, to qualify as a *paysan*.

"Herr Koch," Katzau welcomed Robert, "you should have been here half an hour ago. You would have met Signora Emma Turolla."

Robert had read about the beautiful young Italian opera singer, a rising star who had received flattering reviews in "music tsar" Richard Pohl's *Badeblatt*.

"A delightful lady, very anxious to practise her German. She can't be over twenty-five. Her great ambition is to sing Wagner. She told me she made her debut in Tiflis five years ago singing Rossini's *Semiramis*. Both her parents had been singers engaged by the imperial opera there. Her father was the director. So I sold her the baton that Maestro Henry Panofka used when he performed Rossini's *Stabat Mater* here, with first-class soloists he brought over from Paris. That was in 1842, before my time. The signora was delighted. I asked for two hundred marks."

"Which she happily paid?"

"She certainly did not," Katzau laughed. "She wanted it for half the price. We settled for hundred and fifty, on the understanding that I get two free tickets for *La Juive*, for Wednesday. She will sing Rachel. For you and me."

"What a good idea," Robert. "Thank you. I've always been a little afraid of that opera."

"So have I," Katzau confessed. "Now I must tell you," he lowered his voice, "I have a very important new idea. Let's go to my office. I want to show you something." To his customers he said, "Please excuse us for just a moment."

They went to the office at the back of the boutique and sat down.

"You've heard the Comte de Chambord died last Friday, in exile in Frohsdorf in Austria?"

Yes, Robert had heard the news. The Count, of the elder Bourbon line, born in 1820, the son of the assassinated Duke of Bordeaux, was a grandson of King Charles X, who had lost the French throne in 1830 and had been forced to flee when his cousin Louis-Philippe seized the throne. He was a strong Catholic, a strict traditionalist, an obstinate, austere man who believed in the divine right of kings. His claim to the French throne as Henri V was "Legitimist," and was disputed by the "Orléanist" claim made by Louis-Philippe's grandson, Philippe, the Comte de Paris, who was eighteen years younger than his bitter rival. They were the two irreconcilable "branches of the Bourbon lily." One reason for their passionate hostility was the memory, on both sides, of the events in 1830, when Louis-Philippe, to whom Charles X had entrusted the ten-year-old Prince on his abdication, made himself king. The other reason was the Comte de Chambord's rigidly high-principled intransigence.

"Look at this."

Katzau handed Robert a copy of today's *Badeblatt*.

Paris, August 20.

> The testament of the Comte de Chambord is being hotly discussed here. Many papers believe that it will give the Orléanists the *coup de grâce* and cause their party the kind of embarrassment the testament of the late *prince impérial* created for the Bonapartists. One may be sure that the Orléanists will not attempt a risky coup, but their intentions, it is said, have not changed in the least. They hope that the Radicals and the Autonomists will topple the Gambettists, after which their friends will come to power through parliamentary means.

Robert looked puzzled.

"Don't worry. It will become clear to you in a minute or two," Katzau assured him in a hushed voice. "There is something else that has not been reported in the press. There may or may not be a connection. Listen. This morning I had a letter from a business colleague of mine in Paris who drew my attention to a burglary of Josephine's Château Malmaison. Many of her clothes, including the gown she wore during her coronation, were stolen, as well as other relics, such as some of her jewellery and powder boxes. My colleague thought one of two of these valuable objects might come my way, and that I should know about them."

"But what could possibly be the connection?' Robert asked, scratching the back of his head.

"My dear Herr Koch," Katzau said irritably, "I did not say there was a connection. I said there *may* be one."

There was prolonged silence while Katzau tried to put the pieces together.

"I have always had trouble with the French Republic," Katzau cried. "All those parties! Who can tell them apart? And all those pretenders to a throne that doesn't exist. Things were easy when there was one throne and when there was just one Napoleon sitting on it." He paused. Suddenly, he jumped up from his chair, galvanized. "I just had a thought. What day is it?"

"Tuesday."

"Perfect! What luck! Tuesday is the day for her salon. Are you free tonight?" Robert nodded. "Then let's go and see Jeanne Archambault, the only person in Baden-Baden who understands French politics. She'll find the connection!"

•　　•　　•

At around five that afternoon, their carriage took them south along the Lichtentaler Allee, passing the Hotel Stephanie-les-Bains, and then along the winding Tiergartenweg up the Fremersberg to Jeanne Archambault's small villa, just to the north of the Swiss chalet that, until 1870, was inhabited by the famous singer and composer Pauline Viardot, the renowned Russian writer's Ivan Turgenev's life-long friend, and her family. Robert was vaguely familiar with both names, but did not know much about them. Katzau pointed out the *Kunsthalle* in the garden, now empty.

"You will be impressed by this witty old lady and her guests," Katzau said. "Usually a few articulate, amusing people drop in when she has open house on Tuesdays. Not the great names with the long titles and the big bank accounts, who never smile. They go to your Duchess on Thursdays. But people from the theatre, and some musicians and poets, and always a politician or two. They prefer Jeanne. She also likes young officers. Even the odd professor turns up. And newspapermen. They come, not only to be with her but also to meet the beautiful women she always invites. Being an old actress, and an old professional courtesan, she believes that whatever it is that goes on between men and women is the most important thing in the world. What fascinates her most is the intimate connection between love and money. I think it was in Jeanne's salon that somebody first said 'the religion of money is today the only one that has no unbelievers'."

"Herr Katzau," Robert said, "did I understand you right? Did you say 'courtesan'?"

"I don't suppose you people in Frankfurt have heard of them. You probably think they are just expensive..." He would not pronounce the word.

"No, but..."

"No need to finish the sentence, Herr Koch. I know, being a jeweller, you are not naive about the many ways in which love can be bought. People like you and me often benefit from such transactions and understand that they are often cleaner and more honest than others that are less straightforward and all too often involve a great deal of lying. We are on the side of transactions that are honest and serious and not what is fake and frivolous, are we not? There are real pearls, and there are imitation pearls. The same in politics. Napoleon I was real. Napoleon III was imitation. There wasn't even a blood relationship between him and the real Napoleon. I am not sure anybody knows who Napoleon III's father was, but it is absolutely certain that his mother, Hortense, who was the daughter of Josephine and the Marquis

Alexandre de Beauharnais, had conceived him with somebody other than her husband, Louis, Napoleon's brother. You see, almost nothing that happened in France, and therefore in Baden-Baden, during those twenty-one years in which Napoleon III was in charge, nominally, was genuine and serious. Everything was frivolous. The serious things had all happened before—the French Revolution, the first Napoleon, the Restoration and the revolutions of 1830 and 1848. In times of frivolity, pleasure and money are the only things that matter. Hence the flowering of courtesans during the *belle époche*. They give pleasure and cost money."

Katzau had every right to be pleased by his *bon mot*.

"So I have observed." Robert was amused. Katzau had done him a grave injustice. Robert explained to him with some satisfaction that he had met several courtesans in his store in Frankfurt, though they were usually called friends, sometimes nieces. "I look forward to meeting the lady."

"Let me tell you her story, Herr Koch. It sounds like a Balzac novel."

This is the story. Jeanne's family was poor. Her father, a farmer in Normandy, beat her. At fourteen, she discovered that men liked her. She also discovered that she liked men, but not quite as much as they liked her. She went to Paris. She was told she was beautiful, she should go on the stage. She did. No doubt she made strategic use of her beauty as she climbed her way up in the world of the theatre. The high point of her career was her performance of Célimène in Molière's *Le Misanthrope*. One thing followed another. Jeanne had learned early that money was power. She was lucky, unlike her colleague in the demimonde Alphonsine Plessis, Alexander Dumas's *La Dame aux Camélias* and Verdi's *La Traviata*, who died of consumption at the age of twenty-three, by which time she had become the Comtesse de Perregaux."

For a moment Robert was deflected by a heavily powdered dowager descending from her coach, outside what was probably the gate to her villa, with the help of a gallant young man, her son or lover.

"Please pay attention, Herr Koch. Jeanne taught herself Parisian French. She was excellent company. She read books. She was interested in politics. She surprised her aristocratic patrons with her *esprit*. She was not shy and had a sharp tongue. Unlike Madame de Maintenon, a singularly plain woman, who became the mistress and then the second wife of Louis XIV and thus the untitled Queen of France, by her intellect alone, Jeanne had beauty *and* intellect. She was ambitious and wanted to play a role in the world at a time of unprecedented economic expansion. Bourgeois wives and mothers do not. Jeanne made her choice and never regretted it. The three of four rich and sometimes noble benefactors she chose in succession were not as bright as she was. One was a director of the *Crédit Lyonnais*, another a successful speculator at the Bourse in railway shares. They were men she could—and did—influence, even dominate, usually for sensible and mutually profitable purposes, not only because she relished the power this gave her but also because she adored the material rewards—the villas, the jewellery from the rue de la Paix, the clothes from Worth and Laferrière—that were showered upon her. She always had affection for her men, and they for her. She would never associate with men she despised. She stimulated their intellect as well as their senses and managed the transitions from one to the next smoothly, with tact and skill, in a business-like manner, without unnecessary pain, scandal and acrimony. They always remained friends. All this was entirely in tune with the spirit of the Second Empire."

"As exemplified by this lovely little château here." Robert, clearly hoping for high praise from his lecturer, pointed to a large, elaborately ornamented structure, behind a row of oak trees, that looked like a bank.

"I am proud of you, Herr Koch. I have no doubt you will go far as long as you understand, as I think you do, the way things change from one era to another. In today's Republic money still counts, of course, but the carnival is over and pleasure no longer comes first. Just before the disaster of 1870 Jeanne's last patron, the elderly Comte Jean-Marc de Marigny, married her. After the war and the commune (he and Jeanne had fled south), they moved to this villa"—the carriage was approaching a small château—"to spend the rest of his life here with her, ignoring the vulgar republic on their side of the Rhine, knowing that she would care for him in this residual outpost of the *belle époche* in his last years. She did so, with tender kindness and affection. In 1880, he died and left all his considerable properties to her." He reached the end of the story just as the carriage came to a stop.

The coachman helped the two friends out the carriage, and then joined the other coachmen to have a beer and a smoke under an old oak tree in the garden next door.

A maid showed them in.

Several groups were engaged in lively conversations while three uniformed waiters were offering hors d'oeuvres and petits fours on golden trays, refilling the guests' glasses. The large salon was dominated by a grand piano covered with framed pictures and photographs, which guests occasionally picked up and inspected. There were occasional bursts of laughter. Katzau and Robert relished the stimulating aroma of cigar smoke and expensive perfumes.

Now in her late seventies, heavily powdered and endowed with a magnificent (possibly genuine) beauty spot on her left cheek, and still very handsome, Jeanne Archambault led them to a group where a spirited French-German conversation was in progress, both languages being used interchangeably.

Before she left them there, Louis whispered to her, "We have a lovely little problem which we want you to solve for us. No hurry."

"I'll do my best, Louis. I'll be back in a minute."

There were no introductions. Jeanne believed more sparks would fly if it was assumed everybody knew everybody else.

"I don't think it will ever be ready in time," Frau von Blankenberg said sardonically, referring to the *Niederwalddenkmal*, the patriotic monument triumphantly celebrating the Prussian victory over France and the unification of the Reich that was to be inaugurated in four weeks' time on the west slopes of the Taunus Mountains, near the Rhine at Rüdesheim, provocatively facing France. The celebration was to be performed in the presence of Kaiser Wilhelm and Prince Otto von Bismarck and an assortment of German princes including Grand Duke Friedrich of Baden. Frau von Blankenberg was the wife of an anti-Bismarck staff officer, a friend of the Crown Prince. "The bronze statue of *War* is in place, so is *Germania*, with a lovely crown on her head. But *Peace* is keeping everybody waiting. I think they'll manage quite nicely without, don't you?"

"They're having a problem casting it in Nürnberg," Herr Norbert Dibelius, a reporter for the *Frankfurter Zeitung*, interjected. "Is that what you also hear in Paris?"

He addressed the question to Gaston Moret, a colleague of *Le Figaro*, a tall man who wore a pince-nez. He nodded emphatically and said "Yes, that's what I heard, too."

"I realize," Dibelius went on, "that it is tempting to see profound symbolism in the delay, *madame*. But I'm afraid that is not quite fair."

"Fairness has never been my forte," Frau von Blankenberg conceded bravely, amidst laughter. "My convictions come first."

"That's what a lot of former *communards* in Paris say at this very moment," Irène Lumeau observed. She was a ravishing beauty, daringly *décolletée*, recently divorced by a left-wing lawyer in nearby Strasbourg. "These people don't want to participate in the inauguration of the monument dedicated to the defence of Paris. Like my former husband, they put their conviction of socialism first. Ahead of patriotism. Disgusting. I still get goose pimples when I remember Bismarck's troops marching down the Champs Elysées."

She turned to Robert, putting her face close to his. "I hope you weren't among them?"

"*Madame*," Robert found his thought processes clouded by the perfume exuding from her *décolletage*, "I come from the formerly free city of Frankfurt," he replied. "It was free until Bismarck made it unfree, in 1866. No, we did not fight for Bismarck."

Katzau was proud of his new friend.

"And you, Herr Katzau," Irène Lumeau turned to him—

they had met before—"you are a Hungarian. You have no convictions?"

"We Hungarians worship beauty. That is a full-time job." He gave her a low bow.

"As you will see," Jeanne Archambault overheard this remark, "when you visit Louis Katzau's boutique. But you must bring a lot of cash. He raises his prices every day. Come with me." She dragged him away to find out what his "lovely little problem" was.

She took him to a potted palm near the front window. Katzau told her at great length about Josephine's jewels, the last will and testament of the Comte de Chambord and the burglary of Malmaison. In the meantime Robert went to the piano to inspect the pictures.

First, he picked up a photograph of the Comte de Morny, the intelligent and gifted son of Hortense and her lover the Comte Charles de Flahaut who himself was, so he wanted everybody to believe, the illegitimate son of Talleyrand. It may even have been true. As Napoleon III's half-brother, he was a pillar of the régime until his death in 1865. It was Morny who had engineered the coup in 1851 that made Louis Napoleon Prince-President. It was also Morny who had, in collaboration with Offenbach, dashed off (between a diplomatic reception and a public speech) the libretto of a one-act *opérette-bouffe* that turned out to be a considerable success. It was called *Monsieur Choufleury restera chez lui.*

Irène Lumeau resumed her conversation with Robert.

"Old-timers here still talk about this man's many visits to Baden-Baden." She pointed to Morny's photograph. "He usually came with Cora Pearl. Once, when she was thrown out of the casino because of her outrageously eccentric behaviour, he escorted her back in triumph. No one would refuse to admit a lady at the arm of the Comte de Morny, the half-brother of the French Emperor, even though everyone knew he was a prominent member of the demimonde and had no more right to call himself Comte than you have."

"Alas, I only have ambitions," Robert observed sadly.

"And you will achieve them, I have no doubt. Yes," Irène reminisced, "Cora Pearl certainly knew how to choose her men. When you go to a bordello, monsieur, you do the choosing, do you not, not the ladies?"

"I do indeed, *madame*."

They smiled at each other.

"You see," Irène continued, "Cora Pearl belonged to a profession that allowed the ladies to do the choosing. Of all the *grandes cocottes* she was possibly the most successful, judged by the lavish wealth her lovers bestowed on her. Her breasts were world-famous but Alphonse Daudet thought her mouth was like a sewer. Cora rode like an Amazon and was much, much kinder to her horses than to her lovers. The truth is that she detested all men as a result of a humiliating experience she had suffered early in life. Some of her lovers may have found this exciting. Perhaps Morny did. He certainly showered presents on her. Did you know her real name was Eliza Emma Couch and she came from Plymouth?"

"I don't think she is at all my type, *madame*. Who is this?"

Robert picked up a photograph of smiling boy, about five years old, in an embroidered sailor's suit. Irène explained that it was the *prince impérial*, the only son and heir of Napoleon III and Eugénie. Had it not been for his birth after a long waiting period, Eugénie might well have suffered the same fate as Josephine—divorce for failing to produce a male heir. (Since the early days of her marriage, she thought her fate might one day be that of Marie-Antoinette, a lady with whom she a deeper sense of affinity than with Josephine. Marie-Antoinette had always remained *l'Autrichienne* at the French court, just as Eugénie never got over being *l'Espagnole*). The Prince died in the South African jungle four years ago, in 1879, six years after his father's death, fighting in the Zulu war as a volunteer for the British. He was twenty-four.

"One does not have to be a Bonapartist," Irène said, "to shed a tear for the family. Do you know who this is?"

She pointed to a drawing of Princess Mathilde Bonaparte,

an elegant middle-aged lady whose vivid dark eyes and round Italian face bore a remarkable resemblance to Napoleon's.

Robert detected a distinct family resemblance to himself.

"An illegitimate daughter?" he asked.

"On the contrary! The very opposite!" Mathilde, she explained, was a niece, the daughter of Jérôme, Napoleon's youngest brother, and Catherine of Württemberg, the fruit of perhaps the only marriage arranged by Napoleon with a German princess that was happy from beginning to end. Before Napoleon III was married, Mathilde acted as his hostess in the Tuileries. That was after his other cousin, Stephanie of Baden, had declined the role. Mathilde, *Notre Dame des Arts*, was a much admired, generous patroness who conducted a brilliant literary and artistic salon. She was a friend of Jeanne Archambault's but not of Eugénie's, whom she detested and whom she blamed, among many other things, in 1870, for ignoring the evidence of her husband's deteriorating health and driving him into war, or at any rate not dissuading him from going to war. She even blamed Eugénie for indirectly causing her son's death because he preferred becoming a soldier, and dying for the British, to living with her.

"And who is that?"

It was a photograph of a tall man with a round face, beardless, in full ambassadorial uniform, his chest covered with decorations.

"I hope you are not disappointed, *monsieur*," Irène laughed, "but this time the child *is* illegitimate! It's Comte Alexandre Waleski."

Robert noted, with peculiar satisfaction, an uncanny resemblance to himself.

"You may have heard of his mother, the beautiful, blue-eyed Polish patriot, Countess Marie Waleska, who opened her bedroom door to Napoleon in Warsaw because allowing him to seduce her would free her country from Russian oppression. Her husband encouraged her."

"Yes," Robert said. He happened to be very, very familiar with that kind of situation.

"You know, after that they really did fall in love," Irène continued, slightly puzzled by Robert's somewhat unusual response. "She went to see him in Elba, with Alexandre, who was four at the time, which is more than his wife Marie-Louise did with their legitimate son. And Marie visited Josephine just before Josephine died. It's all very, very touching. She even went to Boulogne with their son to say goodbye to Napoleon before the English shipped him off to St. Helena."

"And so a few decades later Alexandre became his nephew's ambassador," Robert said, his eyes on Waleski's portrait.

"Yes, in London. And President of the Chamber. But that was not his only contribution to the Emperor. His wife, the beautiful Florentine Marie-Anne Ricci, became one the Emperor's innumerable mistresses, triggering the historically correct observation that every Bonaparte in power sleeps with a Countess Waleska. When her husband died in 1868, the Emperor said, sadly, perhaps Alexandre had not been a great statesman, but on the other hand France had none. One of Waleski's mistresses was this amazing woman. She was the mother of one of his children."

Irène pointed to a little watercolour in a gold frame of the great tragic actress Rachel, the illegitimate daughter of a Jewish peddler. *Moi toute juive*, she used to boast. Her promiscuity was legendary, unlike that of the heroines she played who invariably preferred death to dishonour. Jeanne Archambault had shared the stage with her at the *Comédie-Française* more than once.

"Let me tell you a story." Irène was evidently having a splendid time enlightening Robert about Jeanne's friends. "While Louis Napoleon was still a mere plotter and ladies' man in London, in 1846, Rachel was there, too, playing a season at the St. James Theatre. They were having an affair, off and on. One day he accompanied her on a tour to the provinces, by train. He took his cousin Prince Napoleon along—Princess Mathilde's younger brother—to keep them company. Louis Napoleon fell asleep near Birmingham. When he opened his eyes, Rachel and his cousin were making love on the opposite seat. He closed his eyes again. The next day he returned to London, without a word of explanation, leaving the two together to consummate their passion for each other in comfort, undisturbed. What do you think of that, *monsieur?*"

"Self-sacrifice, discretion and a complete absence of jealousy," Robert responded, "have always been family characteristics."

Once again, a slightly peculiar answer, Irène thought, but not peculiar enough to dwell upon.

"Ah, here's a picture of Plon-Plon. That was the name they gave Prince Napoleon later."

Robert would have recognized him as a relative anywhere.

"A very eloquent face," he remarked.

"The *enfant terrible* of the Second Empire," Irène said, "but Napoleon liked him, and always forgave him for the trouble he caused him by his undiplomatic behaviour. As a left-wing progressive, calling himself Citizen Bonaparte, he had opposed the *coup d'état*. But Louis Napoleon did it anyway. When he was his ambassador in Madrid accredited to the Bourbon court, Citizen Bonaparte told everybody he thought all Bourbon dynasties should be kicked off the thrones of Europe because they were reactionary. No wonder Queen Isabella demanded his recall! After the Second Empire was established, the Prince became heir to the throne. After all, he was a first cousin. He was given a wing of the Palais-Royal as his official residence and a million francs a year from the civil list and became a bitter enemy of Empress Eugénie, whom he regarded as a right-wing bigot. And whom he never forgave her doing her duty and producing the *prince impérial*, thus putting an end to his role as heir to throne. However, this *Caesar déclassé* on one occasion did his duty to the Emperor."

"Only once?

"Let's say, on one important occasion, when he married Clotilde of Savoy. She was the saintly fifteen-year-old daughter of Victor Emmanuel, King of Piedmont, and he married her in order to help forge a French-Savoy-Piedmont alliance as a prelude to Napoleon III's contemplated armed intervention in the *Risorgimento*, as liberator, following in his uncle's footsteps. This marriage had been engineered by Camillo Cavour, Italy's counterpart to Bismarck, the diplomatic unifier of *his* country. The Prince's sister, Mathilde, referred to the marriage as a means to put 'the devil in a holy water bowl.' The not-so-young husband of course found diversion in the arms of many less holy ladies. Clotilde, on the other hand, remained fond of him and comforted herself with good works. Soon he was universally known as Plon-Plon. As Commander of the Third Division during the Crimean War, he had been accused of fearing *plomb*, which, as I'm sure you know, referred to the lead in their cannons. That is how he earned the nickname. Much later, after nine years of marriage, Plon-Plon asked to be introduced to—guess whom?"

"Cora Pearl."

"You are brilliant, *monsieur*! Did you know that?"

It was beneath Robert's dignity to reply.

"Plon-Plon established her in a *palais* of her own, on the rue de Chaillot, which became known as Les Petites Tuileries, and paid her twelve thousand francs a month. Later, he gave her a second house, on the rue des Bassins. He maintained Cora in grand style for nine years. During early evenings *à deux* in the Palais-Royal they sometimes heard Princess Clotilde talking to the children next door. This embarrassed Cora but apparently not him."

Jeanne Archambault had arrived while Irène was still talking, with Louis Katzau in tow.

"We've solved your lovely little problem, with the help of the great journalist Gaston Moret," Jeanne announced to Robert after she had finished. "He has come through triumphantly. And one of the children Irène just mentioned turns out to be a key figure in the solution. It's a small world."

"What little problem?" Irène asked.

"Come with us and you'll find out."

Louis Katzau took Robert by the arm.

"Once again, our hostess has outdone herself," he whispered to Robert.

Jeanne, Irène, Katzau and Robert wove their way through the smoke-and-perfume-filled room to Gaston Moret, the tall, elegant journalist of *Le Figaro* who, with his pince-nez, looked like a Sorbonne professor. The two ladies sat down on a chaise longue, Katzau and Robert found chairs. Moret preferred to remain standing, waving his hands as he talked.

"Mesdames et messieurs," he began, "I was asked to find the connection between the theft of Josephine's earrings in the Palais Hamilton, a similar theft at Malmaison and the death of the Comte de Chambord in Austria. That connection is crystal clear. Grasping it, however, requires a short lecture on French politics."

Moret did not like his location and moved a few steps towards his left.

"Thank heavens," he resumed, "that the Third Republic is now securely in the hands of Republicans. This has not always been the case, and there are still people in the country who dream of restoring the monarchy. They are, on the one hand, the Bonapartists, whose support comes mainly from a few hundred sentimental Napoleon worshippers in all classes, some of them influential journalists such as Frédéric Masson, and others peasants. Which is not unimportant since France is primarily a rural country. And, on the other hand, the Royalists. Let's talk about Bonapartists first.

"One would have thought that Bonapartism had been largely discredited by the humiliation of 1870. But, strange to say, it was not. For a short time in 1872, there was even a serious danger of a return of Louis Napoleon's odious régime. Bismarck found negotiations with the Republican leadership exasperating and used the threat of supporting the return of Louis Napoleon, who was his prisoner in Germany, as a bargaining tool."

"Not very nice of our man Bismarck," Louis Katzau pulled down the corners of his mouth, "considering that his prisoner was near death."

"Was it not Bismarck who coined the word *Realpolitik?*" Moret asked rhetorically. "May I continue? Bismarck was being entirely realistic. He thought it would be easier to establish a reasonable relationship between France and Germany if he had to deal with the Second Empire than with the Third Republic. A shadow cabinet was quickly drawn up. But fortunately none of this materialized. In the following years there were Bonapartist demonstrations every August—we called them 'August scares'—on the anniversary of Napoleon's birthday on August the fifteenth. Sometimes the *prince impérial* made speeches in Chislehurst, where he lived with his mother, Eugénie."

"Not very happily, I understand," Irène observed.

"True," Moret agreed. "It is hard to live with one's mother if one is a restless young former heir to the throne. May I now proceed to say a word about the Royalists?"

"Just a second, *monsieur*," Jeanne Archambault stopped him. "You have said nothing about Plon-Plon nor about his son Victor, one of the children playing next door with his saintly mother while Plon-Plon was enjoying himself with Cora Pearl."

"Please, *madame*, do not rush me. I was coming to that later. I am now going to say something about the House of Bourbon, the Royalists. They are divided between the moderate Orléanists, led by Philippe, the Comte de Paris, the grandson of the Louis-Philippe whose advice to one and all was *enrichissez-vous*! And then there are the strictly traditional Legitimists, who, until his death this week, were headed by the devout Comte de Chambord, the grandson of Charles X, who hoped to become Henri V. The Legitimists' support comes from sections of the military and from those in the noblesse nostalgic for the *ancien régime*. The revolutionary former *communards* in the big cities—Marxists, syndicalists and anarchists—are outside the system. Trade unions are illegal."

"Why don't the two Bourbon parties work together?" Robert asked.

"Excellent question, *monsieur*. At one time there was actually a possibility that they might do that, in which case they would have become a major factor. But they became irreconcilable largely because of the high-minded stubbornness of the Comte de Chambord. He insisted on restoring the flag of Henri

IV if and when he came to power. When asked whether under the circumstances a compromise with the *tricolor* might perhaps be expedient, he replied, 'I have neither sacrifice to make nor conditions to accept.'"

"Are you saying," Louis Katzau asked, "that the Count's death strengthens the more flexible and realistic Orléanists?"

"That is what I am saying."

Gaston stopped, took off his pince-nez and slowly wiped it with his handkerchief. He then turned to address Jeanne.

"*Madame*, at last the time has come for me to say something about Plon-Plon. For the Bonapartists to make a comeback, they needed a popular leader. But the leader they had, Plon-Plon, was universally detested, so much so that the *prince impérial*, shortly before embarking on his fatal trip to Zululand, wrote a codicil to his will in which he had appointed him official heir, substituting his son, Victor, a good Catholic, unlike his detested, freethinking father. Plon-Plon refused to accept this and publicly fought back—thereby dividing the Bonapartists between the *Jérômists*, named after Plon-Plon's father, Napoleon's youngest brother Jérôme, and a larger number of Victor's followers, named, naturally, *Victoriens*. Plon-Plon refused to yield an inch. Last year he drew up a letter for Victor to sign. In it Victor renounced all the rights conferred upon him by the *prince impérial*. Victor was tired of the family quarrel and nearly signed. At the last minute he was dissuaded by his followers. They pointed out to him that he deserved to be their leader because he had not followed the example of his detestable father but that of his saintly mother, Princess Clotilde. They insisted on honouring the last wishes of the *prince impérial*."

Robert had no idea what all this had to do with Josephine's jewels, but left it to Louis Katzau to follow through.

"So what you are saying, *monsieur*," Katzau asked, "is that the death of the Comte de Chambord brought things to a head?"

"That is what I am saying," Moret replied a little irritably. "Surely it is obvious that it strengthened the Orléanists under Philippe, the Comte de Paris. And now that the Bonapartists have a respected leader, Prince Victor, what do they need to outmanoeuvre the Orléanists? The answer is obvious. They need sacred relics—relics from the Golden Age of Napoleon the First. And who was the one undisputed goddess of that Golden Age? Josephine! Every Frenchman's heart beats faster when he think of her. And every French woman's weeps for her because Napoleon had to abandon her to fulfil his destiny. Her relics must be obtained at any price, even if it means stealing them from her château in Malmaison, *and* from that of her granddaughter, by adoption, in the Palais Hamilton here in Baden-Baden."

Chapter 8

Under normal circumstances Robert would by now have given up hope to find Josephine's earrings within the time available to him. So many brilliant theories and possibilities, so many excellent reasons for stealing them, and not a single concrete clue! The Russians had good reasons to believe the jewels really belonged to them; the heirs of Queen Victoria's half-sister may well have been tempted to snatch them; the Duchess of Hamilton was vulnerable to extortion by idealistic revolutionaries; her delinquent and unpopular late husband had a claim to a title that was being challenged, a situation crying out for retribution if not self-help, and the Bonapartists in France needed a relic of Josephine. When would there be a breakthrough which would prove one theory correct and all the others false, so that he could at last retrieve the jewels, present them to the Duchess and conquer the world?

But, surprisingly, Robert was far from despondent. This was largely due to Louis Katzau's infectious exuberant personality and Robert's own growing conviction, so far unspoken, that in the overwhelmingly likely case that there would be no breakthrough, he would still be able to make some kind of business arrangements with Katzau for the summer seasons to come.

In the morning of Wednesday, August 29, Robert arrived in Katzau's boutique at about ten. In the evening they had tickets for the opera *La Juive*, starring Emma Turolla.

A tall, garrulous, overdressed lady arrived. She carried an

umbrella although the sun was shining and said she wanted something for her daughter-in-law's birthday, making it clear that she was not very fond of her daughter-in-law. Guessing the customer's political views, Katzau suggested a plaster head of Bismarck.

"Oh, what a good idea. Did you read in the paper that he is leaving Bad Kissingen today?"

"No, I hadn't seen that," Katzau replied absent-mindedly while looking for a box to put Bismarck in. He found one and wrapped the bust. The lady with the umbrella left happily.

The next customer was Countess Mary Festetics, the Duchess of Hamilton's daughter. Together with Princess Wolkowsky and Princess zu Fürstenberg and fourteen other prominent ladies, she was organizing the Bazaar for the Poor, which was to open tomorrow in the electrically illuminated Gartensaal of the International Club. The ladies hoped the bazaar would yield at least six thousand marks. In the evening three male choirs would perform *Aurelia, Hohenbaden* and the *Turnverein*. There would also be folk dancing by the *Schwarzwälder Hochzeitszug*.

Countess Mary asked Katzau whether he might be prepared to lend them six vases for flower arrangements.

Katzau said he would be delighted.

"How is Her Highness?" he asked.

"To be frank, Herr Katzau, she can't wait for the Prince of Wales to leave. Today she has to go with him to the photographer Kunzemüller to have pictures of him taken, together with his friends, and yesterday she had to arrange a meeting with Signor Corrodi, who, years ago, had taught the Princess of Wales painting. I am sure you know him well."

"I do indeed."

"A good thing the Prince is leaving on Monday, so she can enjoy the rest of the season with my brothers and me without having to speak English to the Prince's friends all the time. I know how she feels. Learning Hungarian is bad enough."

Katzau knew that Countess Mary had grave difficulties speaking Hungarian to her new husband's friends in Budapest. He served in the Imperial Guards in Vienna.

There was general laughter while Katzau said something incomprehensible in Hungarian.

"By the way, Countess," he continued in German, summoning Robert from the shadows, "I would like you to meet my new friend, Robert Koch. He is a rising new jeweller in Frankfurt."

They shook hands.

"I hope," he continued, "that at an opportune time I will have the pleasure of presenting my friend to Her Highness."

"I have no doubt," Countess Mary smiled politely, "my mother will be glad to meet you, Herr Koch."

Your word in God's ear, Robert prayed silently.

The next visitor was Signor Enrico Montelli, a flamboyant writer from Florence with pink cheeks and a heavy mustache. True to his profession, he wore a cape, even though it was a hot day, and carried a silver-topped cane. Montelli was the author of a number of melodramas that had been moderately successful on various stages in Italy and France and had had a number of well-publicized encounters with censors in both countries. He came to Baden-Baden occasionally to see Louis Katzau to try out new ideas on him. He had great respect for his judgement.

Katzau introduced Robert.

"What bring you here this time, Enrico?"

"You and Emma Turolla."

Montelli was sometimes called Florence's reply to Venice's Casanova.

"You mean...?"

"Not yet." Montelli made a mournful face. "I adore her. I saw her two weeks ago in Paris, and I am dining with her again tomorrow."

Katzau told Montelli that he and Robert were looking forward to hearing his friend sing Rachel in *La Juive* tonight.

"Good. She wants to spend some time in Germany to learn the language, so that she can sing Wagner and ruin her voice. I can't talk her out of it. She has sung everywhere, in Warsaw, at La Scala in Milan, and in Rome in front of the King and Queen.

In Prague, her admirers were so enthusiastic that after the performance—I think it was *Don Carlos*—they disbanded her horses and pulled her carriage to her hotel themselves, to show their appreciation. Isn't that amazing?"

Katzau and Robert agreed that it was.

"Now I have to talk to you about something else, Louis," Enrico continued. "Urgently. May I make a suggestion? Close your shop this afternoon and visit me at my hotel. We'll go to a café opposite and talk. You've already got too much money. You can afford to lose an afternoon's sales for a good cause. Come at three, both of you. I am staying at the Hirsch Hotel in the Lange Strasse. What about it?"

Katzau and Robert exchanged glances.

Robert nodded.

"We'll be there," Katzau promised.

.　　.　　.

When they arrived, Enrico Montelli was in the lobby, so deeply absorbed in a conversation with two fellow Italians that he could only greet his visitors with a dramatic welcoming gesture of the hand. His compatriots had just arrived from Florence where, as Enrico was finding out, they had attended a meeting of the central committee for the organization of a pilgrimage to the Pantheon in Rome, under the chairmanship of Senator Finoschiette, to celebrate twenty-five years of Italian independence and to observe the forthcoming fifteenth anniversary of the death of Victor Emmanuel II, King of Piedmont and Sardinia and first king of a united Italy. At the meeting General Cadorna, who had commanded the troops in Rome in 1870, was named honorary patron of the pilgrimage. Fifty-two provinces had already agreed to participate and the Italian railway system had announced that they would charge the pilgrims only twenty-five percent of the usual fare.

"Did a spy from the Vatican attend your meeting?" Enrico asked with a wink.

His two friends thought this was highly amusing and laughed uproariously.

Enrico turned to Louis Katzau and Robert.

"I am so pleased you came. I can hardly wait to tell you what is on my mind. May I invite you to come to the café with me and have lemon ice cream?"

After saying goodbye to the two Italian pilgrims, Enrico shepherded Katzau and Robert across the street.

"Let me first tell you what happened two weeks ago in Paris," he began. "Emma Turolla had told me she would only smile at me if I wrote a libretto for a full-scale opera for her. I should choose the subject, she would choose the composer. She suggested two Italians who were not yet established, Giacomo Puccini and Ruggiero Leoncavallo. Both were exactly her age—twenty-five. She knew them both and respected them. I racked my brain. After a long time I came up with a subject that she found immensely exciting—the conquest of Napoleon III by the Contessa Virginia Castiglione. Of course, she would sing Virginia. I then dreamed up a title for the opera. *The Patriotic Bed*. She liked it a lot, which I consider promising. As I say, I took Emma to Paris to meet the Contessa. You see, Emma wants to be involved in the creation of the libretto. Naturally, I favour this. It will bring us close together."

Katzau stroked his whiskers.

"Hm. The subject is not easy, Enrico. True, passion and politics are the very stuff of opera. And, of course, it is an advantage that this would be the first time in the history of the world that an opera is performed while the heroine is still alive."

"Let's cross our fingers," Enrico said. "Today the lady is only forty-eight years old. Though she says she's forty-three. But I know better. So you think it's a bad subject?"

"I'm not saying that, Enrico. All I am saying is that it is difficult. If I remember the story correctly, it has a beginning but no end."

"Oh, I don't think so at all. I've worked out all the scenes. Especially the last one."

Robert had to confess that he did not know what they were

talking about. He had never heard of the Contessa. Louis explained to him that Virginia sprang from an ancient Tuscan family somehow related to Piedmont's prime minister Count Camillo Cavour, the Bismarck of Italy, that her maiden name was Oldoini Verasis, that already as a thirteen-year-old girl she was a stunning beauty and that in 1854, when she was nineteen, she married Count Francesco Verasis di Castiglione, whom she detested. Her husband played a modest role at the court the King of Piedmont and Sardinia, Victor Emmanuel, who was a constitutional monarch like Queen Victoria and a member of the House of Savoy, the future Hohenzollerns of Italy. Turin was the capital. *La divina contessa* soon found herself at the centre of Turin court society and naturally very quickly in the King's bed. He was a great ladies' man often described as, literally, the father of his people.

"Northern Italy," Louis Katzau continued, "was mostly under the control of the Austrians, with the exception of Piedmont, the papal states in Central Italy were governed by the Pope and Southern Italy and Sicily were in the hands of the Spanish Bourbons. Napoleon I had liberated Italy. Napoleon III was ideologically committed to the Principle of Nationality and wanted to do the same. But he needed coaxing. France had by far the largest army on the continent. Cavour understood that without French help he could not achieve his aim to throw out the oppressors and unify Italy under his king, Victor Emmanuel. In 1854, to win Napoleon's favour, and to have a say in future peace negotiations, Cavour contributed Piedmontese troops to the French and English forces against Russia in the Crimean war. The *Risorgimento* was in full swing at the time and secret societies all over Italy were plotting to overthrow of the foreign occupiers from below.

"In February 1856, Cavour dispatched his luscious relative to Paris where the Peace Congress to resolve 'The Eastern Question' was being held. He gave her specific instructions to seduce the Emperor." He paused. His eyes twinkled as an amusing thought occurred to him. "Of course, if Bismarck had had the wit to send a beautiful relative of his to Paris in 1870 with the same mission, instead of provoking a terrible war, even if it lasted only six weeks, the world today would most definitely be a happier place. Especially Baden-Baden. That's the difference between civilized Italy and barbarous Germany. In any case, Virginia's husband Francesco came with her. 'I am a model husband' he told Princess Mathilde. 'I never see or hear anything.' No Prussian husband ever said *that* in similar circumstances!"

With that wise observation, Katzau concluded his background briefing to Robert. He turned back to his Italian friend.

"So you actually visited the Contessa in Paris, Enrico?" Katzau asked "I haven't heard a word about her for years. I don't think she has ever been here."

"She stays at home in Paris. I won't tell you how I found out her address—it was hard. Then I wrote to her, without an introduction, giving her my reasons for wanting to come to Paris to meet her, together with Emma Turolla. She answered right away, quite graciously."

"Does she still have a husband?"

"No. I don't know how that marriage ended. She fell into disfavour at court around 1860, for reasons I don't know. Since then she has been out of the public eye."

"Where does she live?" Robert asked. He had never been in Paris, but had a general idea of its social geography.

"In the *entresol* of 26, place Vendôme. In an apartment between the first and second floor. She only has two maids. There is one staircase inside and one outside, directly facing the column in memory of the *Grande Armée*, with the bas-reliefs made of Austrian cannons and depicting the campaigns from 1805 to 1807, with Napoleon as Caesar on top. One has to ring two different bells to be admitted. It is rumoured she never receives more than one gentleman at a time."

"Emma Turolla must have raised an eyebrow or two when she heard that," Louis Katzau smiled..

"She certainly did. The Contessa is still very beautiful. No doubt her beauty is her profession, but please don't ask me for details. I have been told that the duc d'Aumale, the fourth son of Louis-Philippe and leader of the Orléanists, is one of her friends. I dared not ask her any questions that she might have considered indiscreet. By the way, I had been told she never talks to other women, so I was relieved that she was nice to Emma. You see, the idea that the famous Emma Turolla might impersonate her on the stage flattered her immensely. And she found it fascinating that Emma was born two years *after* Cavour dispatched her to Paris. By the way, Emma was born in Turin, which established a certain bond between them right away. The Contessa even showed her some of her jewellery."

Robert pricked up his ears.

"Yes, she showed Emma the emerald the Emperor had given her, worth many hundreds of thousands. When we left she gave Emma a few 'worthless trinkets,' that's what she called them, to wear when she played her on the stage."

Robert and Katzau each made a mental note. One person's 'worthless trinket,' each thought in his own way, was another person's...Hope Diamond...or...

"Let me tell you what worries me." Katzau pulled himself together. It was time to concentrate on Enrico's problem. "The way you describe her is perfectly in line with what I heard about her at the time. Of course I suppose I shouldn't trust my memory. In 1855, I was fifteen. I remember hearing that her beauty was stunning but that she had absolutely no personality and no intelligence, and that at court she was universally disliked. Seducing the Emperor had been ridiculously easy. He never confused business with pleasure. He did not have the slightest intention of allowing her to influence him in any way, for which in any case she had no talent. He liked her in bed, that was all. If she followed Cavour's instructions and at crucial moments whispered to him 'Sire, do not forget Piedmont,' he would no doubt reply, every time, 'I will never forget Piedmont, *ma chérie*, I promise. Let us continue.' He soon got tired of her. By the end of Act One she was dismissed. Her compatriot the Contessa Waleska took her place. She was brighter and more amusing. I don't quite see, Enrico, how you can manufacture an opera libretto out of this."

"No, no, no, Louis. Waiter! Some more ice cream please!"

Enrico flapped his hand at the waiter loitering at the back of the café. "You are quite wrong. That's not at all what I have in mind. I want an opera in which the seduction is the culmination, the end of Act Three!"

"And how do you propose to keep the audience awake until then?" Katzau asked.

"Everyone is interested in the way a young lady learns how to make profitable use of her beauty. Maybe I will invent a secret love affair, with Cavour in the background, wondering how to make use of her when the time comes. And then the usual marriage to a man she does not love. I understand the Contessa spent much time in front of a mirror every day, naked, admiring herself, and dreaming. I will stage her half-naked, hoping that the censors will be so dazzled by her beauty that for once they will leave me alone. A great scene. Lovely, sensuous music. Just right for Emma. I don't know yet what I will do about the black satin sheets which the Contessa used to serve as contrast to the whiteness of her skin. But I know I can solve that little problem without being arrested. That is no more difficult that staging the court ball scene where she appears daringly exposed, as the Queen of Hearts, wearing a conspicuously shameless dress, a heart affixed to an interesting place not usually advertised, driving men frenzied with desire and women red-hot with moral indignation, making Eugénie remark to her, 'My dear, you are wearing your heart a little low.' And the Emperor quietly twirling his waxed mustache devising his napoleonic strategy."

Katzau turned to Robert.

"What do you think, Herr Koch?"

"This is not my field," Robert replied, "but it seems to me this would make a splendid plot for an opera. I wish I could compose it!"

"You are probably right." Katzau turned to Enrico. "I may be worried about nothing. What concerns me is the character of your heroine. *If* you are faithful to the real person. Which of course in opera you don't have to be. Nobody has ever asked for *verismo* in opera. Not so far, anyway. She is a heroine who is only beautiful and vain, nothing else, who has no personality, no brains. How can one sympathize with a person like that? Heroines like Carmen, or Violetta in *Traviata*, or Aida, have qualities other than beauty. And they have their tragic fates to move us to compassion. But your Contessa isn't a tragic heroine but a stupid heroine. And her fate? Her mission was ended, just before the final curtain, in the patriotic bed? I very much doubt whether either she or the Emperor would find this finale very satisfying. And the public certainly knows that the beautiful Contessa's patriotic mission was only half-fulfilled. In the end, the great liberator Napoleon III backed out. Your composer will have considerable difficulty inventing the right music for such a dubious finale. You should not be misled, Enrico, by your very understandable wish to have Emma Turolla sing the part!"

Enrico Montelli took out a green handkerchief and noisily blew his nose.

"Don't answer, Enrico. Herr Koch may be perfectly right that your idea will work well and that I see difficulties where there are none. But you took the trouble to come to Baden-Baden to ask me for my opinion. So let me give it to you. I think your beautiful stupid Contessa is the perfect centrepiece for a witty satire exposing the vanity, the shallowness, the fakery, the cynical pretentiousness, the spiritual hollowness of Louis Napoleon's fifth-rate circus, his hair-raising effrontery, his ultimately doomed efforts to emulate the real Napoleon. Emma Turolla's two young composer friends may have all the talent in the world for writing grand operas, but they are not Jacques Offenbach. You should go to him."

"You think so?"

"Yes, I think so. Very definitely. And you need a second plot to contrast with the first. The Contessa's pursuit of the Emperor by itself is not interesting enough to sustain a full-length opera."

Enrico pulled down the corners of his mouth.

"Oh, I don't know," he said. "I would want Cavour to be a major character. He pulls the strings."

"I understand. He's also a major character in the plot I'm

going to suggest to you. The parallel plot I'm thinking of is the conquest of Princess Clotilde by Prince Napoleon. I am sure you have heard of those two characters. That plot was also engineered by Cavour, for the same patriotic reasons as the Contessa's conquest—to involve France in the liberation of Italy. Never mind that it occurred three years later. In opera you can do anything if the music is right."

Enrico scratched his chin.

"Yes, I know about those two," he said.

"Plon-Plon is perfect for opera. Of course he has to be a bass. Infuriatingly tactless and willful, always going his own way, erratic, idealistic, he is invariably forgiven by his long-suffering imperial cousin. You can have Plon-Plon trying to intercept the Contessa before she lands in his imperial cousin's patriotic bed. And the lily-white fifteen-year-old Princess Clotilde, the devout daughter of the very king who had already enjoyed Virginia's favours—isn't she the precise counterpart to the Contessa? Then there is Plon-Plon. Cavour's plot suits him perfectly. It enables him—so he thinks—to play a dominant role in the forthcoming struggle as the husband of the King's daughter. So with a heavy heart, Victor Emmanuel agrees. At his and Cavour's urgings the obedient and patriotic Princess sacrifices herself and in record time marries the lascivious ogre from Paris who is twice her age. You might even hint that, against all expectations, this marriage lasts and in the decades to come Clotilde will be the only member of the imperial family who is truly devoted to the welfare of the common people and becomes popular. What about it, Enrico?"

"And how would you end the opera?"

"Easy. Total success. Or rather, so it seemed for a day or two. Remember you are doing a satire. The two plots seem to have met their objective. Everybody's off to the Battle of Solferini, where at last the French army helps the Piedmontese crush the Austrians. The liberation of Italy is on the way. Your audience knows very well that soon afterwards Napoleon left the Italian freedom-fighters in the lurch. You can leave that for your next opera."

Enrico looked unhappy.

"Don't say anything now, Enrico."

Enrico did not say anything now.

"And above all let's not talk about it tonight when we will want to concentrate on enjoying Emma Turolla's performance. You need a little time to think this over."

• • •

Louis Katzau and Robert Koch knew the plot of *La Juive*. The reason they were afraid of seeing the opera was that they found the subject of Christian persecution of Jews painful and embarrassing. They knew that this feeling was irrational and that the underlying intention of the opera could not have been more noble and its effect probably largely beneficial. But they could not be absolutely sure of this. They thought that while the liberal seeds sown by Napoleon at the beginning of the century had at last begun to sprout after the long period of reaction following his fall in 1815 and that there was, generally speaking, good reason for optimism, nonetheless true harmony between Christians and Jews had not yet been achieved by any means. Any public expression of Christian hostility to Jews was therefore fraught with danger. They did not advertise their own Jewishness but they never denied it. If they were ever confronted with the choice the protagonists of the opera had to face in the fifth act—conversion or death—they would have chosen conversion. They were afraid that sermons on the virtues of tolerance, even in the form of grand opera, might have unintended results.

The composer of *La Juive*, Fromental Halévy, was the teacher of Charles Gounod and Georges Bizet and married Bizet's daughter. He was much admired by Richard Wagner. Its first performance by the Paris opera took place in 1835, five years after the revolution of July 1830, which had brought Louis-Philippe to power and ended the régime of Charles X. In that régime the clergy had exercised strong influence. *La Juive* represented the spirit of Louis-Philippe's more freethinking bourgeoisie. It had been commissioned by the entrepreneur Louis Véron and financed by the banker, the Marquis d'Aquado.

Louis Katzau and Robert were relieved that most likely they did not have to talk about the opera with Enrico Montelli tonight. He sat downstairs in the front row, in the centre, while their seats where upstairs on the balcony.

On the strength of Emma Turolla's interpretation of Leonore in *Il Trovatore* of three moments—the only three moments when she could show what she could do—Richard Pohl's *Badeblatt* had called her *prima donna assoluta*. These three moments were, the music tsar had written, the finales of the first and second acts and the first scene of Act Four. At the end of the entire performance, cries of Bravo! had emanated from many places in the theatre, he had written, including the loge of His Royal Highness, the Prince of Wales. Turolla's soprano voice had a warm, southern timbre—it was "high, soft and controlled." She was, in sum, an extraordinary, truly dramatic singer, with a great future ahead of her.

The performance, by the Italian Opera Company of the Grand Ducal Hoftheater of Karlsruhe, took place in the elegant Kleine Theater am Tummelplatz, which had five hundred seats, far less than the number of people involved in the production of *La Juive*, which included a *corps de ballet*.

The theatre was less then ten minutes from Katzau's boutique. For its inauguration in 1862, the director of the casino Édouard Bénazet, who had financed the construction of the building out of his own pocket, had commissioned Hector Berlioz to compose *Béatrice et Bénédict*, which Berlioz produced and conducted himself, having brought with him from Paris a troupe of first-class singers. Before the opera, the orchestra played the *Jubelouvertüre* by Carl Maria von Weber. Few remembered that in late July 1810 Weber had come to Baden-Baden at the age of twenty-four to give a piano recital but had to abandon his plans because there was no piano in the place. Conditions were so primitive, Weber wrote at the time, that the *Denglersche Truppe* had to give a performance of *Don Giovanni* with an orchestra containing three and a half men. What better proof could there be, in view of the première of *Béatrice et Bénédict* in Baden-Baden fifty years later, that the nineteenth century was an age of progress?

However painful to see it on the stage, Louis Katzau and Robert admitted, the spectacle of a cardinal as the anti-Jewish villain was a step in the right direction. And what a spectacle! The action took place at the beginning of the fifteenth century during the Council of Constance in Switzerland. The punishment for love between a Jewish man and a non-Jewish woman was death, unless the Jew gave up his faith. It was impossible not to be moved by the story of doomed love, jealousy, mistaken identity and filial devotion. One surprising revelation followed another. The music was magnificent. In the end, the two main characters were thrown into a cauldron of boiling water, a fate they could have avoided by conversion to Christianity. Emma Turolla's Rachel was one of the two. The other was her father, Eléazar, a goldsmith.

For Louis Katzau and Robert, this tragic conclusion did not have the shattering effect it had on others, not only because they knew about it beforehand. The main reason was that their minds were on something else. In Act Two, during the Seder at Eléazar's house, Emma Turolla anachronistically wore what seemed to be a pair of Empire ruby earrings, which—they could not be absolutely sure from where they sat in the balcony—may very well have been among "the trinkets" Napoleon III had given to the Contessa Virginia di Castiglione, and which the Contessa so generously passed on to Emma. If so, it was entirely conceivable that Josephine's jewels had found their way into Louis Napoleon's possession, perhaps without his ever knowing that his grandmother had worn them at her coronation. Katzau and Robert could not wait to ask her to show the rubies to them after the performance.

Turolla's room was filled with admirers, mainly men, first among them Enrico Montelli. There were flowers everywhere. Not a trace of fatigue showed in her face.

Enrico introduced them as men of high standing in Germany's operatic world.

"It is most generous of Signor Montelli to flatter us," Katzau said, "although it is true that I have been close to the operatic scene for many years. But my young friend is a jeweller—like Eléazar."

"Oh, really?"

It was not a new experience for Robert to note that his profession was appealing to beautiful women.

"And," Katzau continued, "Herr Koch has a sharp eye for rare and beautiful jewellery."

Emma Turolla turned to Robert.

"I wish I had some pieces to show to you, *monsieur*."

"But you do, *signora*," Robert responded. "I could not help but admire the earrings you wore during the second act. I was wondering whether you might allow me to have a closer look at them."

Turolla went to her dressing table and picked them up.

"I'm always afraid," she said with a *coloratura* laugh, "that I may forget to take them off before they put me in the cauldron."

The two men examined the rubies.

The setting was clearly modern, not at all Empire.

"Very beautiful." Robert concealed his acute disappointment with superhuman bravery. "Please let me know, *signora*, if you ever want to sell them."

Chapter 9

Thursday was the third *Renntag*. There was only one more day's racing, on Saturday, before the Prince of Wales and his retinue were to leave for Bad Homburg. Robert had a good reason to go. When he had reached the Pension Luisenhöhe late the night before, still bleeding from the wounds inflicted by Signora Turolla's disappointing Empire earrings, a letter was waiting for him. It had been delivered in the afternoon.

Baden-Baden,
Wednesday, August 29, 1883

Dear Herr Koch,
Please forgive me for approaching you in this direct manner. I was given your address by Haushofmeister Edmund Jenkins, who, in great confidence, informed me of your current concerns. You will find it useful to meet me at Iffezheim on Thursday afternoon, August 30, at three o'clock, at the park bench outside the Tribüne. I regret I cannot see you earlier. I have not told Monsieur Jenkins of the purpose and content of this communication.
Yours respectfully,

Count Richard de Léon

P.S. It will pay you to place a bet on Lothario in the Saint-Léger Handicap. The prize is 10,000 marks.

So early on Thursday morning, while he still pondered Count de Léon's somewhat puzzling letter, Robert lined up at the wicket at the Iffezheim race track and put ten marks on Lothario. The weather was splendid, the atmosphere festive, the music bracing and the stakes high. The Saint-Léger Handicap, with its generous prize, was one of the five main events.

Robert had rarely placed a bet and had little experience as a gambler. The other races were the Preis von Merkur (Herren-Reiten) (2,000 marks), the Preis von Sandweiler (2,000 marks), Kosmopolitisches Handicap (4,000 marks) and the Grosse Badener Jagdrennen (10,000 Marks). Robert noted that the Duke of Hamilton's horse Fénélon was running, and so was Count Tassilo Festetics's Frangepan.

The only unshakable piece of information contained in the letter was that the Count played the horses. But so did everybody else in Baden-Baden. The rather ordinary handwriting told him nothing. Louis Katzau, whom Robert had asked in the morning before setting out for Iffezheim, did not recognize the count's name. It sounds like Richard the Lion-Hearted, he said, but that was not of much use. Robert decided against going to the Palais Hamilton to see the *Haushofmeister* to obtain an advance briefing. He hoped he would soon need him for something more important.

• • •

Count Richard de Léon was waiting for him on the park bench at the far left of the Tribüne, as announced. Could this unsavoury character, Robert wondered, this man who smoked an offensively smelly cigar, really be a count? He did not know that characters such this were commonplace at race tracks, and often assumed whatever fanciful titles appealed to them.

But once Robert had recovered from this unpleasant first impression, he noticed something quite extraordinary, something amazing, unprecedented, something for which he could not have been prepared—the man was—how should he put it?— *an unpleasant mirror image of himself!*

Richard de Léon was—no, surely this was the wrong word—his *Doppelgänger*.

The same general size, only Count Richard de Léon had a hunchback. The same round face, only it was unshaven. The same hair, only it was unkempt. The same high forehead, only there were ugly scars on it. The same brown eyes, only their expression was insolent. The same nose, only it needed blowing. He did so noisily into a dirty handkerchief. There were dark stains on his trousers.

No doubt, Robert thought, his alter ego was going to announce that he had stolen the earrings and would be delighted to sell them for a hundred thousand marks.

"Ah, there you are, Herr Koch."

"Count."

Richard de Léon did not rise. "Do take a seat."

There was no alternative but for Robert to sit so close that he could not help inhaling the fumes emanating from the man's body.

The "Count" produced a bottle of schnapps from his hip pocket and offered it to Robert. Robert took it.

"Did you follow my suggestion?" Richard asked. "Did you place the bet?"

Robert swallowed the mouthful of schnapps—he was surprised how good it was—and said "Yes."

"Have some more. I want you to be in a good mood, Herr Koch, so that you will say yes to the proposition I am about to put to you. I suppose by now you have looked me up in the *Almanac de Gotha*?"

"I am sorry, *monsieur*. I did not. I hoped you would volunteer some essential information."

"I certainly will not. Ask the Grand Duke about me. 'But let's not waste time now. The next race will start in ten minutes. The earrings you are looking for belong to me and are in my possession."

"I see."

"If you wish, you may tell the *Haushofmeister* about this. Or the police. Nobody will believe you. Take another drink."

Robert took another drink.

"Are you saying, *monsieur*," he asked as the second intake made his inner system glow, "you will let me have them at a price?"

"I most certainly will not. I told you they really belong to me. By natural inheritance. I will not part with them, certainly not while I am on a winning streak. As I am now. No, I am going to offer you something much better. I am thinking of you, and, I won't deny it, of myself."

"To what proposition am I to say yes?"

"The *Haushofmeister* told me why you were a talented, ambitious young jeweller from Frankfurt, on the way up, and you wanted to find the earrings for a specific purpose. You wanted the Duchess of Hamilton to demonstrate her thanks to you for returning the lost or stolen rubies by making you her court jeweller and introducing you to all her noble and rich friends. Is that right?"

"Yes, that is right."

"Since the earrings are now safely in my possession, there is no need for you to waste your time any longer. I can do much better than the old lady. All the people she knows I know. And hundreds and hundreds more. Nowadays it is not only her crowd that has the money. The world is changing before our very eyes. The Duchess only knows one level of society. But I know them all, from top to bottom. Mention any name that comes to your head, and I will introduce you. After that, you're on your own."

"King Umberto of Italy"." It was the first name Robert could think of. As soon as he said it he regretted it. It was far too easy. He should have said Alfred Krupp or the King of Siam.

"Well now, let me see," Richard de Léon once again took out his dirty handkerchief and blew his nose. "The last time I was His Majesty's guest in Rome was in February, after an audience with the Pope. Herr Koch, let us stop playing games. Let us be serious. This is my proposition. You let me introduce you to a list of people of means and standing, which I shall submit to you. Once we have agreed, and you begin doing business with these people, you will let me have thirty percent of the profits flowing from these transactions. For five years. The profits you earn from other transactions, of course, remain yours. We will have a normal legal contract drawn up and properly notarized. I do not believe in gentlemen's agreements. I have burned my fingers with them far too often. You think it over. You don't have to associate with me. No need to worry that I come to your store in Frankfurt uninvited, with my bottle of schnapps, and frighten away your customers. You can always contact me through the *Haushofmeister*."

The fanfares sounded for the next race.

Before leaving the race track, Robert learned that Lothario had paid ten to one. He made one hundred marks.

· · ·

Robert gave a summary of this conversation to Louis Katzau and described the "Count's" manner and appearance in gruesome detail, naturally without mentioning the striking resemblance to himself. Before turning down his proposition, it would only be sensible to try and find out something about the man.

After a short pause of deep concentration, Katzau at last recognized the name. Why had he not thought of it before?

This man was a grandson of Napoleon.

His grandmother was none other than Eléonore Denuelle, Countess of Laxburg, who had been good customer of his before she died two years ago. Her third husband, the Count of Laxburg, had been Minister of State for the Grand Duchy of Baden. In her old age, Eléonore Denuelle had been a friend of Jeanne Archambault's who had told her many times about her love affair, in 1807, with Napoleon.

At that time Eléonore Denuelle was eighteen and married to an adventurer recently imprisoned for forgery. The union with Napoleon, in her husband's involuntary absence, produced a son, who became Count Charles Léon and who looked very much like his father. "Richard de Léon was one of that count's three sons. That count—Napoleon's son—had entered history only because he had become a dreadful nuisance to his cousin Napoleon III.

The *Haushofmeister* knew all about him.

Edmund Jenkins could not see Robert until Friday morning, August 31, 1883, at ten o'clock, in his office on the second floor of the Palais Hamilton. When requesting the appointment Robert had declared that the subject of his enquiry was Count Richard de Léon.

After receiving Robert, the tall, elderly, bearded *Haushofmeister* was concerned that Robert might want to reproach him for having given out his name and address to the "Count" improperly.

"I only did so," he explained to Robert in his Cockney German, "only because the theft of the Grand Duchess's jewels is by now common knowledge. The "Count" said he thought he could help with the search."

Robert smiled.

"He did not say that they were now in his possession?" he asked.

"Most certainly not," Jenkins replied with heat. "I would immediately have taken appropriate action." He hesitated for a moment. "Although, of course, my first thought would have been that the man is lying."

"What would he have gained by that, Mister Jenkins?"

"That I cannot answer. With the kind of upbringing he had, I suspect telling the truth was never a high priority." The *Haushofmeister* took off his gold-rimmed glasses and slowly wiped them. "Since you have met the son, no doubt you would like to hear something about the father. I come from Wimbledon, which is a small town south of London. I don't suppose you have heard of it."

Robert had not.

"In early March 1840, when I was not yet twenty, there was a great commotion in Wimbledon. There was to have been a duel on the Common early in the morning between two men. One man was this man's father, who claimed to be—and no doubt was—an illegitimate son of Napoleon and whose full name, so he said, was Count Charles Léon Denuelle de la Plaigne. The Count had started life as a well-mannered little boy, much admired for his resemblance to the King of Rome, Napoleon's son by his second wife Marie-Louise. In 1815, when Léon was seven, he went to Malmaison to say goodbye to his father, who was off to St. Helena. But soon he turned into an awful, dissolute person, partly no doubt because he was shamelessly neglected by his mother, whom he hated and whom he later sued for fraud. He had become a compulsive gambler who quarrelled with everybody, a frequent duellist, perhaps a pimp, always in money trouble, having lost the large sum Napoleon had left him. When he arrived in England in 1840, he had just spent time in debtors' prison in Clichy, from which he was unexpectedly released. King Louis-Philippe's security police gave him instructions that were very much to his liking. He was told to go to London and provoke a duel with Prince Louis Napoleon and kill him. Once in London, Léon stayed at Fenton's Hotel and claimed to be a commercial traveller in lamps. Prince Louis Napoleon, the man who later became Napoleon III, was at the time living in romantic exile in London, lionized by high society, hoping that next time he staged a *coup d'état* he would topple Louis-Philippe's throne instead of bungling the *coup*, as he had twice before, and land in prison."

"How did Léon challenge him?" Robert inquired.

"Very simple. He wrote several letters to him, calling him 'dear cousin,' insulting him, accusing him, among others things, of not having a drop of French blood in his veins, and demanding an interview. As Léon hoped, Louis Napoleon refused. So Léon did what he was paid to do. He challenged him. Duelling was illegal. Louis Napoleon alerted the police. Once the two arrived on Wimbledon Common with their seconds, the two parties started bickering whether they should fight with pistols or sabres. The police arrived. Both parties were arrested, charged with unlawful assembly and taken to Bow Street. But all this happened three weeks after Queen Victoria's wedding and everybody was in a good mood. They were only cautioned.

Léon returned to France and continued his dissolute life. When the soft-hearted Louis Napoleon became emperor, Léon begged him for a pension, got it and then, again and again, demanded increases. The long-suffering Louis Napoleon usually yielded, but he would never receive him at court."

"And after all these years, Mister Jenkins," Robert shook his head in amazement, "you still remember the excitement in your hometown? Amazing."

"Yes, I have never forgotten it."

"And Count Léon presumably married," Robert said, "and had three dissolute children. Of whom I have just met one. And hope that I will never see him again."

Robert told Jenkins about the proposition the "Count" had put before him, and added that he had every intention of turning it down.

"Suppose," the *Haushofmeister* said after a moment's thought, "that for once the man is telling the truth and he really has the earrings, then I suppose the ones stolen from the Duchess are copies."

"Or the other way round," Robert observed. "It would make no difference."

"And suppose," the *Haushofmeister* mused, "the man really has those connections?"

"Nothing will induce me to have any more to do with him," Robert replied firmly.

·　　·　　·

This time Robert was alone with Jeanne Archambault in the retired courtesan's little villa in the Tiergartenweg, drinking tea in her salon. In one corner was the grand piano covered with framed pictures. He conveyed to her that he had met Count de Léon in Iffezheim. Louis Katzau had told him, he said, she had been a friend of his grandmother's, the Countess von Laxburg, who had died two years ago.

"Ah yes, I was fond of his grandmother. One of my more

colourful colleagues. She was nearly ninety when she died. And only eighteen when she caught her biggest fish. The only woman in Napoleon's life who lived that long, she always said."

"Did you ever meet their son?" Robert asked.

"Oh no," Jeanne replied. "They were not in contact. Eléonore had nothing to do with him. Léon detested her. And she detested him. No doubt Léon knew something about the unusual way he was conceived."

"Unusual?"

"That is what Eléonore told me. Napoleon's sister Caroline was Queen of Naples. Her husband was Joachim Murat, perhaps the most brilliant of Napoleon's marshalls. They had an estate in Neuilly. In the spring of 1806, the empire was at its zenith. Its future—and Caroline's—hinged on Napoleon at last fathering a male heir with Josephine. By then, Napoleon and Josephine had been married for ten years. Josephine had two children from her previous marriage. Caroline had always been Josephine's adversary. She now decided to prove something that had not yet been proven, that Napoleon was perfectly capable of procreating with women other than Josephine. If that could be proven beyond a shadow of a doubt, then, if the empire and the dynasty—and Caroline as Queen of Naples— was to survive, he had no choice but to divorce Josephine and marry somebody with whom he could produce an heir."

"So Caroline procured Eléonore?"

"Exactly. She decided to conduct an experiment. But first she had to obtain her brother's consent. He gave it—for *raisons d'état*. Eléonore was the perfect candidate. She was experienced, attractive and more than willing. Her husband was in jail for forgery. Perfect. She was placed in a pavillion on the Neuilly estate, under close supervision to make sure that no man got near her, and from time to time was conducted to the Tuileries. In his encounters with her, Napoleon was even more perfunctory than usual and always—so Eléonore reported—had one eye on the clock. By September, she was pregnant. Josephine heard about it in no time and became resigned to the inevitable."

"Am I right," Robert pointed to the photograph of Count

Alexandre Waleski on the grand piano, "that soon after Napoleon gave another proof—in Poland?"

"You are absolutely right," Jeanne agreed. "But Marie had a husband who was elderly but not in prison, and therefore there *was* a shadow of a doubt."

Robert rose and once again examined the picture.

"But I would have thought the striking resemblance with Napoleon would disperse any doubt."

"I don't think one should put too much stress," Jeanne observed, "on what one imagines to be a family resemblance."

She narrowed her eyes and looked at Robert.

"I mean, for that matter, one could even imagine that you, Herr Koch, were a grandson of Napoleon!"

Chapter 10

Preparations were already under way for the birthday celebrations for Grand Duke Friedrich, who was to be fifty-seven on September 9. In a special proclamation Mayor Gönner invited all citizens of Baden-Baden to participate. The phrase "all highest" was used, although one would have thought it would have been reserved for the Kaiser and not wasted on a mere grand duke. The celebrations meant flags everywhere, a concert by the Kurorchester, religious services, fireworks and a special dinner in the Conversationshaus. The evening before there was to be Reunionsball, beginning at nine o'clock, to which no one not dressed in the prescribed evening toilette was to be admitted.

For Robert, these and similar matters were the subject of modestly irreverent discussions after breakfast with Fräulein Fröhlich in the Pension Luisenhöhe on the Werderstrasse. This elderly, well-educated amateur pianist, who had been governess for Robert and Clara Schumann's seven children, had already impressed him with her knowledge of music and musicians, which was not at all his field. He liked her, and she clearly preferred him to her four other guests. He was particularly drawn to her soft and expressive local Baden intonation and also appreciated her sensible, sober-minded detachment from the extravagant superlatives (and the spirit behind them) about titled personages used in official and semi-official communications, language invariably conveying fawning submissiveness. The worst of these were contained in the *Badeblatt*. She knew and respected the musician Richard Pohl but could not abide the tone of his publication. But she understood the political purpose of his obsequiousness, namely to gain support from those in power for the "New Music" of Wagner (who had died in Venice last February), Liszt and Berlioz. Fräulein Fröhlich told Robert that Pohl's critical writings, and especially his biography of Liszt, were entirely free of such servility.

On Tuesday, September 4, the morning after the Prince of Wales had departed for Bad Homburg, after breakfast, Robert and Fräulein Fröhlich had a memorable conversation. She had nearly collided with one of her guests as she rushed into the dining room to ask him with some agitation:

"Why didn't you tell me you were looking for Josephine's earrings?"

"Who told you that?"

"Ludwig Weiler. You know, the jeweller on the Gernsbacher Strasse. I had heard earlier they were missing. You should have told me, Herr Koch, instead of keeping it a deep dark secret. I know quite a lot about the earrings."

"You do?"

"Yes, Herr Koch. I do. You see, I could be useful you. Of course, I don't know where they are *now*. But you never can tell—one thing may lead to another. I understand you want to find them to get into the good graces of the Duchess, for your business reasons. That's a smart idea. Once you have her on your side, that whole crowd will follow. We're never allowed to forget for a moment that the Grand Duke is the son-in-law of the old Kaiser himself."

"I have not forgotten, Fräulein Fröhlich." Robert smiled. "Well, what is it that you know?"

"I know that on September the thirteenth in 1864—I always remember the date, even though, Heavens! it is nearly twenty years ago—we had a joyous celebration, right here—I mean, over there"—she pointed vaguely in a southerly direction—"in Lichtental, in that lovely chalet in which we lived, on the banks of the Oos. Near the *Aubrücke*. Have you seen it, Herr Koch?"

"I am afraid not yet."

"Oh, how delighted Frau Schumann was with her idyllic chalet in Lichtental," she continued. "You see, she had bought it in the spring the previous year, after travelling and playing the piano at concerts all winter. You know, she was a great artist in her own right, not only famous for being Robert Schumann's widow. The children called the chalet *unsere Hundehütte*, our doghouse. Frau Schumann often relished the sight of the green meadows and the dark forest behind the house, with its beech, elm and fir trees, breathing in the invigorating Black Forest air, to restore her spirits after her strenuous concert tours. She often stood on the balcony for five, ten minutes at a time, just breathing in the air. When they were older, the children often said this had been the happiest time of their lives. They had three grand pianos to practise on, by the clock, never for long stretches at a time. But their mother insisted on regularity. I had to keep an eye on them. Only the two oldest daughters, Marie and Elise, were taught by Mama. They, in turn, taught the younger ones. Of course, they're now all grown up and another family lives in that house."

Robert did not wish to be rude, but obviously he had to help Fräulein Fröhlich a little to find her way forward to the earrings.

"Was it Frau Schumann's birthday?" he asked. "And somebody gave her the earrings as a present? I assume they must have been copies. After all, the real ones were in the possession of the Duchess of Hamilton. Her mother, Stephanie, had left them to her when she died in 1860."

"I suppose so." Fräulein Fröhlich was not interested in such subtle distinctions, nor did she wish Robert to deflect her. "This may have been the first reasonably happy summer for her since Herr Schumann's death eight years earlier. I think she was forty-five. Many great musicians were there. Anton Rubinstein, who also had a house in Baden-Baden, and Joseph Joachim and his new wife Amalie, and of course Johannes Brahms. As you know, Brahms worshipped her. Did you read in the *Badeblatt* this morning that he was moving from Vienna to Wiesbaden?"

No, Robert had not read it.

"Oh, you should have seen him then, Herr Koch. He was not thirty yet, the most handsome man on God's earth, with his high forehead and soft, curling blond hair and a complexion so pure that it seemed he never had to shave. He wasn't very tall, but that didn't matter, for in his music he was a giant. Brahms had rented two rooms in Lichtental in the upper story of a house belonging to Frau Becker, about twenty minutes walk from our chalet. Behind it was the forest, where he went for long, long walks, composing in his head. On this occasion, on Frau Schumann's birthday party, he was in particularly good spirits."

Robert chose not to interrupt when Fräulein Fröhlich paused, as she recalled one particular moment.

"I'll never forget the time when the young *Kapellmeister* Hermann Levi arrived from Karlsruhe and sat down at one of the pianos. He pretended it was out of tune and played a Strauss waltz—what was it? It wasn't *The Blue Danube* he played because Strauss hadn't yet composed it. I don't remember, but he played the right hand a semitone lower than the left. It was so awful that Brahms had to escape to a clothes cupboard and from deep inside he proceeded to sing O Freunde, *nicht diese Töne...* Oh, you don't recognize that?" Fräulein Fröhlich finally noticed Robert's bemused look. "It's from Beethoven's *Ode to Joy*, the recitative that introduces it: 'O friends, not these tones!' Brahms himself often performed extraordinary feats of transposition, you know. Once, when he was to play Beethoven's *Kreutzer* Sonata with the Hungarian violinist Édouard Reményi—I think it was in Göttingen—he discovered, just before the concert, that the piano was tuned a semitone too low. He simply played his part a semitone higher, from memory! And he often enjoyed playing musical jokes with his friends. Another violinist who often performed with Brahms once told me he never knew what key Brahms was going to start in."

Robert sensed that Fräulein Fröhlich knew very well that he wanted her to come back to the point, but enjoyed keeping him waiting. But the time had come for him to say something.

"And it was Brahms," Robert asked gently, "who gave Josephine's earrings to Clara Schumann?"

"Oh no, that would have been quite out of character. He did not approve of any extravagance. Remember he was a sober North German, quite different from us southerners. Not only that, but I also remember him saying he had no use whatsoever for Napoleon, nor for his wife, ever since he heard his mother reminiscence about Napoleon's siege and occupation of his native Hamburg, one of the bitterest chapters in the city's history, he said. No, it was not Brahms who gave her the earrings."

Fräulein Fröhlich clearly found it amusing to play her little game with Robert.

"It must have been one of the seven children who found them in the gutter. Right?"

"Oh, Herr Koch," Fräulein Fröhlich chuckled, "you're such a tease! Oh, all right. I won't keep you guessing any longer. It was Joseph Joachim. He was at the birthday party, too, together with his new wife, Amalie."

"And who is Joseph Joachim?"

"Oh, forgive me, Herr Koch, I forgot you are not one of us. Joseph Joachim is our greatest violinist. At the time he was *Konzertmeister* for the King of Hanover and he was hugely excited about being able to give Frau Schumann the historic earrings. He made a solemn speech in which he said Empress Josephine wore them at her coronation and he had such warm admiration for Frau Schumann that he had decided only imperial treasures would be worthy of her. You can imagine how the children enjoyed that! So, naturally, everybody was disappointed when Frau Schumann did not seem to be sufficiently impressed. At the centre of her life was the memory of Robert Schumann, and the world of music and poetry, and her own art. And, of course, her family. That was enough. She had little feeling for other things. I often wondered whether she remembered that when she was a child prodigy she had played for Goethe himself, in Weimar, not long before he died. She was always worried about one thing or another. Including money. She never had enough time for composing herself, for which she had a great talent. Few people know this. The whole world considered her one of the best pianists of our time, and respected her for being one of the few women artists, perhaps the only one, able to support a large family from her own efforts alone. But she was occasionally criticized for a certain lack of humour."

Robert nodded full of understanding.

"I wonder, Fräulein Fröhlich," he asked, succeeding splendidly in concealing his impatience, "whether anybody asked Joseph Joachim how he got hold of the earrings?"

"Of course." Fräulein Fröhlich laughed. "He told everybody, at great length. It's such an extraordinary story. Let me clear the dishes so that Minna can wash them."

Robert waited as patiently as he could while Fräulein Fröhlich cleared the dishes, delivered them to Minna and returned to the table.

"Now let me tell you the story. It seems Napoleon had a younger brother, Jérôme. He made him King of Westphalia and found him a wife, Catherine of Württemberg. They had a daughter, Princess Mathilde."

"Who became *Notre Dame des Arts* and whose younger brother was nicknamed Plon-Plon."

"Herr Koch," Fräulein Fröhlich was awed, "you amaze me."

"I amaze myself." Robert lowered his eyes and inspected his fingernails.

"Your modesty does you credit, Herr Koch. Let me go on. In 1838, Princess Mathilde lived in exile, in Florence, Joachim told us. She was eighteen, lonely and miserable, worshipping the memory of her uncle Napoleon and going to the opera to hear Rossini and Donizetti. Suddenly her life was turned upside down. She heard Franz Liszt play. The great genius was twenty-seven and already universally known as the Paganini of the piano. But that is not the point. The point is—now, listen well, Herr Koch, this is astounding—Franz Liszt reminded the sad, lonely romantic young Princess of her uncle when he was young, of Napoleon in 1796, during his Italian campaigns, pale and intense, with long hair and big dreamy eyes. She said the likeness was absolutely astonishing. Of course, she could only have seen portraits of the young Napoleon."

Robert was indeed amazed, but also a little puzzled.

"But from the pictures I have seen," he said, scratching the back of his neck, "Liszt was considerably taller than Napoleon."

"Who are we to argue with the eighteen-year-old Princess Mathilde?" Fräulein Fröhlich asked rhetorically. "She was so enchanted with Liszt that in a moment of overpowering emotion she gave him her aunt Josephine's precious earrings. Please don't ask me how she got the earrings in the first place."

"No, I won't. But, as you say, this is a strange story. You don't have to be a jeweller to know that women don't usually give men jewellery."

"With Liszt nothing was usual," Fräulein Fröhlich replied. "Women adored him. They looked at him and swooned. They would do anything for him. *Anything*, Herr Koch. His mistress at the time was the Comtesse Marie d'Agoult, who had left her husband and two children to live with him, publicly, delighted to shock the world. She was born in Frankfurt—you must have heard of her."

Robert had not.

"Well, you should have, since her mother was a member of the Bethmann family, the bankers, and her father a French aristocrat. A few years later, after the Countess and Liszt had three children of their own—one of whom was to become Cosima Wagner, you've heard of her, no?—the Countess discovered him making love to another woman during an intermission at a concert he was giving in London. It was not the first time. So she threw the earrings back at him said she had enough of that "dandy"—yes, that is what she said, whatever that means, somebody who heard her say it told me—and they split up. For twenty years Liszt forgot about the earrings. They were probably lying in a silver jewellery box in some château or other, together with hundreds of other trinkets his female admirers had given him. Of course, none of them unique, like Josephine's rubies."

"So when Liszt found them and remembered who had

owned them, and how he got them, he gave them to Joseph Joachim?" Robert asked.

"Not so quick, Herr Koch. When the Countess from Frankfurt called Liszt a dandy, Joachim was still a little boy, though already a *Wunderkind*. Imagine, Herr Koch, in 1844, when he was only thirteen, he played Beethoven's Violin Concerto in London under the direction of Felix Mendelssohn! Wouldn't you like to have been there? And then he played it again at a concert in Windsor before Queen Victoria, Prince Albert, Tsar Nicholas I of Russia, the King of Saxony and the Duke of Wellington. At that time, he had not yet heard Liszt play. But with the arrogance of youth, he thought a man who was said to have such a fabulous technique could not possibly be a great musician. When Mendelssohn heard him say that he gave him a little lecture to convey to him how seriously wrong he was— he called him *Mein Söhnchen*, my little son—and arranged that he would play soon, somewhere or other, his own, Mendelssohn's, violin concerto, *with Liszt accompanying him on the piano*. In due course, this was arranged, in a room in the Hotel London in Vienna. Later, Joachim often described the scene. Liszt was holding a cigar in his right hand, between his index and his middle fingers, right through the performance. Joachim was overwhelmed by the sensitivity and expressiveness with which Liszt played the accompaniment. He took back every unpleasant thing he had ever said about him. They became friends. So what was more natural than, when twenty years later Joachim married Amalie, Liszt gave her Josephine's earrings as a wedding present? After finding them, he probably wanted to get rid of them anyway because they reminded him of Countess Marie d'Agoult."

To Robert something seemed to be wrong with that story.

"And Frau Joachim did not object," he wondered, "when her new husband simply took the earrings and gave them to another woman as a birthday present?"

Fräulein Fröhlich waved a finger at Robert. "You certainly seem to know a lot about women, Herr Koch," she said. "Normally she most certainly would have been upset. But something had come between Joachim and Liszt, so that the new Frau Joachim did not mind at all that he would part with the present Liszt had given her. The two men remained good friends—Liszt was the most generous of men and never held a grudge—but there had been a rupture, not with Liszt the man, nor with Liszt the pianist, but with Liszt the composer. That is no doubt the reason why Amalie Joachim seemed to be quite willing to relinquish the earrings. Already in 1860, Frau Schumann, Brahms and Joachim had publicly criticized Liszt's works. They considered them a threat to the integrity of their art. This criticism was not directed at the New Music as such—it was not directed against Wagner, or Berlioz. Only at Liszt. At the time, Brahms still had great respect for Wagner. They had met in Vienna, in February 1864. Brahms played his "Variations on a Theme by Handel" for him. The piece greatly impressed Wagner. The world had not yet become divided between Wagnerians and Brahmsians. And the young conductor Hermann Levi, who had played the Strauss waltz at the birthday party, was still a great friend and admirer of Brahms and of Frau Schumann, and had not yet crossed over into enemy territory to be rewarded ultimately with the supreme prize—the first performance of Wagner's *Parsifal*. Am I boring you, Herr Koch?"

"Oh no." Robert was not very good at lying. "Of course not. How could you think of such a thing? But I am sure you were going to tell me what Frau Schumann did with the earrings after they had been given to her. You say she did not appreciate them. Did she give them away?"

"She did."

Fräulein Fröhlich paused for a long time, wondering how long it would take Robert to ask the obvious question.

"To whom?" Robert asked, finally.

"To Pauline Viardot."

Chapter 11

Next morning, Wednesday, September 4, 1883, three talkative Hungarian ladies assembled in Boutique Number Five to invest their considerable Iffezheim earnings in generously priced souvenirs. Louis Katzau assumed busts of Bismarck and of Grand Duke Friedrich were of limited interest to them. This assumption proved correct. They did, however, like his English silver teapots and his Russian Easter eggs. Then the handsome, slightly rakish William, the twelfth Duke of Hamilton, dropped in to inspect Katzau's collection of gold cigarette cases. He said he may buy one "for a young lady I know who enjoys smoking." He stayed for a few minutes to practise his rudimentary Hungarian on the ladies. After all, he said, Count Tassilo Festetics was his brother-in-law.

"I am surprised to see Your Grace." Katzau said in Hungarian English. "I would have thought you would have accompanied the Prince of Wales to Bad Homburg."

"How could I?" the Duke asked. "How can I leave my horses alone? Unless you would like to look after them for me?"

Just as Katzau was trying to think of a suitably witty reply, Robert came in. Katzau introduced him as a young jeweller of promise from Frankfurt.

"You must know the Rothschilds," the Duke said.

Robert did not wish to admit that he did not.

"It is always highly gratifying to us Frankfurters," he replied, "that they have spread the good name of our city to the four corners of the earth."

Louis Katzau gave him a congratulatory smile.

He turned to the Duke.

"Her Highness must be pleased that the Prince seemed to have a splendid time while he was staying with her."

"She is indeed, Herr Katzau." The Duke got ready to leave. "But it always takes her a week or two to recover from these visits. Of course, you will not tell her I said this," he added, with a rakish smile, as he gave Robert a quick nod and shook hands with Katzau.

The Hungarian ladies left soon after him.

At last Robert was able to tell him that Fräulein Gertrud Fröhlich, the owner of the Pension Luisenhöhe, had given him potentially sensational new information. In 1867, Clara Schumann presented a copy of the earrings to Pauline Viardot, right here in Baden-Baden.

Louis Katzau whistled through his teeth.

"This may well be the moment we have been waiting for. The Duchess will never know whether you return to her the real thing or a copy. You remember we talked about Pauline Viardot on the way to Jeanne Archambault's villa—we passed her house on the Tiergartenweg. I am told she now lives near Paris, in Bougival, just west of Paris, on a forested hill overlooking the Seine. Very close, by the way, to Josephine's Malmaison. Maybe that's a good sign."

A dark cloud suddenly appeared on his face.

"Normally," he went on," I would have suggested you ask the *Haushofmeister* for a letter of introduction to Madame Viardot. You would take a train to Paris and call on the lady. If she did not still have the earrings, she might know where they are. I have never met her but obviously she is a remarkable person. But this is not the time. The papers say Ivan Turgenev is close to death. She is sure to be looking after him. So we have to think of something else."

There was a moment's silence.

"I think I've got it!" Louis Katzau cried. "Richard Pohl!"

Robert happily recognized the name.

"The music tsar who owns the *Badeblatt*?"

Katzau was duly impressed

"You've learned a lot, Herr Koch, in the week since you've arrived. Just wait a few moments."

Louis Katzau went to the back room and, after two minutes, arrived with an old issue of the *Badeblatt*.

"I've kept this," he said, "because I found it remarkable. Pohl used to be a friend of both Pauline Viardot and Turgenev. And of Clara Schumann. Like Clara, he comes from Saxony."

Baden, July 1, 1883

... His Royal Highness Karl Alexander, the Grand Duke of Sachsen-Weimar-Eisenach, has graciously deigned to award to the publisher of this paper, Richard Pohl, the Knight's Cross First Class, His Own Highest House Order of Vigilance and the Order of the White Falcon.

At the same time he sent him a hand-written letter, dated Weimar, June 25, 1883:

"... You, my dear Herr Pohl, have done me the honour to dedicate your work about Franz Liszt to me, an honour I accept because I am certain that the portrait you draw of the man (whom I may call my friend) with so much understanding and empathy will serve as a monument to this great human being and artist..."

They both laughed.

"Before we go on," Katzau explained, "let me remind you that His Royal Highness is the grandson of Karl August, Goethe's life-long patron and friend, and the brother of Augusta, the wife of our Kaiser. He is the man who single-handedly revived Weimar as the Athens of the North. Pohl lived there for ten years, until 1863 when he moved to Baden-Baden. Liszt had invited his wife, an excellent harpist, to play in his orchestra. Pohl was already well known as music critic and a leading

Wagnerian and went along with his wife to Weimar to write poems, articles and books. We must go and see him."

Katzau sent a courier to Pohl's house to ask him when he might be permitted to visit him for an hour or so, with a friend. The answer was characteristic. Katzau had often noted with amusement that Pohl, who crusaded so valiantly for the *avant-garde* "Music of the Future," was so old-fashioned in his social relationships. It would be great joy to receive him, Pohl had scribbled on a note. Any friend of Katzau's was a friend of his. He was fired with curiosity as to the reasons why Herr Katzau would give him this rare pleasure, somewhat surprisingly, in the middle of the week. He was looking forward to find out.

Pohl may very know quite a lot about Clara Schumann's gift of the earrings to Pauline Viardot, Katzau explained to Robert as they walked along the Lange Strasse up to Richard Pohl's villa in the Hirschstrasse. Viardot was one of the great singers of the century, a composer as well, a brilliant all-round musician, a woman of high intellect and unique social gifts. Little had gone on in her wide circle in Baden-Baden, and that of her lifelong friend Ivan Turgenev, the greatest Russian writer since Pushkin, that Pohl did not know.

Turgenev, Robert should know, had been living in voluntary exile in the West, but occasionally gone home on short visits to look after his estates and maintain contact with other writers such as Leo Tolstoy and Feodor Dostoevsky, and with his publishers. His relations with the authorities in St. Petersburg were often strained. Turgenev had fought hard for the emancipation of the serfs. This had been achieved by Tsar Alexander II in 1861, but Turgenev, a strong liberal and westernizer, was still under a cloud.

Pauline, her husband Louis Viardot and Turgenev had lived side by side in the Tiergartenweg from 1863 to 1870, and in the early seventies people were still talking about the assumed *ménage-à-trois*. Pauline Viardot and Clara Schumann both conducted musical salons, to which Pohl was frequently invited. As was, incidentally, the Duchess of Hamilton.

Pauline's Sunday matinées were held either in Turgenev's château or in her own garden next door in which she had built a theatre-art-gallery-concert-hall, the *Kunsthalle*. To these she attracted High Society, her great friend the German Kaiserin Augusta, also Queen of Prussia, whom she had first met in Berlin in 1847 when Augusta was still Crown Princess. Augusta's husband Wilhelm, now Kaiser, usually stayed behind in the Maison Messmer. He only liked military music, and was quoted as saying, 'When I am at a concert I never know why the music begins and why it stops.' Their daughter, the Grand Duchess Luise of Baden, and her husband, the Grand Duke Friedrich, were also frequent guests. Prince Bismarck and Field Marshall von Moltke attended several times. So did the Prussian ambassador Alfred von Flemming and his wife Armgard, the daughter of Goethe's friend Bettina von Arnim, whom Turgenev had greatly admired when he was a student in Berlin. And, of course, many musicians. Hector Berlioz and Charles Gounod were often there. Katzau did not remember whether it was here in Baden-Baden or later in Paris, but at one of her private concerts Pauline was said to have given goose pimples to her guests when she sang Schubert's *Erlkönig,* with Camille Saint-Saëns at the piano.

Another favourite guest was Boris Ivanov, an old friend of Turgenev from their student days in Berlin, in 1838, when they both made friends with the fiery revolutionary agitator, the dashing, aristocratic, cheerful Mikhail Bakunin with his thick mane of brown hair and piercing gaze. All three had been excited by Hegelian philosophy, with its assurance that the world obeyed intelligible laws that experts could discover, laws identical with the development of spiritual forces, and that therefore progress was possible. For a short time, Ivanov (whom Katzau also knew well) followed in Bakunin's footsteps and, after long discussions with another student of Hegelism, Karl Marx, became a passionate anarchist who believed that before building any new institutions all existing ones had to be torn down, and that a system of anarchist communism would then automatically appear. Ivanov did not remain an anarchist for long and soon became a convinced liberal, like Turgenev, who wrote a novel about Bakunin—*Rudin*—a novel about a weak, ineffectual, idealistic dreamer and phrase-maker. This novel turned out to be not merely about Bakunin, but also, in a strange way, a kind of self-portrait, although not in ideological terms. Turgenev's way of thinking—always fixated, above all, on the future of Russia—was far too skeptical to go along with any passionate ideology. He preferred the views of Alexander Herzen, who was firmly opposed to any doctrine proposed by idealists in the name of altruism and believed that the central problems of Russia were far too complex to be solved at all in the foreseeable future. Ivanov was just as stumped by the immensity of the task of creating a new, decent Russia. After an uncle had left him a considerable sum of money, he bought the hotel *Der Russische Hof* in the Sophienstrasse in Baden-Baden, mainly to please his wife, Margaret, a voluptuous Scottish beauty from Glasgow half his age whom he adored and who wanted to run a hotel. Thanks to her, the Duke of Hamilton, a fellow Scot, gave some of his more extravagant parties in the Ivanovs' establishment.

But Richard Pohl would no doubt tell them more.

The only really important thing that Robert wanted to know before meeting him concerned the historic *Tonkünstlerfest* three years ago. That musicians' festival, at which Kaiserin Augusta received Franz Liszt like a fellow sovereign, was largely Pohl's achievement. Some may have thought it was a consolation prize for his failure, long ago, to persuade his idol Richard Wagner, who always called Pohl the "oldest Wagnerian," to pick Baden-Baden rather than Bayreuth as the site of his Festspielhaus. Whether Pohl ever had a real chance, Katzau did not know. He rather doubted it. But, years ago, he had heard stories about a secret meeting in the Zähringer Hof, allegedly attended by Wagner, Liszt and Berlioz, to discuss a way to serve the cause of the New Music in a common Festspielhaus in Baden-Baden. But they failed to reach agreement. Wagner had probably already received a better offer from King Ludwig, for him alone. Later, there actually was a formal exchange of letters between one of the city fathers and Wagner, inspired by Richard Pohl. All in vain. When the foundations to the Festspielhaus were finally laid in Bayreuth in 1872, Wagner asked Pohl to join him there for good, but by then Pohl was having too good a time in Baden-Baden as music tsar to consider such a move. Perhaps he was also afraid—no doubt with some justification—of being swallowed up by a considerably bigger tsar.

Pohl was a kindly, bespectacled, beardless, professorial gentleman, fifty-seven years old, bald but with strands of white hair hanging over his ears, a long nose and a pointed chin.

A maid showed the visitors to the library. Piles of manuscripts and scores were heaped untidily on every table in the room. On the walls were pictures of composers, poets, and performers, many with dedications.

"A jeweller?" Pohl asked, with his strong Saxonian accent, after Louis Katzau had introduced Robert. "Are you two forming some sort of duet?"

"Who knows?" Louis Katzau replied—a reply that was music to Robert's ears. He then proceeded to tell Pohl about the theft of Josephine's rubies from the Palais Hamilton, of which Pohl had heard rumours, and of Robert's efforts to retrieve them, or at least copies of them, in order to win the Duchess's favour.

"How clever of you," Pohl gave Robert a warm smile. "And I suppose you want me to put something in the *Badeblatt*?"

"Oh no!" both men cried *unisono*. "That would be a grave mistake," Katzau declared. "We only have a chance if we conduct ourselves with—how shall I put it?—the utmost discretion. No, Herr Pohl, we came here to test your memory. Do you remember Clara Schumann giving Pauline Viardot a pair of earrings as a birthday present, sixteen years ago, in 1867?"

Richard Pohl scratched his nose as he tried to collect this thoughts.

"Yes, I think I do remember the occasion," he said. "But you will have to give me a little time to put the pieces together." He closed his eyes. "Yes, I think it is all slowly coming back. Ah yes, the magic earrings that used to belong to Empress Josephine. Magic, like the magic love potion in *Tristan*. Or am I just imagining that they had magic qualities?"

"Oh," Robert smiled, "I don't think anybody ever mentioned that. It's an interesting new thought."

Katzau thought that perhaps the mention of *Tristan* was worth pursuing.

"I wonder why you are associating the earrings with *Tristan*, Herr Pohl. Is there any connection?"

"Not with the earrings as such, no, but with Pauline Viardot. Did you know that, in a private performance in the salon of Madame Kalergie in Paris, Pauline Viardot *sight-read* the role of Isolde, and Richard Wagner himself sang Tristan, with Karl Klindworth at the piano? The whole second act? Pauline had never seen the part before. I don't think she liked it very much, and she held back, she did not use her full voice. Her husband could not abide Wagner, and I think she never told him. Turgenev also had great reservations about Wagner, but I never held it against him. Pauline herself later became quite fond of Wagner's music, especially *Die Meistersinger*, and wrote a letter, which he appreciated very much. In his letter of thanks he asked her to send him a copy of her husband's translation of *Don Quixote*. I don't know whether she ever sent it." He shook his head. "Back to the private performance of the second act of *Tristan*. Wagner had imported Klindworth from London, at his own expense. Madame Kalergie had been very generous to him and he wanted to impress her. You know, she was the niece of the former Russian foreign minister, Count Nesselrode. This was the first time any part of *Tristan* was heard in Paris."

Louis Katzau and Robert were not overwhelmed by this information.

"Oh, forgive me," Pohl said, "you must be patient with me. I want to tell you something else, before we get back to the earrings. It has to do with Richard Wagner."

He swallowed hard as he thought of his dead friend.

"I think it was a little after that memorable *Tristan* performance in Paris when I was Wagner's guest at a dinner party at an inn in St. Gallen. Franz Liszt was there, too, with Carolyne von Wittgenstein. So was Hans von Bülow, Liszt's daughter Cosima's first husband, and Joseph Joachim and, I think, Hermann Levi, who many years later was to conduct the first performance of *Parsifal*, and I forget who else. We were all in high spirits. On such convivial occasions no one was more captivating, more witty, more seductive than Richard Wagner. He was the greatest entertainer imaginable—a man of the theatre all through. Suddenly I had a dreadful migraine and had to sneak away from the table, hoping that nobody would notice. I suffer from these attacks from time to time. I went to my room, took off my clothes and went to bed. After a little while Wagner noticed my absence. There was a knock at my door and there he was, to express his concern and to wish me a speedy recovery. I was so touched that I immediately felt better. I jumped out of bed. He helped me get dressed. Together we went downstairs to join the party again."

"Memories like that," Louis Katzau remarked, "must help you get over the grief over the loss you have suffered. As have we all."

Robert nodded sympathetically.

"So Joachim was a great friend of Wagner's?

"Oh, yes."

"He was also a good friend of Brahms."

"As a matter of fact," Robert said, remembering what Fräulein Fröhlich had told him, "it was in Brahms's presence that Joachim had given Clara Schumann the earrings as a birthday gift. She was not comfortable with them and handed them on to her friend Pauline Viardot."

Richard Pohl gave this a moment's reflection.

"Do you happen to know," Louis Katzau asked, "whether Pauline Viardot and Clara Schumann were close friends?"

"An interesting question, Herr Katzau. Clara first met her in Leipzig when she was just nineteen and Pauline seventeen. Clara was completely captivated. She had never met a singer before who was truly interested in music, not just in singing. That was in 1838. Six years later, Pauline arrived in St. Petersburg just as Pauline was completing a most successful tour.

In her farewell press interview, she said, 'I am leaving you Clara Schumann. Her singing on the piano is better than mine.' They sometimes said they were the oldest friends of the century. Clara was always amazed by Pauline's intellect. Pauline, Clara had discovered, read a great deal and had wide knowledge about many things unrelated to music. Clara was envious of such talents, and also admired Pauline's seemingly carefree way of life. She often said Pauline was the most gifted woman she had ever met. But for Pauline, Clara was a little too earnest. Pauline sometimes did not invite her when she entertained royalty. Then Clara invariably felt snubbed. Sometimes when Clara called on her, Pauline would run away to write a letter in the middle of a conversation, or talk to somebody else."

"From the way you describe Clara Schumann," Louis Katzau said, "it would seem to me to make perfectly good sense that she would think the earrings would mean more to Pauline Viardot than to her."

"You are quite right. I am coming to that," Richard Pohl said. "Please be patient with me. Turgenev had written a libretto in French for an operetta, which Pauline set to music to give her students and her children an opportunity to perform something entertaining on the stage before a small audience. She was an excellent composer, you know. She had already published two volumes of songs, some with verses by Turgenev. Over fifty songs altogether. This operetta was called *Le Dernier Sorcier*. They invited me to the dress rehearsal in the theatre in Turgenev's château. I subsequently translated it into German and it was produced two years later in Weimar, with full orchestra. I remember exactly what Grand Duke Karl Alexander said about it when he saw it first. He said, 'It made Turgenev grow in my estimation, if that was possible. It had his distinctive touch—simple, original, poetic and totally French." He gave a little laugh. "I remember how amused I was to hear him say that he thought the great Russian had written something that was totally French.. But he was quite right. After all, the Grand Duke's childhood had been shaped by Goethe, as he often told us, and he was a man of taste. Liszt also was enthusiastic. What

Goethe had been to Grand Duke Karl Alexander's grandfather, Liszt was to him—the jewel in his crown. Liszt wanted to do the orchestration, but I think in the end Édouard Lanner did it. It was also produced in Jena, Karlsruhe and London, and just last year, in 1882, in Bougival, once again in a private performance, in Viardot's home. By the way, Turgenev saw to it that the original French text was never published. He insisted that not a single line of his written in a language other than Russian was ever to be printed. Anybody who published a text not written in his mother tongue was, he said, 'a scoundrel and a wretched swine without talent,'"

Richard Pohl did not seem to notice that Louis Katzau had taken out his watch from his waistcoat and was looking at it.

"Even if *Le Dernier Sorcier* was initially only a modest student's exercise, you must understand what an extraordinary event it was, this production of a French operetta written by a Russian of wide European reputation, performed in a French château on German soil, set to music by a celebrated Spanish singer. It was a true Concert of Europe."

"A Spanish singer?" Louis Katzau asked. "I thought Pauline Viardot was French."

"Oh, no! Pauline Viardot was the daughter of Manuel Garcia, the famous singer and impresario who lived in Seville. No one was more Spanish than Manuel Garcia, even if he did not know who his father was—perhaps a gypsy, perhaps a Moor, perhaps a Jew. It was he who had created the role of Count Almaviva in Rossini's *Il Barbiere di Seviglia*. Garcia was the entrepreneur who, with his company, first introduced Italian opera to the United States. He was responsible for the production of *Don Giovanni* in New York in 1825. There he made friends with the old man who had written the libretto forty years earlier, Lorenzo da Ponte. He was living there."

"Pauline Viardot also met da Ponte?" Katzau asked. Robert wondered who da Ponte was and what he had to do with the earrings.

"Probably. Garcia had taken the whole family to

America. But I never heard her talk about da Ponte. No wonder—she was only four at the time, taking singing lessons from
her father and already speaking four languages."

Unless we are careful, Louis Katzau thought, Richard
Pohl will tell us the full story of Pauline Viardot, Louis Viardot
and Ivan Turgenev. He had heard it many times before, including her encounter with Charles Dickens who had journeyed to
Paris just to hear her sing Orphée, shortly before she left the
operatic stage. Dickens was moved to tears. After the performance he went to see her husband Louis Viardot, his face still
wet, and asked him to take him, please, to the great singer's
dressing room to pay homage. Viardot did so and introduced
Dickens with the words "Permit me to present a fountain."

It had been George Sand who had introduced Pauline to
Louis Viardot because she thought Pauline needed a husband
who was both cultivated and rich. In George Sand's Chopin
novel *Consuela* a character modelled on Pauline plays an important role.

When she was over forty, her voice began to deterio-
rate. She did not want to live in Paris any more, the scene of her
greatest triumphs. So she and Turgenev moved to Baden-Baden
where she was to teach and compose, give a few recitals and
produce little plays and operettas with him.

Undoubtedly, Louis Katzau knew, the nature of the relationship between Pauline Viardot and Ivan Turgenev was remarkable. When Pauline was twenty-one, Turgenev twenty-
five, she sang Rossini in St. Petersburg. That is when he fell in
love with her. That was fifty years ago. Since that moment, she
had held him in thrall. There had never been any doubt that
Turgenev's lifelong devotion to her was deeply romantic and
intensely emotional, that it was at the very centre of his being.
It was often assumed that at least one of Pauline's four children
was Turgenev's. But at the same time it was a strangely formal
relationship. Turgenev always addressed her in the second person plural—*vous*, never *tu*. One thing remained fundamental
throughout. She was the dominant partner and he, the gentle
giant from barbaric Russia, from the first moment on, worshipped

her from below. Many of his novels were studies of weak, indecisive men and their relationships with strong women. On one occasion, Flaubert called him a "soft pear." The nickname stuck. He always took it in good humour.

The second time Louis Katzau looked at his watch Pohl noticed it.

"Oh yes," he said, "*Le Dernier Sorcier.* Josephine's earrings. That is why you came to see me. You see, it was during the dress rehearsal that Clara Schumann gave them to Pauline. I can now remember it quite clearly. Let me set the scene. It happened in the theatre in Turgenev's little château—*le château enchanté,* some of us called it—in the Tiergartenweg, half way up the Fremersberg, next door to Viardot's Swiss chalet. I suppose I should not really call it a theatre—it was a salon, divided in the middle by a plain green curtain. I don't think it had more than thirty seats. Turgenev had the château built for fifty thousand francs by a French architect in the style of *Louis Treize,* a mixture of gothic and Renaissance, complete with turrets, slate roof, glass doors, a large salon also intended to be used as a theatre and a semicircular terrace. Those who built their residences in the *Louis Treize* style did so as a political gesture. They were in opposition to Napoleon III, as Turgenev and Louis Viardot were. Viardot in particular considered him an abomination. Turgenev had not yet moved in. He was not comfortable with its grandeur and still lived in his small apartment in the Schillerstrasse. Clara Schumann often sat at the centre of the first row. Johannes Brahms was sometimes with her, but he rarely felt at ease in such elegant company and was usually grumpy."

"So you say Clara Schumann," Robert asked, "handed them over during the dress rehearsal?"

"Not *during,* Herr Koch, just *before* the overture. Clara Schumann had not yet taken her seat. I don't think Brahms was with her, on that occasion. She walked straight to Pauline Viardot, who was sitting at the piano, looking at the handwritten score and frowning. Perhaps she thought she should make a last-minute change. That is when Clara handed her the earrings. Of course I did not hear what she said. Pauline shook her head, smiled politely, and made a gesture with her right hand indicating clearly that she did not want to accept them. But in the end Clara talked her into it."

"Did she put them on?" Robert asked.

"No. She held them in her hand, as if she did not know what to do with them."

"Do you happen to remember what the earrings looked like?"

"I think they were red. With quite large oval stones. They must have been rubies. Later, Pauline told us what Clara had said. She said they had been given to her, but they were wrong for her. She thought they were more Pauline Viardot's taste."

"From the pictures I have seen of Madame Viardot," Louis Katzau observed, "she was not at all pretty. *Une jolie laide.*"

"That is true. She was not good looking. Not in the usual way. But the brilliance of her personality always shone through."

"Did you ever find out whether Clara Schumann told Madame Viardot anything else about the earrings?" Robert asked.

"Yes, I did, Herr Koch. She said she had been told the Empress Josephine had worn them at her coronation. I remember what Turgenev's reaction was. He laughed and said next time his friend Leo Tolstoy came to Baden-Baden to gamble they should give them to him because he was working on a book in which Napoleon played a certain role."

"Oh yes. Of course. *War and Peace.* And what did Pauline Viardot reply to that?" Louis Katzau asked.

"She said she was too superstitious to wear them herself. She then wondered whether they would suit any of the performers. Her daughter Louise, a mezzo soprano, sang Prince Lélio, in trousers, a *travesti* role, so obviously that was out of the question. Stella, the sorcerer's daughter, was sung by a student with a very round face. Pauline thought women with round faces should never wear long, drooping earrings. Fifteen-year-old Claudie was the Queen of the Elves, and thirteen-year-old Marianne was the Principal Elf. No self-respecting elf, Pauline decided, would ever wear earrings."

"What is *Le Dernier Sorcier* about?" Robert wondered out loud.

"It's a rather profound Russian fairy tale about a wicked sorcerer who lives in a forest and whose name is Krakamiche. In the Baden-Baden performances, he was played by Turgenev himself, who spoke his lines because he could act but not sing. The part required that he spent some time clowning and grovelling on the ground, which some of his Russian compatriots found undignified and humiliating. So, by the way, did the Crown Princess of Prussia, the daughter of Queen Victoria. Krakamiche delivers a throne speech that parodies the orations of Napoleon III, which, an observer wrote, provoked 'thick laughter' from the King of Prussia. Three years later Napoleon was to surrender to the King."

Pohl leaned back in his chair, enjoying having an audience. "Krakamiche has a dim-witted servant called Perlimpinpin, who never finishes a sentence and gets many laughs. Long, long ago Krakamiche had been terrifying but now his sworn enemies, the elves, are systematically depriving him of his power. They use a magic blade of the grass *Moly,* which is mentioned in the *Odyssey,* to make him believe that he will be restored to his former strength and then trick him out of it. The elves also employ Prince Lélio, who always appears with a magic rose in his hand and who loves Krakamiche's beautiful daughter, Stella, to chase the old sorcerer out of the forest. The story is full of dark, pessimistic ironies. The elves represent Nature, Will and Unreason, and the wicked sorcerer Reason. Turgenev must have been reading Schopenhauer."

Louis Katzau brooded over this story for a few moments.

"You mention Tristan's magic love potion, a magic blade of grass and a magic rose," he said. "And you slipped in the word 'magic' when you first mentioned the earrings. Perhaps you didn't notice it. As Herr Koch has observed," he nodded to Robert, "nobody we talked to about the earrings had done that before. I am beginning to wonder—was Pauline Viardot superstitious?"

"Every artist is," Richard Pohl replied with a smile. "And surely," he continued, addressing himself to Robert, "so are the people who buy precious stones from jewellers like yourself. Why else spend all that money? Obviously you don't have to be a great artist to believe that rubies, especially if they had belonged to Empress Josephine, have certain—how shall I put it?—metaphysical powers."

"You must have a reason for saying that, Herr Pohl," Robert replied.

"Yes, I do. Pauline Viardot took the earrings home and deposited them in her golden jewellery box. Soon afterwards, Dostoevsky, and his new wife, the nineteen-year-old Anna Grigorievna came to Baden-Baden. He was about forty-five or -six. He had already spent some weeks in the West to escape his creditors in St. Petersburg who were about to throw him into the debtors' prison. What better place to restore his finances than in our casino? As you no doubt know, Dostoevsky was, for a time, an addicted gambler. He stayed in cheap lodgings in a blacksmith's house on the Gernsbacher Strasse. The blacksmith was a friend of mine. Two or three weeks after Dostoevsky had left Baden-Baden for Geneva, having lost everything he had won, and more, the blacksmith visited me—I think I was his only friend who knew how to read—and gave me a dossier containing two notebooks, one containing the sketch of a story obviously written in haste to make money, the other a long letter drafted in Geneva after the Dostoevsky couple had left Baden-Baden, but sent—probably by mistake, there simply is no other explanation—to my friend the blacksmith. Neither has been published. They will help you see for yourselves whether—and, if so, in what way—Pauline Viardot was superstitious."

Richard Pohl pulled out the dossier from the lower drawer of his desk.

Chapter 12

JOSEPHINE'S RUBIES
by Feodor Dostoevsky

I was not pleased to have been assigned a miserable room on the fourth floor of the Hotel Bellevue in Baden-Baden, next to those occupied by the valet and the maid. But my mood changed quickly for the better when, just before lunch, my employer handed me two thousand-franc notes and asked me to go downstairs to the hotel counter and get change in the form of twenty-one hundred-franc notes. This was not a task normally assigned to a tutor entrusted with the education of two children of noble birth but humble talents—Sasha, age nine, and Maria, age seven—but I was delighted to perform it anyway because I wanted to enjoy the invigorating sensation of having money in my hand again, after having lost my last franc in the Casino the night before. Moreover, the assignment indicated to myself, to the world—or at least to that part of the world that witnessed the exchange of banknotes in the lobby—that I was in a position once again to engage in financial transactions. It was not written on my face, even if the concierge knew it, that I was a mere employee of General Yegor Illyich Rostanev and his *souffrante* wife, Natasha Glafira, and that the money was his.

Perhaps my relationship to money, and to the related subject of gambling, requires a little explanation. My father was a

147

doctor and a miser. When I was a child in St. Petersburg he never let me have any money of my own at all. Once I was away at school, I was allowed only a fraction of the money I needed. I had to beg my father for it and he always made me feel guilty whenever I spent any of it. Later, at the university, I was an intellectual, a free spirit and a bohemian and I hated the greedy and often crooked shopkeepers from whom I was compelled to borrow. They always charged exorbitant rates of interest

On my first trip abroad—to Wiesbaden—I discovered roulette. Since I played with a mixture of aggression, guilt and anger, I invariably lost. My companion, Dasha, to whom I had promised marriage, drove me wild by insisting that in my heart of hearts I really wanted to lose. I later broke my promise to her, thus causing her to return to her drunken father who regularly beat her.

I knew General Rostanev was waiting for me as I climbed the stairs to his room on the second floor to hand him his change. Taunting me was one of the main pleasures in his life.

"I suppose," he said, "you want to take the children to the Casino with you to teach them how to lose."

"I am afraid, sir," I said, "when the time comes they will have to learn it by themselves."

The General gave me no credit for the speed and brilliance of my reply.

"I know it's none of my business," he continued, "but I watched you last night. You're on your way to becoming an addicted gambler. No one will be able to save you once you've crossed the line."

"There is no need for concern," I declared firmly. "As I have told you before, sir, I have a system and I always know when to stop. Besides, I don't have any money left."

So far, whenever the General lectured me, I had carefully refrained from explaining my system to him, knowing very well he would dismiss it as "silly." But merely because it was so elementary it was far from silly. My system was, to put it in its simplest form, never to get excited, to keep my head the whole time, to play calmly, with calculation, with *sang froid*, whatever the state of the game. That was the most difficult thing in the world to do, but it was essential and the system was infallible. Whenever I lost, I knew it was because my attention had strayed. I envied those who had no need to prove to themselves that they were capable of such superhuman self-control.

"You seem to have forgotten, Dmitri" the General said as he walked to his dressing table to pick up two one-hundred-franc notes of the money I had just handed him and give them to me, "that I owe you one month's wages."

"No, sir, I certainly had not forgotten," I replied. "But they are not due until tomorrow."

"So you have money for one more day," he said gruffly, "to make a fool of yourself. I will be watching you."

"Thank you, sir," I said. "I will see you tonight."

On the stairs down to the dining room, I encountered the older Rostanev daughter, Tatyana, aged twenty-one, carrying her whip and wearing her riding costume, going upstairs to change for lunch. Tatyana was a student of literature in St. Petersburg and had come along with us to spend her second semester at the University of Heidelberg, very close to Baden-Baden. If I had not been infatuated with the intoxicatingly beautiful soprano Katarina Alexandrovna I would not have hesitated to yield to Tatyana's many invitations to become her lover. Naturally Tatyana was jealous of Katarina, and there had been a number of embarrassing scenes.

Katarina was the daughter of a ship builder in Odessa. She had recently left her husband, right here in Baden-Baden. By pure chance she had seen him and the wife of her singing teacher embracing behind a tree in the gardens surrounding the Alte Schloss. The two couples—Katarina and her husband, and the singing teacher and his wife—knew each other well and were frequent guests at matinées in Turgenev's little château in the Tiergartenweg and at soirées in the Palais Hamilton, the residence of the Duchess of Hamilton, the daughter of the Grand Duchess Stephanie.

Tatyana's various attempts to seduce me need not be spelled out in this account. She never gave up. She liked to sit near me at the *table d'hôte* because she said I reminded her agreeably of her fiancé, Prince Aleksey Petrovsky, whom she was to marry in November. It was part of her strategy to remind me from time to time that she was a woman of the world who had no intention, during her forthcoming wedding night, to learn anything she had not already learned from men of lower birth. She was by no means averse to continue her learning experience with me. *Au contraire.* Her German fellow students, she usually added, were no good as lovers—they were mechanical, uninspired and lacked imagination. Of course, once she was married she had every intention to remain faithful to her husband. I indicated to her that, although tutoring was, for the time being, my profession, tutoring her in the art of love was not the purpose for which her father General Rostanev had engaged me.

As soon as we sat down at the *table d'hôte* and the children had folded their napkins on their laps, a fading beauty named Irena began telling Tatyana and me in a deliberately neutral voice that, according to a letter she had just received from St. Petersburg, her grandmother, who was over ninety, was not likely to live another two days.

Tatyana expressed her sympathy.

"She is only my step-grandmother," Irena explained. "No blood relation. But she was very fond of me and I am certain the old lady has remembered me in her will. On the strength of a word from home, Monsieur de Grieux has promised to lend me ten thousand. Do you know Monsieur de Grieux?" Irena asked me.

"I regret I do not," I said. "Obviously I should," I added, "since he appears to be a man of wealth."

"That is not the only reason," Irena observed. "He is a most interesting man. I discovered the other evening that the French officer who took my father prisoner in 1812 just outside Moscow was Monsieur de Grieux's father."

"That is amazing," I exclaimed. "What a coincidence!"

Tatyana, too, found it extraordinary. "Tell us more," she said. "This is far more interesting than what I heard yesterday at the Conversationshaus from a man of about seventy. When he was ten, in 1812, he said, a French soldier had fired on him, merely for the pleasure of discharging his musket. But, fortunately, he had missed."

"Impossible!" a French guest sitting opposite us exploded. "No French soldier would fire on a child!"

Tatyana shrugged her shoulders. "I'm merely repeating what he said."

"May I go on?" Irena said, visibly annoyed at being interrupted. "Monsieur de Grieux's father has written his memoirs, and so has mine," Irena said. "His father had been a lieutenant in Napoleon's army during the Italian campaigns, and during every one of his campaign after them, and never recovered from the humiliating retreat from Moscow. After Waterloo he would have liked to have shared Napoleon's exile in St. Helena, but the English would not let him. He died in his bed in 1818, a broken man. His memoirs are very moving. And so are my father's."

"I wonder if it's too late to show both of them to Count Lev Nikolayevich Tolstoy," Tatyana said.

"Who's he?" Irena asked. Tatyana explained that the Count was a writer who was working on a novel about Napoleon's campaign in 1812, and was doing extensive research. Most of the book was finished. He had made his reputation, she added, for writing a personal report on the Battle of Sebastopol in 1856 that was so gripping that Tsar Alexander II had it immediately translated into French. The Tsarina had wept when she read it."

"Did you say Tolstoy?" an old Russian in a red waistcoat asked. "I remember him. He was staying in the Holländische Hof in the Sophienstrasse. It must have been—let me see— exactly ten years ago. It was the first time he was outside Russia."

"How on earth do you remember that?" Irena asked.

"Because that year I was staying in the same hotel. I

remember that a banker named Ogier brought him home one evening from the Casino after the Count lost all his money, and stayed with him until three in the morning, talking about literature. I also remember the Count telling me at breakfast that on the Promenade he was astonished to encounter—I still remember the names—Prince Obolenskii, Prince Nicholas Trubetskoi, Count Olsufiev, Prince Menschikov, Count Orlov-Denisov, Count Brobinskii and the Princess Shcherebatov. They all meet regularly to gossip with other compatriots under the so-called 'Russian Tree'—a magnificent birch tree—outside the Conversationshaus."

"What an amazing memory you have, sir," Irena shook her head.

"I also remember," the man went on, "what he had to say about losing all his money, plus the money he borrowed from Ogier. He said 'I was surrounded by imbeciles. But I was the biggest imbecile of them all.'"

I was pondering that remark on my way to the Casino after dinner, dressed in my best evening clothes and carrying two hundred francs in my pocket. Surely, I thought, Tolstoy cannot have said anything as foolish as that. Serious gamblers gamble not because they are imbeciles but because they have to, not because they want to. Does a man who has sprained his ankle choose to limp? Whenever I am asked why I have to gamble, rather than choose to gamble, I am stumped. I write stories like these in order to find out. Who knows the reason? Who can understand the mechanism? To erase my guilt for breaking my promise to Dasha? I am sure I was not the only person who often pondered why, when at the gaming tables we confront the Irrational, as it were, raw and naked, we do so in formal dress. We do so in places designed to replicate the Palais de Versailles, and in rituals designed by masters of etiquette and protocol, to impose the severest restraints of civilization, as though we were in the presence of kings and queens—which sometimes we are, though they usually come incognito. Otherwise we would all cut each other's throats and subject the croupiers to torture and death. Those of us who do not follow a proven system when gambling often suspend their religious beliefs in favour of some absurdly atavistic superstitions. I think, however, it is perfectly rational of me if, before approaching a table, I ask myself whether or not this is a lucky day for me. Asking myself whether this is a lucky day for me is just as rational as it was for Napoleon to have asked his officers, before appointing them marshall, whether they were lucky. If I feel well and am able to concentrate, I know I will be lucky and will not, by losing, add a single franc to the already overflowing treasury of the Grand Duke of Baden, the owner of the Casino, who rents it out to Monsieur Bénazet. If I have any doubts about it, I stay away.

At ten in the evening, Tatyana and I walked into the crowded, hushed Casino. In the centre of the table was a large polished wooden basin with a moveable rim. Around it there were thirty small compartments, red and black, in irregular order. The moveable rim was set in motion by hand. The marble was released to move in the direction opposite to that of the rim. For the public, it was impossible to predict where the marble would stop.

There were about hundred fifty to two hundred people in the room, several rows deep. Those who had succeeded in squeezing their way right to the tables stubbornly stayed there—until they had lost. People who came just to watch were told to leave. Though there were chairs placed around the long green table few of the players sat down. They preferred putting down their stakes standing up—*pair, impair, passé, manqué*. People relentlessly pressed forward from the back, waiting for their turn. Sometimes a hand from the second or even third row would put down a stake. Every few minutes there was a scene. Officials usually settled disputes quickly. Sometimes police officers in plain clothes had to intervene. But they main job was to catch pickpockets, for whom the Casino was paradise.

Tatyana and I squeezed our way through the crowd close enough to the table to see a man we later found out was a French marquis win and lose ten thousand francs, cheerfully, within two minutes, without a murmur. Then an Italian won five thousand. Another person—let us call him Herr X—stretched out his hand and added the Italian's winnings to his own pile. The Italian began shouting. There was an uproar. Fingers were pointed at Herr X, who denied everything. "Prove it," he said. "Produce witnesses!" An official soon appeared from nowhere, said a few things quietly to both, and everybody calmed down. The two were probably bribed into silence.

What happened next was a severe test to my *sang froid*, but I was happy to note that I passed the test with flying colours. First, I felt some one touching my sleeve. I turned around. It was Katarina who had squeezed through the crowd to greet me. I held my breath. She looked absolutely stunning, in a blood-red dress, with a very low décolletage, exposing a large area of her exquisite skin. She wore a pair of ruby earrings I had not seen on her before. Obviously she had chosen her dress to match her new earrings.

"Good evening, Dmitri," she said, ignoring Tatyana, who, visibly annoyed by the snub, turned around and left to look for her father. "You're trying again?"

"Last evening I lost," I said, "because of you, Katarina. You distracted me and you know it."

"Then tonight, my friend, I will commit the ultimate sacrifice," she announced, laughing. "I will keep out of your sight. And I will do one more thing," she said, taking off her rubies. "I will lend you Pauline Viardot's earrings. She predicted they would bring me luck. She is convinced they have metaphysical qualities. Obviously she is right. I made a hundred thousand francs. I know they will bring you luck, too, Dmitri. Put them in your pocket. But stop playing the moment you have won a hundred thousand. We will add your hundred thousand to my hundred thousand and spend an agreeable week or two in Florence, and after that—who knows?"

My throat was dry.

I put the earrings in my pocket

"The Empress Josephine," Katarina continued, "wore them

during the coronation in Notre Dame."

The pistol that killed Pushkin is exactly like any other pistol of the same make. But it is sacred. There is a halo, too, over Josephine's earrings, whatever one may think of Napoleon. However, I was certain I would succeed tonight because of my system, not because of the sacred earrings in my pocket. I would not yield to primitive superstition. But who was I to say no to her offer?

"May I really borrow them?"

"Yes, Dmitri. I am serious. As I told you, they belong to Pauline. I must return them tomorrow."

"How did she get them?"

"The pianist Clara Schumann gave them to her. There is no question they are authentic. Promise to stop playing the moment you've made one hundred thousand. I will be in the lounge."

I promised.

My employer, General Rostanev, with Tatyana at his side, watched me closely from across the table as I staked two hundred francs on "even." That is how I started. My eyes never strayed from the marble, my heartbeat never accelerated, my hands remained dry, my breathing even. I won a hundred thousand francs in six and a half minutes.

General Rostanev and Tatyana walked around the table and made their way through the crowd to congratulate me. He shook my hand. For the first time he treated me like a man who deserved respect. Tatyana kissed me on both cheeks.

Somebody told Katarina, who soon emerged from the lounge.

"Congratulations," she beamed, throwing her arms around me.

I shook her off. I no longer felt the slightest desire for her. The fulfillment I had just experienced exceeded a thousand times any joy she could ever give me. I had won because I had remained unexcited. There was no question I had to return to the table.

I put my hand in my pocket, took out Josephine's earrings

and gave them back to her.

"I'm delighted," Katarina said, "Josephine did not distract you."

"Thank you."

I did not want her to think I owed my reversal of fortunes to the earrings. It was entirely due to my system.

"Please excuse me."

I began the push my way back to the table.

"Dmitri," she called out, an edge of hysteria in her voice. "Don't be an imbecile! You promised!"

I did not turn round.

That night, I was among the last to leave the Casino. No wonder I lost the hundred thousand francs. I simply could not keep my eyes on the marble, however much I tried to stick to my system. I kept thinking of the other promise I had broken, the promise I had made to Dasha.

"You always lose," Dasha used to say, "because in your heart of hearts you want to lose."

Extracts from draft letter from Feodor Dostoevsky to the poet and literary critic Apollon Maykov, written in Geneva on August 16, 1867[7]

... For what a long time I've been silent and not answered your letter, dear and unforgettable friend Apollon Nikolaevich. How much I have lamented your absence! You know the circumstances that forced me to leave and made me have more and more attacks of my cerebral disorder of which you know. It was either debtors' prison—or leaving the country. To tell you the truth, I would not have minded debtors' prison. It would have provided me with enough material for another House of the Dead, which brought me between four and five thousand rubles. But I had my young bride to think of, my guardian angel Anna Grigorievna. So we left on our travels.

Now, after six weeks of hell in Germany, we have landed in another alien land where there is not a Russian face, not a Russian book, not a Russian thought. How can one spend one's life abroad? I have not been in my native land for more than a year, without knowing when I can return. I need Russia. I need it to write. I need it to breathe.

In Germany, I heard that my creditors have started proceedings against me for recovery of the money I owe them. I didn't even have enough money to live on! I wrote to Katkov, the editor of *The Russian Messenger*, and described to him my situation. I asked for an advance of five hundred rubles. And what do you think? He sent it! What a wonderful person he is!

So we had enough to set off to Switzerland. I wanted to show it to Anna Grigorievna to amuse her. I wanted to travel a bit with her. Dear Apollon Nikolaevich, you're a person with a heart. I have always valued your judgement. It's not painful for me to confess to you. I will now begin describing to you my vile and shameful deeds.

My dear friend, you, of all people, know that my nature is passionate. Everywhere I go, and in everything I do, I go to the last limit. I have done so all my life. No, it's even worse. I always go *beyond* my last limit.

Once I was in Dresden, it occurred to me to go to Baden-Baden. I felt an overpowering temptation to sacrifice two hundred francs and win two thousand—that is living expenses for four months. The awful truth is that on previous occasions I won. Let me tell you what my guardian angel Anna Grigorievna has told me about my gambling. She says my rationalizations about the possibility of winning at roulette by using my gambling system are entirely correct. I would succeed without a doubt, she told me, if only I were a cool-headed Englishman or a German and not a nervous and impulsive Russian who always goes beyond the outermost limits in everything.

Of course, she is absolutely right. To give you an idea of what an angel she is—she has never reproached me for my losses. She has never quarrelled with me. She gave me the last of her money without a word—realizing that, most likely, I would lose it.

We went to Baden-Baden. The devil immediately played a prank on me. In three days I gambled one hundred francs and won four thousand, with extraordinary ease. Anna Grigorievna implored me to be satisfied and leave town immediately. But I had just seen people win twenty thousand, thirty thousand francs! (Of course, one never sees the losses.) ' Well—I need money more badly than they do.

I lost my four thousand. I started pawning my clothing—but not my dinner jacket, which I needed to enter the Casino again. Anna Grigorievna pawned everything she had. Then she tried to comfort me. What a treasure she is!

Oh, how detestable the Germans are, what usurers, scoundrels and cheats they all are, every one of them. Our landlady, sensing our situation, raised the rent! I wrote to Katkov again. And do you know—he sent another five hundred rubles! But more than half of that went to the interest and the renewal of the pawning of our furniture in St. Petersburg.

With one hundred francs in my pocket I went back to the Casino. Just as I was about to sit down at the table, a tall, gaunt man (whom I had seen before) touched me on the shoulder and introduced himself as Nikolai Konstaninovitch, a friend of Ivan Goncharev. Goncharev—the author of *Oblomov*—was in Baden-Baden. I had spoken to him a few times.

"I've been observing you," Nikolai Konstaninovitch said. "I don't need to ask you whether you are superstitious. All gamblers are."

Since he did not ask me, I did not answer. If I had answered I would have said that as a person I was very superstitious, but as a gambler I was not superstitious at all. I had a rational system that was absolutely fail-safe. My only problem was that I was not always able to follow it.

Nikolai Konstaninovitch pulled out of his pocket a pair of earrings, with blood-red stones, which I suppose were rubies.

"Do you see the man over there?" He pointed to a pink-faced, white-haired man standing behind the table, smoking, talking to someone with his back to me.

"These earrings earned him thirty thousand, less than an hour ago. He is an opera singer. He held them in his hand while he played. I have instructions to pass them on to you."

"Instructions from whom?"

"From Ivan Turgenev."

A violent spasm seized the pit my stomach. Oh no! Turgenev! The man to whom I owe fifty thaler! The idol of my youth whom I now disliked so intensely! The famous writer who helped me launch my magazine when I was still completely unknown! The atheist whose cool self-assurance and so-called "charm" infuriate me every time I meet him! The man whose views on Russia are the opposite of mine! The author of a new novel *Smoke*, which I despise!

Of course, I knew he lived in Baden-Baden. That is where the new novel takes place. Two years ago, in Wiesbaden, when I was desperate, I asked him for a loan of hundred francs. He sent me fifty.

"And is that opera singer over there"—I looked at the man behind the table who had thirty thousand francs in his pocket—"a friend of Pauline Viardot?"

Like everybody else, I knew about Turgenev's relationship with the famous singer.

"He is indeed," Nikolai Konstaninovitch said. "She lent the earrings to her colleague, to bring him luck. They belong to her and have already brought luck to her friends. She now wants you to take them. Turgenev suggested it to her. You see, they are very special earrings. The Empress Josephine wore them at her coronation."

"They did not bring *her* much luck," I cried. "They brought her divorce and death!"

"But to others, as the opera singer over there can testify," Nikolai Konstaninovitch continued calmly, "they bring good luck. But if you prefer to do without..."

I suddenly remembered something.

"Pauline Viardot is a witch!" I whispered.

He stared at me. "Why do you say that?"

"Because in his new novel *Smoke*," I went on, my voice very low, "Turgenev wrote that Irina, who was obviously Pauline Viardot, had hypnotic powers. She was a member of an ancient family, he wrote, that had been accused of witchcraft. It was thanks to these inherited powers that the hero, Litvinov, was obsessed with her. Litvinov, of course, is Turgenev."

"So much the more reason for you to take them, " Nikolai Konstaninovitch insisted. "And once they have done their job, you must return them to me, not to anybody else. Oh, and one more thing. Turgenev would like you to pay him a visit. Of course, when you go, not a word about this."

I took the earrings.

First they brought me luck—forty thousand.

Then they brought me total, irrevocable, irretrievable disaster.

Oh, my dear *unforgettable* friend Apollon Nikolaevich, how I *loathe* Ivan Turgenev!

I went to see him at noon the next day in his pretentious villa on the Tiergartenweg, which he has built himself and calls his *château enchanté*. His valet who wore a frock coat opened the door and showed me in. Turgenev had just started his breakfast. He jumped up from his antique chair, wiped his mouth with a linen napkin with the expression of the purest, most beatific joy, embraced me as though I was a general and offered me his cheek, which I was forced to touch with my lips. My blood curdled. He wore a dark grey short jacket with little mother-of-pearl buttons and did not cover his prominent belly. A woollen checkered rug, which had been covering his knees trailed to the floor, although it was warm in the room. He offered me breakfast, which I declined. But I accepted a cup of coffee. I sat down at the table while he continued eating his rolls, on which he spread butter and raspberry jam.

We started talking. No reference was made to my gambling, nor to my debt to him. I had no doubt he had heard about my loss at the Casino and knew that I had my back against the wall. Rather than offer me another loan, which he certainly, very obviously, could well afford, he talked about literature. We discussed some of the articles and books a few of our common friends had recently published (some had been forwarded to me) and then he mentioned *Smoke*. Very pointedly, he did not ask me what I thought about it. He knew it without having to ask. He told me about the lashings he had received everywhere in St. Petersburg and Moscow. Why did he tell me? I was not surprised. He deserved them. He certainly could not have wanted me to commiserate with him. Surely, there were enough people in Baden-Baden only too happy to do that. So, in order to say something, I said I wasn't sure I had grasped the main point of the novel. He was eager to enlighten me. The main point, he said, was that it would be no loss to mankind whatsoever if Russia disappeared from the face of the earth. Of course I remembered that shameless phrase in the book. I managed to look puzzled. He greatly enjoyed my discomfiture and said the character in the novel who said this spoke for him. It was obvious he wanted to provoke me into an argument. I did not say a word. I just bit my tongue. So, in order to enrage me further, he said—I know, my friend, you won't be able to believe it—"I am an atheist through and through."

Yes, my dear Apollon Nikolaevich, that is what he said. Can you imagine? Ivan Turgenev actually boasted about being an atheist! But my God, deism gave us Christ, such a lofty notion of man that it cannot be comprehended without reverence! One cannot help believing that this ideal of humanity is everlasting. And what have these atheists put in its place? Instead of the loftiest divine beauty, which they spit on, they have nothing. They are disgustingly selfish, flippant and proud. What could I say?

I certainly did not tell him that I have been thinking for some time about writing a novel to be called The Atheist. But before sitting down to write it I will have to read almost a whole library of atheists, Catholic and Greek Orthodox theologians. I have invented my chief character. A Russian of our set, middle aged, not very educated, but not uneducated either, a man of quite good social position who suddenly loses his faith. He pokes his nose among the younger generation, the pan-Slavs, the fanatical sects, the hermits and priests. Please, don't breathe a word about this to any one.

He took another roll and covered it with butter and raspberry jam. I said I was not in the least surprised to hear he was an atheist, and that I really had nothing to say about that. Then I returned to *Smoke*. I said my impressions of the Germans were clearly very different from his. He said he had respect for the Germans, but the important thing he wanted to get across was that there was one correct path available to everyone and that was the path of civilization, and that all attempts at Russianism were swinishness and stupidity.

I told myself, this man knows nothing about today's Russia. He has been away too long. So I suggested him he should order a telescope from Paris.

"Why?" he asked.

"To train it on Russia. To see what it is like. I really had no idea, Ivan Sergeevich, that all that criticism of *Smoke* has got so much under your skin. Why don't you rise above it? It's really not worth it. Forget about it."

"I don't know what you are talking about," he snapped. "I don't pay any attention to it at all. Let's talk about something else."

I told him what I thought about the Germans, a people of rogues and swindlers. The common people here, I said, were far worse and far more dishonest than our people at home. Why talk about civilization in connection with the Germans? What had civilization done for them?

My dear Apollon Nikolaevich, Turgenev turned pale when I asked that question. He literally turned pale. I am not exaggerating.

"When saying these things," he retorted, "you offend me personally. You should know that I have settled in Germany for good, that I consider myself a German. I am no longer a Russian. I am proud of that."

I could not believe my ears. I rose from my chair.

"Please forgive me for having offended you." My voice was ice cold. "I hope I will soon be able to pay you the debt I owe you."

"That would be very nice," he said with a frigid smile.

I turned around and, without shaking hands, left.

He remained seated.

The next day I went back to the Casino, to return the earrings to Nikolai Konstaninovitch. To my horror, there was Ivan Turgenev, talking to him. He saw me, our eyes met, but we did not exchange greetings. He made his excuses and left.

I handed the earrings back to Nikolai Konstaninovitch and thanked him. I managed to refrain from commenting sarcastically that regrettably Pauline Viardot's witchcraft did not work for me. He had words of comfort for me.

"Turgenev just told me," Nikolai Konstaninovitch said, "that you and Tolstoy were the only writers in Russia he took seriously."

"That was indeed generous of him," I replied. "I hope the earrings will do more for Tolstoy than they did for me. I understand he comes here from time to time. As the author of *War and Peace*, he is closer to Napoleon's first wife than I am"

Oh, to hell with them all. Listen, my friend. Here's my request. I am asking you for hundred and fifty rubles. Send the money to me in Geneva. My address: Monsieur Theodore Dostoevsky, Suisse, poste restante. In two months, The Russian Messenger will send you five hundred rubles addressed to me. Take the hundred fifty rubles out of that sum, and send the rest to me.

In any case, I beg you most earnestly to write to me as soon as possible and let me know all the news about all our people, about what's going on, what's current, what you yourself are doing. In a word, water my soul which has become dried out in the desert. I am completely isolated in Geneva and have not seen any of the Russians here.

If you don't help me, I will perish! Save me! I am a drowning man!

Chapter 13

Badeblatt des Stadt Baden-Baden,
Wednesday, September 5, 1883

PARIS—Ivan Turgenev died yesterday
in Bougival near Paris where he has been living
for some time. Until the moment of his death
he was fully conscious. A memorial service
will probably be held on Friday in the Russian
Church.

Turgenev was born on November 8, 1818,
in Orel, and studied in Moscow in 1833 and
in Berlin in 1838. An essay about Gogol
brought him into serious conflict with the authorities. Since 1848, he has been living first
in Germany (for more than ten years in Baden-
Baden) and then in France. His poetry attracted
less attention than his prose. His *Sportsman's
Sketches, Nest of Gentlefolk,* and *Virgin Soil,*
which described conditions of life in Russia,
triggered considerable excitement in Russia
and abroad and were immediately translated
into German and French. His short stories have
much in common with the work of Prosper
Mérimée, who, in 1863, wrote the preface to
the French edition of Turgenev's novel *Fathers
and Sons.*

Turgenev's recent publications were
greatly admired in Germany and France by

reason of their exemplary form. Moreover, his pessimistic assessment of the higher echelons of Russian society was much discussed. Among Russian novelists Turgenev will always occupy a high rank.

In the summer of 1871, Turgenev, in despair over the course of events during and immediately after the Franco-Prussian war, spent several weeks in Baden-Baden to sell his and the Viardot's properties. He was suffering at the time from a severe attack of gout, which, however, did not prevent him from writing *Spring Torrents*, a novel about a man caught between two women illustrating a remark made by Potugin, his mouthpiece in *Smoke*: "Man is weak, woman is strong, chance is all-powerful." He had hoped to spend the rest of his life in Baden-Baden. Later that year, he joined the Viardot family in England and subsequently they all settled again in France.

Turgenev left behind an assortment of notes, letters, newspaper clippings and bric-a-brac. It was not clear whether he did so deliberately or whether he was in such a state of emotional turmoil that he was not paying attention. In any case, his old friend from his student days in Berlin, Boris Ivanov, the owner of Der Russische Hof and husband of the voluptuous Margaret, gathered them and put them in two white shoeboxes. Some time later, in the mid-seventies, just after Louis Katzau had opened his boutique in the Promenade, Ivanov, after buying a silver comb as a birthday present for his voluptuous young Scottish wife, on the way out, mentioned these boxes to Katzau.

"One of these days," Boris said, "we will invite you over, open a bottle of red wine and see what's in them."

But he never did.

When Louis read the notice of Turgenev's death in Thursday's *Badeblatt*, he suddenly remembered them. "What if, among the bric-a-brac...?"

He could not finish the sentence, even when talking to himself.

"You see," he told Robert when he arrived, "nothing makes better sense. Turgenev despised Napoleon III. Louis Viardot detested him. Before leaving France, right through the 1850s and early '60s, they told themselves that they simply could not abide living under an autocratic régime of adventurers, impostors and profiteers, but that they had to stay there for Pauline's sake. This was a rationalization because in truth they did not really find it as unbearably hard to stay as they pretended to themselves. They finally left in 1863, not for political reasons but because Pauline did not want to remain in Paris, the city of her greatest triumphs. Her voice was in decline and her career on the opera stage was over. So they all left for clean, honest, music-loving, free Baden-Baden where she could teach, compose, enjoy the life of a great celebrity and accept occasional invitations to give recitals. The Prussian victory in 1870 and its consequences put an end to this idyllic interlude. By 1871, France was a republic again. Why take relics of the hated Bonapartes to Republican France?"

"Even copies of the relics," Robert observed dryly. "If *they* could bring good luck, imagine the power of the real things!"

"We may have to forget about ever finding *them*," Louis Katzau declared. "But don't worry, Herr Koch. Our Duchess will most definitely open her doors to you once you present the copies Turgenev left for us to find in one of the shoeboxes in the Russische Hof!"

•   •   •

Boris Ivanov received Louis Katzau and Robert in his sumptuously furnished residential suite on the second floor. On the way up, they had caught a glimpse, through the open door, of his beautiful young wife's more modest manager's office on the first floor, to the right of the entrance, with a gold-framed photograph of her friend and benefactor William, the twelfth Duke of Hamilton, on the wall.

Boris was a rugged giant of a man of Tartar stock, with

a round, pink face, heavy bags under his dark, almond-shaped eyes and a drooping black mustache. His gentle manner was in agreeable contrast to his fierce looks. It was not difficult to think of him as a former friend and associate of the anarchist Mikhail Bukanin, whose writings inspired terrorists like those who two years ago, in 1881, assassinated Tsar Alexander II, the man who had emancipated the serfs and the most broadminded monarch who had ever ruled Russia. The Tsar was dismembered by a bomb in the street, in broad daylight, on his way back from a military inspection, an act that had so horrified Turgenev and Ivanov that they considered it a deathblow to Russian liberalism.

Ivanov had put the two shoeboxes on a small table near the window.

"I have no doubt there will be a state funeral in St. Petersburg," he said after they sat down on comfortable easy chairs. "It will be an event of national importance. There will be demonstrations against westernizers. In Russia, great writers matter more than in the West."

Robert's eyes were on the shoebox, which, perhaps, contained his key to the Duchess.

"I am sure you regret not being able to attend, Boris," Louis Katzau said sympathetically. It was clear they were fond of each other.

"Oh, I don't think it is too late. I would still get there in time if I take the train tonight. But, no, I don't feel the need. Let us remember him by opening these boxes. I understand you have your own reasons."

"Yes, we do," Louis Katzau said. "But we won't tell you what they are until the end, if you don't mind, Boris. It's kind of a game. It's not a matter of life and death. We are just curious."

Boris lifted the first shoebox and shook it. There was a rattling noise made by the objects at the bottom. He inspected a few yellowed papers at the top, found them unrewarding and put them aside. Then, at random, he picked up an old letter dated Baden-Baden, August 20, 1817, signed by Roxandra

Stourdza, evidently one of the ladies in waiting of the Tsarina Elisabeth Alexievna, Tsar Alexander I's estranged wife. She was *née* Elisabeth of Baden, the sister-in-law of Grand Duchess Stephanie of Baden and aunt of the Duchess of Hamilton.

"This looks promising," Ivanov exclaimed, running his eye over the first page. "I wonder how Turgenev got hold of it."

He began reading a passage. "'At the time of the Restoration, after Napoleon had been safely dispatched to St. Helena, there was widespread hatred in Europe. But in Baden-Baden friend and foe, Germans, Russians and members of Napoleon's family and loyalists managed to live together in harmony. The Russians in particular had been welcomed by Grand Duchess Stephanie, who was exercising considerable diplomatic skill at a time when everyone was trying to undo the real and imagined damage the exiled Emperor had done, forgetting that Baden had enjoyed immense benefits from his activities in the early part of his career. In fact, without the generous and moderating presence of the Russians the universal reaction against Napoleon and everything he had stood for, the reaction symbolized by both Metternich and by Louis XVIII and his court, would have exercised a disastrous influence not only on France but on the rest of Europe as well.'"

"Doesn't this fit in with Turgenev's thinking about Russia's civilizing mission in Europe?" Louis Katzau asked. "Could that be the reason why he had kept the letter?"

"You may well be right," Boris Ivanov said, nodding. "I recall him saying once that, in spite of the unspeakable suffering Napoleon had caused, the war against him had a good effect on Russia because it brought the army officers from the landowning class into contact with the European Enlightenment. Also, it was a good thing for these officers to fight side by side with their men, in a common patriotic enterprise. And, of course, Tsar Alexander emerged as the liberator of Europe. It is in that light that we have to think of him taking the salute of Baden troops in Karlsruhe in 1813, thereby in a roundabout way opening up nearby Baden-Baden as a Russian summer resort. And visiting Josephine in Malmaison soon afterwards, just before she died."

Ivanov disposed of another batch of papers. Then a letter from a friend of Turgenev caught his attention. He did not recognize the signature. It was written after the Franco-Prussian war.

He began reading.

"'I am not surprised you expected the French to cross the Rhine and occupy Baden-Baden at the beginning of the war. You say the place was completely empty, but you stayed, asking yourself what could they do to you. By now we all know why the French did *not* come. By the way, I was struck by your description of Helmuth von Moltke in Berlin on the day on which France declared war. Remember, you happened to be there on the way home from Russia. The Chief of the Prussian General Staff, you say, was dining with a distinguished-looking lady at a table opposite yours in a restaurant. Perhaps his wife, perhaps not. You exchanged a few words. You had met before, after a performance of *Le Dernier Sorcier*. You said you were impressed by his cool demeanour and professorial brow. This raised your hopes for a German victory, despite your sympathies for the land of Gustave Flaubert and George Sand. Soon after that, back in Baden-Baden, you heard cannon fire in the distance. Reports of Prussian victories reached the town and set the bells ringing. You hoped the bells were the death knells of the Napoleonic empire, which you considered incompatible with the progress of freedom in Europe. You thought another battle of civilization against barbarism had been won. I just wonder at what stage you changed your mind...'"

Boris placed the letter on the table, next to the box.

"Well, I know the answer to that one," Ivanov said. "May I tell you, or are you too anxious to find what you are looking for?"

"No, please tell us," Louis Katzau said.

Robert reluctantly nodded agreement.

"Turgenev had always thought of Germany as the land of poets, composers and scholars. He now discovered another Germany, a Germany that was brutal, domineering and greedy for conquest. He deplored the burning of Strasbourg and was appalled by the plan to annex Alsace and Lorraine, which he thought would be to Germany what Poland was to Russia. He thought the Prussians should have made peace after the French were defeated at Sedan on September first, Napoleon captured, and two days later the Republic proclaimed. But no, the Prussians had a different plan. They continued the war against the new Republic and were not satisfied until they had laid siege to Paris, proclaimed the German Empire in Versailles on January 18, 1871, and, by now joined by Baden and the other German states, forced Paris to surrender. Here in Baden-Baden the Viardots were being called names and scratchy music—*Katzenmusik*—was played outside their windows. It was clear they could not stay in Germany. So they moved to England where Pauline had a brother and where she could give concerts and teach. Turgenev followed them. There they stayed for a while and then, after the Commune, they returned to Paris, where Turgenev joined them late in November 1871. There they recovered their house at 48, rue de Douai, their furniture, their friends and their bank account. The house soon became a rallying point for all Russians living in Paris. Turgenev was widely regarded as the 'ambassador of intelligence.'"

Boris Ivanov uttered a deep sigh.

"Baden-Baden has never recovered," he said as he went to work on what was left in the first shoebox. He poured out three bundles of Russian newspaper clippings, tied together in black ribbons. He put them aside as of no immediate interest and continued rummaging.

"What a surprise! I haven't seen this in years!"

He picked up the poem *Die Noth*, by Richard Wagner, written in March 1849, printed on two separate pages.

"Could this be what you are looking for?" he asked hopefully.

Ivanov passed it to Louis Katzau and Robert. They obediently glanced at it and sadly shook their heads.

"Too bad. I wonder why Turgenev kept it. Perhaps as a reminder of his happy days in Berlin with our friend Mikhail Bukanin—who later became Richard Wagner's friend, too—

long, long ago. The old order going up in flames. Cities reduced to skeletons. Life springing up anew after total destruction. That is what *Die Noth* is about."

"Did you say Richard Wagner?" Katzau raised his eyebrows.

"Yes, I did. You probably don't know that in Dresden, during 1848 and 1849, Bukanin and Wagner were fellow revolutionaries. By then Bukanin and I had parted ways, but I must confess to you I've always remained fond of the cheerful old anarchist, until his death a few years ago. Wagner and Bakunin, who was already in flight from Prague, went on the barricades in Dresden. Or at least so they said. Bukanin had rented a room from Wagner's disciple August Röckel. Wagner was working on *Siegfried's Death*, which later became the *Die Götterdämmerung*. He was in the mood for total destruction. He was thirty-six at the time and deeply in debt. He knew his career in Dresden was at an end. So naturally Bukanin's message came just at the right moment, satisfying both his personal and, far more important, his artistic needs. He saw himself as a romantic hero redeeming a doomed materialistic world. Alas, the insurrection failed. Wagner eluded capture, indictment and a possible death sentence, and made his way to Weimar to join Liszt. But Bakunin, a much more generous man who deserved better, was arrested in his sleep and handed over to the Russian authorities who sent him to Eastern Siberia for life. However, he managed to escape to London after six years. He was a convinced atheist, not—so he emphasized again and again—merely an agnostic. He never claimed that God had saved him."

Ivanov had nearly reached the bottom of the shoebox. There was only one large green envelope left, with reviews of concert performances by Pauline Viardot in Copenhagen and Amsterdam.

"I'll look at these later."

He poured out the bric-a-brac at the bottom of the shoebox.

Robert took a deep breath.

All that fell out were keys of various sizes, silver cuff

links, a gold watch with a gold chain and a pair of scissors.

Ivanov had not noticed the barely suppressed excitement and, following it, the grave disappointment on the faces of his visitors. He proceeded to open Shoebox Number Two.

"Oh, now I remember. I marked it *Bazarov*. I hope you find what you are looking for among these papers."

His guests were too polite to say they were not looking for any papers.

"Who is Bazarov?" Robert asked.

"Don't Frankfurt jewellers read books?" asked Louis Katzau, smiling. He knew very well that Robert never pretended to be a reader. "He is Turgenev's most famous character in his most famous—and most controversial—novel, *Fathers and Sons*."

Robert was silent.

"Do you mind if I try to tell him the bare bones of the story, Boris? After that you may tell Herr Koch what it is really about. It's the story of the angry young radical Evgeny Vasilev Bazarov, a bright medical researcher with meagre prospects, the son of a poor army doctor, who describes himself as a nihilist and who, like Bakunin, believes the whole rotten corrupt old world had to be raised to the ground before something new could be built on it. He rejects everything that cannot be established by the rational methods of science. Everything else, he believes, is untrue and 'romantic nonsense.' Now, Bazarov is invited by his fellow student Arkady Kirsanov to visit his father's house in the country. The father is a kindly, unassuming gentleman who loves poetry and the beauties of nature. The father's brother is a retired army officer, a touchy man, very elegant, a westernized dandy. All kinds of interesting things happen in the novel—including a duel between this elegant uncle and Bazarov, and an unhappy love affair with the cold, clever society beauty Odintsova, who rejects him, a fascinating woman of paradox. In the end Bazarov dies. The description of his death—he was infected while dissecting a corpse in a village autopsy—is one of the most moving passages I have ever read in any book. There was no other way to end the story. Bazarov had already failed in his personal and social encounters. No rebellion was possible.

He had nowhere to go. Now you take over, Boris."

"Obviously," Ivanov responded, "this is a novel of confrontation between the old and the young, between the liberals and the radicals. At the same time, it is an attempt to breathe life into the image of the mysterious new men Turgenev sensed all around him whenever he went to Russia, an attempt to try and understand them. And everything that has happened in the twenty-one years since the book was published—significantly, the year after the Emancipation of the Serfs in 1861—confirms how clearly he saw the new men. The remarkable thing, and no doubt the reason why the book unleashed such a storm and caused him such pain, is that he came to love Bazarov while at the same time being terrified of him. This he had not expected when he started writing the novel. Many years later he asked me how anybody could be offended by being compared with Bazarov. Did I not agree that he was the most sympathetic of all his characters? He said he shared almost all of Bazarov's views except those about art and nature. He wished he had not used the label 'nihilist' Bazarov used to describe himself. It gave the reactionaries an easy weapon with which to hammer him."

"I must read the book," Robert said.

"You must," Ivanov said. "Now, let us see what we have here."

He picked out a clipping from a radical review so obscure that it must have escaped the attentions of the censor.

"'What are we supposed to think?' the writer asks. 'Is this a hero or a devil? Does he stand for Freedom and Progress? Bazarov has no faith in the people. He thinks such faith is irrational. He does not believe in anything he cannot perceive with his senses. A man should rely on himself alone, he says, on his own strength. How can we make a revolution with men like him who have no faith in the people?' Good question," Ivanov said.

He glanced at the next paper, a letter written by a man who introduced himself as a friend of Mikhail Katkov, Turgenev's publisher. He read at random from the second page.

"'This glorification of nihilism is nothing but grovelling

at the feet of the young radicals. Don't you see that your man Bazarov is nothing but a propagandist for crude materialism? He is not interested in scientific truth at all. He is not a scientist. That species does not exist in Russia in our time. Bazarov is merely a preacher. He is no better than the ignorant priests from whose ranks most of his fellow nihilists spring. And they are much more dangerous! How can you glorify such people?'"

"Poor Turgenev!" Louis Katzau observed. "I wonder why he kept these letters."

"Well, he did, and he did not. After all, he left them behind when he left Baden-Baden, didn't he. Listen to this. 'Your Bazarov is a Mongol, a Genghis Khan, a wild beast symptomatic of the savage condition of Russia, who has read a few translations of third-rate German books. Are you, Ivan Turgenev, intending to become the leader of a political movement? Or do you not yourself know how to take your Bazarov, as a fruitful force for the future or as a disgusting boil on the body of hollow civilization?'"

"Strong stuff," Robert commented.

"Look at this! Here is a copy of Alexander Herzen's last essay. 'I do not believe in the seriousness of men who prefer crude force and destruction to the development and arriving of settlements. One must open men's eyes, not tear them out. Wild cries to close books, abandon science and go to some senseless battle of destruction—that is the most violent and harmful kind of demagoguery. It will be followed by the eruption of the most savage passions... No! Great revolutions are not unleashed by evil passions.'"

Ivanov noticed the attention of his guests was wandering. He took out a handful of documents and spread them out on the table.

"Why don't you go through these yourselves? Perhaps one of them will catch your eye."

The two men did what was suggested.

"Look at this!" Robert exclaimed, after a while.

This acknowledges receipt of a pair of Empire ruby earrings belonging to Madame Pauline Viardot. They are alleged to have been worn by Empress Josephine at her Coronation in Notre Dame on December 2, 1804.

At the request of Herr Ivan Turgenev, I have undertaken to examine them and give my expert opinion as to the question whether they are copies of those which the Duchess Marie of Hamilton is known to have possession.

Theodor Klammerer

Jeweller
Boutique Number Three
Promenade
Baden-Baden
November 19, 1871

Chapter 14

The festivities to celebrate the twenty-fifth anniversary of the Iffezheim Races were to end on Tuesday, September 11, 1883. There was no question that Robert would stay in Baden-Baden beyond that day, unless, of course, there was a breakthrough. It was remarkable that he had stayed as long as he had. Now, with the breathtaking revelation that Josephine's earrings might be stored, of all places, in a safe right next door to Louis Katzau's boutique, the breakthrough that had slipped through his finger so many times at last seemed imminent.

On the morning of Monday, September 10, a courier arrived at Louis Katzau's boutique to deliver an urgent invitation from Herr Boris Ivanov and the voluptuous Frau Margaret Ivanov. They hoped both Herr Louis Katzau and Herr Robert Koch to do them the honour to attend an improvised dinner that evening at eight in the Russische Hof to celebrate the victory of their friend the Duke of Hamilton's horse Fénélon in the handicap steeplechase at Iffezheim and at the same time mark the end of the festive weeks to celebrate the twenty-fifth anniversary of the races.

For some reason, the Monday edition of Richard Pohl's *Badeblatt* did not carry a report about Turgenev's final journey to St. Petersburg—the coffin did not reach its destination until September 27—nor were there any stories about the preparations for the state funeral. Instead, there was news from Vienna about an illegal workers' meeting in the *Fünfhaus*. When they refused to disperse half a battalion of infantry attacked them with sabres. It was also reported from Vienna that on the occasion of the birth of a daughter to Crown Prince Rudolf and Crown Princess Stephanie (good customers of Louis Katzau), two hundred and two prisoners had been released from prison before having served their full terms. The *Badeblatt* also carried an item from Vienna about a decree ordering eight days of official mourning for the Comte de Chambord.

As for news from Berlin, it was reported that on September 6 the Kaiser had been the guest of the Crown Prince in Potsdam at a dinner in honour of the Duke and Duchess of Connaught. (The Duke was the Crown Prince's brother-in-law.) There was also news that Kaiserin Augusta intended to arrive in Baden-Baden on September 25 for her usual sojourn of two months. The Kaiser himself intended to arrive for a stay of several weeks on September 29. On September 30, they would celebrate Her Majesty's birthday. But first the Kaiser would attend the imperial manoeuvres near Frankfurt, an event at which the Grand Duke and the Grand Duchess of Baden would also be present. Afterwards, most of them would proceed to Rüdesheim to inaugurate the *Niederwalddenkmal*, the monument celebrating the Prussian victory over France thirteen years ago and the unification of the Reich. The triumphant monument faced France across the Rhine.

The amateur philosopher and jeweller Theodor Klammerer and Louis Katzau were good friends and neighbours. Robert had mentioned to Katzau on a number of occasions that he was curious about him. They had nodded to each other but he had not yet formally met. Klammerer's heart, Katzau had told him, was really in Kant, Hegel and Schopenhauer, not in jewels. He did not tell Robert that it had occurred to him that, if things went well between Robert and the Duchess, an amicable, mutually beneficial arrangement of some sort could be contemplated between the three of them, just for the summer months.

Just before they went next door to ask Klammerer what his expert opinion had been of Pauline Viardot's earrings, Robert had a sudden horrific idea.

"Suppose," he said, "like everybody else, Klammerer has heard of the theft, has opened his safe, retrieved Pauline's copies, taken them across the Oos to the Palais Hamilton and said to the Duchess 'Your Highness, look what I found! Please make me your court jeweller'."

Louis Katzau laughed.

"Very good thinking, Herr Koch. It confirms my unbounded faith in you. I know you will go to the top. As you will see, Klammerer is not in your class. His strength lies elsewhere."

They went next door. It was just after eleven in the morning of Monday, September 10. In his leather case Louis Katzau carried Klammerer's signed receipt, which Boris Ivanov had kindly lent him for the purpose. It was a document that, so they had good reason to believe, might very well be Robert Koch's entrance ticket to Paradise.

Theodor Klammerer was a tall, thin friendly man of about fifty. He had an oval face and hollow cheeks, a decorative duelling scar and no fashionable beard, and wore horn-rimmed glasses.

"May I introduce Robert Koch." In order not to arouse any fears of new competition, Louis Katzau did not add "a colleague of yours from Frankfurt." He preferred to describe him as "one of my more pleasant business friends."

"We already have a casual acquaintance," Klammerer said as they shook hands. "Delighted."

"Herr Koch has a somewhat morbid interest in relics of the late Empress Josephine."

"Not another relative?" Klammerer asked with a smile.

"No, not exactly," Robert said in good conscience.

Louis Katzau opened his leather case and pulled out the receipt. Klammerer looked at it.

"Ah, yes!" he exclaimed. "Where did you find it?"

"It was among many papers Turgenev left here in 1871, when he departed from your victorious country. Boris Ivanov gathered them and kept them."

Theodor Klammerer took off his glasses and wiped them

with a silk handkerchief. The initials T.K. were embroidered on it.

He turned to Robert.

"And I suppose now that Ivan Turgenev has left this world you would like to add the historic earrings to your Josephine collection?"

"You mean the copies of the historic earrings," Louis Katzau corrected him. "If indeed you found them to be genuine copies."

"Yes, yes, I did. Well, Herr Koch?"

"Not at all. But I wonder if you would be so kind as to lend them to me for a day or two. I would be happy to explain to you why, at any time that would suit you."

"I see."

Theo Klammerer stared into space.

"I am afraid," he said after a seemingly endless pause, "before I can respond to your request, I see no alternative to your listening to a long, but I promise not uninteresting story. May I invite you gentlemen to share with me a bottle or two of red wine, and maybe even a glass of cognac, across the Promenade in our habitual Café Weber. And a plate of cold cuts and salad."

The Café Weber in the Conversationshaus was already crowded, but a waiter managed to find them a quiet table near a potted palm in a corner. Klammerer ordered coffee for three, to start with.

"Let me try to proceed systematically. Act One. Scene One. The time—April 1878. The locale—over there." He pointed in a vaguely northerly direction. "The Reading Room that our gracious Grand Duke many years ago permitted the late D. R. Marx from Karlsruhe to establish on these very premises, in conjunction with his bookstore and his printing press. As you know, Louis, April is still rather a slow month in Baden-Baden. No one can blame me for spending as much time as I could in Herr Marx's Reading Room, rather than serving non-existing customers. So there I sat, deeply absorbed in a collection of essays, reprinted from newspapers and magazines under the title

Völker, Zeiten und Menschen, by the literary critic Kurt Hillebrand. I had met him a few times and admire him. Do you know him, Louis?"

Louis Katzau stroked his whiskers. "Wasn't he the man who was Heine's secretary in Paris for a few months?"

"Exactly. Let me tell you about him. You will soon understand why he is relevant to my story. After he escaped from Rastatt, where he had been imprisoned in 1849 for having taken part in the Baden revolution, he went to Paris. He had been a student in Heidelberg, radical like so many of us. But he had the bad luck of getting arrested. Once in Paris, after an adventurous flight across the Rhine, he met Heine, who was already quite ill, and did some work for him, enrolled in the Sorbonne and, in due course, after Heine's death, became professor in Douai. When the Franco-Prussian war broke out in 1870, he went to Florence. There he wrote reviews of three early books by the astounding young philosopher, moralist, psychologist and poet Friedrich Nietzsche."

"By whom?" Robert asked.

Klammerer repeated the unusual name. "By April 1878, those early books of Nietzsche's had hardly caused a ripple, except in a few university faculties. But the most recent of them, a book of aphorisms he called *Human, All Too Human* aroused heated indignation in slightly wider circles. By then only the first part had appeared. The second followed soon after. By now, five years and several books later, people are beginning to pay serious attention. As they should. You've read him, Louis?"

"No, I have never heard of him," Louis Katzau confessed.

"Why the heated indignation?" Robert asked.

"Because in this latest book, which had just appeared, this intense and trenchant young writer made a public display of a spectacular reversal. He had begun as a follower of Kant, Hegel and Schopenhauer in his belief that the metaphysical world was inaccessible to us, as opposed to the world we can perceive with our senses, and that the essence of the human experience was the interplay between the two. By 1878, after a monumental crisis, he had come to the conclusion that the metaphysical world was not only inaccessible but also of absolutely no significance to us, and, on a moral and psychological level, that unreason rather than reason guided much of human behaviour. There was, or could be, unity in opposites, he wrote, in yes and no, good and evil, pleasure and pain, truth and illusion. The free spirit had to transcend, *sans* metaphysics, the old romantic dualism while still loving and hating much of what had to be discarded. Consequently, he was denounced as a confused and confusing materialist and nihilist."

"But not by you?" Robert wondered.

"What I understood of it," Klammerer replied, "I welcomed as liberating expressions of an honest and original thinker who was constantly transforming himself and struggling heroically to come to terms with ever new insights. Also, he wrote beautifully. Then there was another dramatic element in this reversal that interested me hugely—his declaration of independence from his former idol and substitute father, Richard Wagner."

"Wagner?" Louis Katzau and Robert were stunned. "Did you say Wagner?"

"Yes, I did. Nietzsche had worshipped him," Klammerer explained. "He himself was deeply musical. He composed. Wagner was thirty years older, born in the same year as his father. In 1866, Nietzsche heard a concert performance of *Tristan*. It was an earth-shattering experience for him. They met. Wagner, already a living legend, began to exercise an almost hypnotic attraction for him. Ten years of visits and correspondence followed. For Nietzsche, Wagner met Schopenhauer's definition of genius. While Nietzsche was a young professor in Basel, Wagner kept two rooms for him in his house in nearby Tribschen, on Lake Lucerne. There was never any real intimacy between them. Nietzsche always addressed Wagner as *Meister*, as in *Meistersinger*, and they adhered to the formal *Sie*. But then there was a change, a transformation. By 1876, the spirit of *Human, All Too Human* was Voltaire's, not Wagner's, and the style was modelled on La Roche Foucauld, not *Tristan*. Nietzsche had turned away from Wagner's romantic pessimism towards a renewed interest in the French Enlightenment. He found it sickening that Bismarck, whose deeds were, in Nietzsche's view, profoundly anti-Christian, would publicly proclaim his Christianity. In short, he felt an overwhelming need to counteract the hypocritical, philistine chauvinism that followed the German victory over the French. These insights later evolved into direct opposition to Christianity as such, and specifically into an attack on Christian compassion."

"All right, Theo," Louis Katzau said, tapping the table with mock impatience. "Back to your story. There you sat in Herr Marx's Reading Room, one lovely day in April 1878, reading Herr Hillebrand's book instead of minding your store. What does this have to do with the Empress Josephine?"

"Waiter," Klammerer called out. "Bring us a bottle of your red Kaiserstuhl '75, please." He turned to Katzau. "Well, you see, the simple reason I am telling you all this is that, in that very Reading Room, next to me sat none other than Friedrich Nietzsche himself, calmly reading *Fathers and Sons*, by Ivan Turgenev, probably because the book was sold out in the stores."

"What?" Katzau cried. "This Nietzsche of yours was here in Baden-Baden?"

"He was indeed. In terrible health. He had come for the cold-water cure in our brand-new Friedrichsbad, which he admired greatly. And also to correct the proofs of the second part of *Human, All Too Human*."

"The cold-water cure for what?" Robert asked.

"Excruciating headaches. Sleeplessness. Gastric troubles of all kinds. Vomiting. He had been appointed full professor of classical philology in Basel at twenty-four. Unheard of. Eight years later, in 1876, he had to give it up. His disastrous health, he said, forced him to live blissfully as a free man and a free spirit. Contradiction was his way of life. The university paid him a modest pension, enough to live on if he confined himself to cheap hotels. He was only thirty-four years old and did not look like a sick man. He had wonderfully clear black eyes, bushy eyebrows and a thick, heavy mustache. He was quite vigorous and went for long walks in the forest. The real cure for his condition was being alone, he said. Cold water was not enough."

"Where was he staying?" Louis Katzau asked.

"The Hotel Stadt Paris. The hotel, he told me, in which Louis Napoleon planned his abortive *coup d'état* in Strasbourg."

"You said he wanted to be alone," Robert observed. "Yet, Herr Klammerer, he seems to have talked to you rather freely."

"Yes, I was also surprised. It was only because of the book I was reading. Clearly, Nietzsche had the same curiosity I have. I am always interested in what other people are reading. I noticed he was reading Turgenev and *he* noticed I was reading Hillebrand. Of course, I had no idea know who he was. He waited for me to stop for a moment to blow my nose and then asked me, right out of the blue, whether I didn't agree with him that there were few authors that came close to Hillebrand's candour and devotion to justice."

"He must have sensed that you were a kindred spirit," Louis Katzau said.

"Who knows? Didn't Hillebrand's essays exhale European air, he went on, and not the usual nationalistic provincialism so common these days? He didn't read newspapers, he said, or magazines, and he added, no doubt forgetting for a moment that he was talking to a complete stranger, that he was so grateful this writer had also written some favourable reviews of his own works.

"So I took him up on that. 'Your own work?' I asked him. 'May I inquire...?'

"When I recognized his name and he saw my reaction, and especially when I told him that I had read his *Birth of Tragedy* and most of his *Untimely Meditations* with great excitement, he said we must have a long conversation. So I invited him to dinner at the Hotel Stephanie-les-Bains."

Theo Klammerer summoned the waiter and ordered another bottle of wine, and cold cuts with salad for the three of them.

"Rarely had I heard such scintillating talk," he resumed. "On many subjects. Nationalism, for example. He had nothing good to say about official, artificial, whipped-up nationalism, which was all too common nowadays, he said. It was like martial law, imposed on the many by the few, in the interest of few royal dynasties, and a few commercial and social classes. But never in the interest of people at large. One should be fearless in presenting oneself as a good European, not as a national of one state. One should encourage cross-breeding and work actively to speed up the merging of nations. The Germans, because of their age-old, proven talents as interpreters and mediators would be well suited to help in this process."

"I would have thought," Louis Katzau observed, "Germans were the worst offenders. Especially these days."

"Not ordinary Germans, he said. Only certain Germans. Then he brought up the subject of the Jews, perhaps because of Wagner's well-known anti-Semitism, which he deeply deplored. Jews were sometimes considered a problem within national states, he said. But if one wanted to produce the strongest possible mixed European race, the Jews would be immensely useful. We should always remember that in the middle ages, when invasions from Asia threatened Europe, we owed it not least to the Jews that the ring of culture that now links us to the Greeks and Romans remained unbroken."

They had finished the salad but were still thirsty. Theo Klammerer ordered another bottle of Kaiserstuhl '75 and three cognacs.

"And may I now at last ask, my dear Theo," Louis Katzau wondered with a smile, "what about the link between the Greeks and the Roman and the Empress Josephine's earrings?"

"Have you not guessed it yet? I would have thought the link was obvious. Wouldn't you agree, Herr Koch?"

Robert had a certain suspicion but he did not wish to shame his friend.

"All right. I won't keep you waiting any longer," Klammerer said. "After all, you've been admirably patient all evening. The link is, of course, Turgenev. I asked Nietzsche, as we walked back to hotel together, whether he knew that Turgenev had lived in Baden-Baden for ten years. No, he did not know that. The reason he was interested in Turgenev was that he, Nietzsche, who was being called a German nihilist, wanted to read once again—he had read the book before, when it first came out—what Turgenev's famous character Bazarov had to say about the world. I told Nietzsche that before Turgenev left Baden-Baden in 1871 he asked me to have a look at a couple of ruby earrings that belonged to his friend Pauline Viardot and give him my opinion whether they were genuine copies of the earrings Josephine had worn at her Coronation. I never had a chance to give him my opinion, which was that indeed they were, and to return them to him. When he left for England he seemed to have forgotten all about them. They were now in my safe in my boutique. Nietzsche was fascinated. The next day he visited me. I showed them to him. Later he told his Basel friend Paul Rée about them. A few weeks later Rée was about to see Turgenev in Paris, to discuss with him the possibility of a French translation of his *Psychological Observations*. Before leaving he wrote him a letter to ask whether it would be a service to him if, on my behalf, he brought the earrings along. Turgenev immediately replied that Madame Viardot and he would be deeply grateful. So Paul Rée came to Baden-Baden on the way to Paris, to pick up Josephine's rubies. They are now in the possession of Pauline Viardot in Paris."

Chapter 15

It was Robert's plan to attend the Ivanovs' "improvised dinner" at the Russische Hof on Monday evening, September 10, 1883, and leave for Frankfurt first thing the following morning. He had gambled and lost. He knew the Duchess's son William, a great friend of the Ivanovs, was likely to be at the dinner, but there was no chance that his mother would also be there, so that he could woo and win her even without having the rubies in his pocket. He knew that relations between mother and son were strained and that therefore she was unlikely to be invited to celebrate the success of her son's horse at Iffezheim. Not only that, but the daughter of a grand duke of Baden, and the widow of the eleventh Duke of Hamilton, the scion of one of Scotland's most venerable families, was not likely to appear in a hotel owned by an ex-anarchist.

Tomorrow was the end of the festive season, and the right psychological moment would have gone.

Robert was right. The Duchess was not invited. No "respectable" woman was. The Russian-Scottish Ivanovs had not improvised a conventional hotel dinner at all, but a bacchanalian feast, for men only, with all the amenities of an exclusive *belle époque* bordello on the Faubourg Saint-Honoré. But there was one difference. In the classical Paris prototype, one of the iron laws was that the guests were not to meet each other under any circumstances, in order to protect their good name in society, whereas in this instance they were to spend the evening, if not the night, together in convivial, public celebration.

EARRINGS

Why the Ivanovs had gone to such elaborate lengths, and such vast expense, to stage this unusual, unprecedented and totally original event was not at all clear to Robert. It may well have something to do with Boris Ivanov's gradual conversion to bourgeois hedonism in reaction to the time when he, Turgenev and Bakunin were friends during their idealistic Hegelian studies at the University of Berlin in 1838.

Whatever the motivations, Ivanov's bacchanalia had profound political and cultural significance. The evening appeared to have been designed to enable his guests to experience once again the refined sensual pleasures of pre-1870 Baden-Baden, to hold before their inner eyes an ideal that, since the brutal Prussian victory over the French and the unification of Germany, seemed as remote as the Florence of Lorenzo di Medici or the Athens of Pericles, in short, to remind them of the time when it was the continent's summer capital, the original site of the Concert of Europe, the home of Johannes Brahms, Clara Schumann and Pauline Viardot, and of Russian aristocrats and *émigrés*. Boris Ivanov must have thought, for his own reasons, that it was useful to remind his guests of the golden days before rival nationalisms and imperialisms were tearing the continent apart, of the era when the only threat to peace and stability came from the Bazarovs of this world, a threat that had so far not in the least disturbed the idylls of Baden-Baden where no one seriously objected to a tacit (and perhaps not always tacit) arrangement stipulating that members of the lower classes—cooks, coachmen, off-duty governesses—were not to promenade on the Lichtentaler Allee during the summer season. Elsewhere one had to be very aware of bomb-throwing terrorists, and of rabble-rousers like the recently deceased Karl Marx. However, such people and their ideas were relatively easy to deal with by the systematic use of the instruments of law and order available to those in power. Still, it was only prudent to remember the few occasions in recent memory when trouble-makers got out of hand—in 1848 and 1849, for example, and again, not very long ago, in 1871, when French Republicans chose to put down the *cummunards* with ruthless efficiency.

There was nothing in Robert Koch's experience in respectable Frankfurt, or in the few stories he had heard about the legendary pre-war Baden-Baden courtesans, to prepare him for the momentous adventure that was in store for him.

He and Louis Katzau were late when they arrived at the Russische Hof. Robert remembered Ivanov's elegant suite upstairs, which had contained Turgenev's two shoeboxes, and Margaret's office on the first floor, but he had not seen the room next to it to which they were being shepherded. It was the anteroom to a large, sumptuously decorated and flower-filled dining room. This anteroom had only one purpose, to help the Ivanovs' guests shake off the heavy yoke of their worldly cares and to put them in the right condition to relish the delights to come.

The crowded and noisy room had no chairs, only tables covered by a dense forest of bottles, pewter mugs and glasses. Three uniformed waiters were busy filling and refilling the guests' glasses. There was heavy cigar smoke, mixed with other, as yet undefinable but decidedly stimulating aromas.

Strange music, not Russian, not Spanish—certainly not German—filled their ears, played by three deliciously young half-naked girls, sisters, as it turned out, one playing a mandolin, another a clarinet and the third a viola. The music was very different from the Strauss waltzes to which the guests were accustomed in hotels and cafés. An ingratiating young tenor in an outlandish costume, a woollen skirt decorated with green and red squares, displaying bare knees and hairy legs, sang a lovely nostalgic melody in an incomprehensible guttural language.

Leaning against a bottle-covered table, Robert glanced at the crowd. He could not easily imagine that, perhaps with one of two exceptions, any of the few men whose faces he recognized—most of whom no doubt happily married, as he was—would normally frequent houses of pleasure, even if they had done so once or twice when they were in their early twenties. But of course one could never be sure of such things, since this aspect of life was not usually the subject of polite conversation, certainly not in Robert's circles. That he suddenly found himself in such a place—or rather, in a normal Baden-Baden hotel that had been converted into such a place probably for this one occasion only—had not been obvious from the beginning. But it became obvious the minute he noticed with a shiver of delight that the fashionable clothes the women wore had one thing in common. They were provocatively, tantalizingly *décolleté*, leaving the provocatively exposed bosom free to display pearl and diamond necklaces which his practised eye immediately established as decorative but false.

A dark-haired young beauty, with marble-white skin, touched him on the sleeve.

"Herr Koch?" she asked.

"How did you know my name?"

"There are certain things one knows, and certain things one does not know," she replied with studied seriousness. "My name is Francesca. I would like to explain these whiskies to you." She had dimples and an alluring Italian accent. "I don't suppose you drink much whisky in Frankfurt?"

"No," he replied "We don't. We drink wine. And *schnapps.*"

" Franzl," she addressed a curly-haired waiter, "please pour a little glass of this Scottish mountain dew for Herr Koch to try. And a big one for me." She pointed to a bottle. "It comes from Glenlivet on Arran, near Glasgow," she explained to Robert, "the home of our victorious Duke."

Robert had never tasted anything as exactly, uniquely right. His interior began to glow.

"You drink this in Italy all the time?" Robert asked.

"Of course." She downed her whole glass, shook herself a little with pleasure, and put her face close to his. Robert lowered his eyes to her magnificently shaped, young, intoxicatingly inviting breasts and inhaled her perfume of fragrant musk and sweet spices. He touched her forehead with his lips.

"Let us have another one," she said, taking his hand and giving it a squeeze. "This time Franzl will fill your glass to the rim, as our Duke does. In Baden-Baden it is bad form to put water or soda in your whisky. Anyway, Franzl comes from Munich and prefers beer."

Before Franzl could protest Louis Katzau approached, at his arm another dazzling beauty, a lady with gorgeous, Slav cheekbones and glorious white shoulders. They had begun drinking earlier than Robert and Francesca. Their faces were shining.

"May I introduce Wanda. She specializes in whisky from the Polish Highlands."

Wanda nodded amiably to Francesca and pinched Katzau's cheeks.

"Herr Koch," she also knew his name, "did you know that Hungarians grow whiskers if they drink a bottle of Polish whisky every day?"

"Every child knows that," Robert said.

"Absolutely." Francesca put her arm around Robert's waist. "And we Italians can't make love without Italian whisky."

People were slowly going in to the dining room next door.

Before they could follow, David MacDonald stopped them, Robert's masseur at the Friedrichsbad, the lively chronicler of the Hamilton clan and their relation to the tragic history of Mary Queen of Scots. Herr MacDonald was holding hands with Dimitrea, a *petite* girl from Salonica who was only wearing a chain of freshly cut dark blue flowers and a long purple skirt. Their drinking was clearly advanced.

Herr MacDonald pointed to the tenor.

"Would you like me to tell you what the song is about?" he asked Robert.

"First—in what language is he singing?" Dimitrea wondered.

"Gaelic, of course. First, let me give you the English version of what he sang when we came in."

> Glenlivet it has castles three,
> Drumin, Blairfindy and Deskie,
> And also one distillery,
> More famous than the castles three."

"And what is he singing now?"
Herr MacDonald cocked his ear.

"He is singing a ballad about a young country lass in Dundee who went to a barn dance with a boy who was shy. After the dance she took the boy's hand and showed him where to give her a gentle massage to give her immediate pleasure and lay the groundwork for his pleasures to come. Oh, by the way, Herr Koch, did you ever find the man who stole those historic earrings you were telling me about? You remember I gave you a number of leads."

Robert shook his head sadly.

"It is too late now," he lamented.

"I will show you later, upstairs," Francesca said *sotto voce*.

"Show me what?" he asked. Evidently, Robert's mind was elsewhere.

"Let's ask Franzl for another drink. Herr MacDonald, will you come with us?"

On the way to Franzl, Robert stopped in his tracks. His *Doppelgänger* was rushing towards him, beaming. Napoleon's hunchbacked grandson, Count Richard de Léon, looked just as disreputable as he had the other day at the racetrack.

"Ah, my friend, the jeweller from Frankfurt. How are you? Are you still looking for rich customers? Do you want me to introduce you to some?"

Francesca stared at the count, her mouth open.

"No, no, no, thank you. I have found more than I can handle."

"Good." He seized Robert by the arm, glanced disdainfully at Francesca, and took him aside. "There are plenty of prettier women upstairs, in Suite Number Seventeen, waiting for you. From all corners of Europe." he whispered. "I've just had one from Corsica. Probably a relative." Of ours, Robert corrected him in his mind. "They've all been paid, including your girl, so you don't have to worry. I don't know why they force these girls on you. A man is supposed to pick and choose."

"I am faithful to Francesca," Robert responded.

The Count shrugged.

"By the way, *monsieur*," he resumed, still keeping his voice down, "the private rooms upstairs have mirrors on the ceiling, just as in Paris. And black silk sheets. All the comforts of home."

"Francesca," Robert said with deliberate gallantry, "before we ask Franzl for some more mountain dew, may I introduce you to a grandson of Napoleon."

She burst into laughter.

"And I am the Pope's wife," she giggled.

"Remember, *monsieur*," Count Richard de Léon pointed upstairs towards Suite Seventeen, and went on his way. Robert was relieved that Francesca did not say "This awful man looks exactly like you."

Franzl filled their glasses.

"I am glad you are faithful to me. I overheard what you said to that awful man." Francesca and Robert clinked glasses. "I like jewellers," she said.

"The whole world does." Robert could not remember a single moment in his previous life when he felt so pleasantly inebriated, in the company of a lovely woman whose charms he was certain to enjoy after dinner—unless there was an earthquake or its equivalent. Earthquakes were unknown in Baden-Baden.

"I am hungry," Francesca said.

"We'll go in in a minute," Robert said. "Let's just see what's happening here."

A group of people were lining up to shake hands with a tall man wearing a solemn black coat and a yellow vest who seemed to be enjoying himself hugely. Somehow, he looked familiar.

"It is our victorious Duke," Francesca said.

Oh yes, Robert had once met the rakish Duke, the son of his elusive Duchess and therefore Josephine's great-grandson by adoption, in Katzau's boutique when he bought a golden cigar case for a lady who smoked.

They joined the queue. Ahead of them was a bemedalled Russian general, with a Spanish girl at his arm, perhaps a gypsy. He turned around to address Robert.

"My friend," he said, "have you read Turgenev's story about Lieutenant Ergonov?"

Robert had to confess he had not.

"You should. It takes place in a house of joy, just like this one."

"I will read it with interest," Robert replied.

When it was Robert's turn to congratulate the Duke on his horse Fénélon's triumph at Iffezheim, he recognized him immediately.

"Ah, the jeweller from Frankfurt, Rothschild's friend." William was in a suitably jovial mood.

Robert presented Francesca to His Grace.

"Herr Koch," the Duke declared with a gallant bow to Francesca, "your taste in women is as exquisite as the Rothschilds' taste in Bank of England bonds."

"Your Grace is very kind," Robert said with a bow.

"I hope you will enjoy the Scottish dinner. Especially the main dish."

"The main dish?"

"Wait and see."

The twelfth Duke dismissed them to receive homage from the next in line.

Robert and Francesca proceeded to the large dining room. The three half-naked sisters had arrived a few minutes earlier to take their place in a corner to provide dinner music, together with the ingratiating tenor whose repertoire of titillating folk-lore—incomprehensible to most, but not to the Duke and the three sisters, who clearly loved the songs—seemed limitless. Four or five inviting whisky bottles had been placed on each of the twenty tables, each set for eight. At the centre of the room there was a large table, covered with a tablecloth but, for an unknown reason, left empty. Soon after they had entered the doors were closed.

Menu

Seaweed Soup or Cock-a-leekie Soup

—

Baked Salmon or
Haddock Rarebit with whisky sauce

—

A Scottish Meat Dish That No Guest Would Dare to Cut or
Haggis or
Boiled Gigot of Mutton or
Minced Collops

—

Atholl Blose Dessert or
Caledonian Cream or
Peaches in Whisky or
Date and Whisky Torte

•   •   •

The Duchess of Hamilton's *Haushofmeister* Edmund Jenkins and Richard Pohl, the Wagnerian music tsar and editor of the *Badeblatt*, were already seated when Robert and Francesca joined them. The companion Herr Jenkins had chosen, or who had been assigned to him, was a real or pretense Bavarian peasant with pigtails and freckles named Bärbl, who wore a very short *Dirndl* dress. By now her robust, lily-white thighs, whose upper reaches she recklessly allowed him to caress, had kindled the poor man's desire for rapid consummation to such an extent that she had to remind him several times, in the half hour to come, of the strict orders given to all the ladies to remain on duty in the dining room at all costs until the main course had been served.

The consort strategically chosen for Richard Pohl was a young lady in sudden, desperate need of money, a ravishing soprano from the Braunschweig opera who had just been devastated by a review for her début as Senta in the *Flying Dutchman*, suggesting that she could only succeed on the German opera stage if her impressive physical endowments, and her much-advertised social talents, could sway a besotted critic to declare, in the face of overwhelming evidence to the contrary, that she was capable of carrying a tune. By the time the soup was served, Richard Pohl was prepared to print in his *Badeblatt* that he had had to wait for twenty-four years, since he first saw the Master's manuscript, to meet a singer capable of singing Isolde. At last he had done so.

At the next table next, Robert recognized Georg, the sixth duke of Leuchtenberg, Josephine's biological great-grand-son via Eugène Beauharnais. The Duke was inflamed by a heavily rouged, bejewelled Rumanian lady, a graduate of one of the more fashionable establishments in Bucharest, who spoke very loud French and was old enough to be his mother, and Prince Hermann von Hohenlohe-Langenburg, the son of Queen Victoria's half-sister, who was being entertained by an enchanting junior member of the Karlsruhe corps de ballet, in need of pocket money to buy food for her starving lover, a struggling impressionistic painter from Riga. At other tables, Robert spotted Signor Enrico Montelli, the flamboyant writer from Florence with pink cheeks and a heavy mustache, the friend of Louis Katzau, who was being entertainment by a singularly attractive blond, blue-eyed actress from Sweden who had just played the *ingénue* in August Strindberg's *Master Olof,* and various familiar faces from the International Club, some of them wearing jockey clothes, as well as the Hungarian Count Tassilo Festetics, the member of the Imperial Guards in Vienna, the Duchess's son-in-law, but Robert could not tell who their ladies were. All the men, their veins dangerously inflated by burning mountain dew, appeared to be in a state of—by now almost insane—anticipation of ecstasies to come.

There was lively conversation and much laughter—and,

to judge by the occasional, very audible admonitions "Please don't!" or "Not yet!"—considerably exploratory fondling under the tables, not only by the *Haushofmeister*—as the unfamiliar soup and fish courses were served and consumed. Those men still able to concentrate on matters unrelated to going upstairs as soon their companions would let them tried to guess what the mysterious main course might be, "A Scottish Meat Dish That No Guest Would Dare to Cut." The most ingenious guess was probably the operatic Enrico Montelli's. He thought most likely it would turn out to be an *agnus dei* from a shrine in the Highlands.

Suddenly there was a droning sound not often heard in Baden-Baden, at first distant and then becoming louder. It was not the sound of an organ, nor of woodwind, nor did it really have the quality of a human voice, although it could have been any of these. The melody was uncannily beautiful, evoking ancient laments and buried memories of battlefields in the deep, dark prehistoric past.

The door from the anteroom opened. Four men marched in slowly, wearing peculiar headgear and woollen skirts decorated with yellow, green and red squares, their knees and legs exposed, blowing strange instruments that combined some of the characteristics of blacksmiths' bellows, spinning wheels and horns. Other than David MacDonald, only the learned music critic Richard Pohl would have been able to identify them as bagpipes if, having consumed an inordinately generous amount of love potion, he had not been paralyzed with lust for his Isolde.

This procession was followed by another four men, dressed in similar costumes, who carried a huge silver salver, solidly covered with a lid, also marching slowly, keeping time with the bagpipes' other-worldly drones. There was no question that the salver contained the main dish.

The music stopped. The world held its breath.

The four men deposited the salver on the empty table in the centre.

The Duke of Hamilton rushed in from nowhere and theatrically lifted the lid.

EARRINGS

A voluptuous woman, smoking a cigarette, stepped out and stood on the table holding up her arms. No woman was ever more naked. No Aphrodite, no Venus, had ever appeared from the sea, from the mountains, from the desert, even from the nearby River Rhein itself, as proudly, as exuberantly, as magnificently, as triumphantly, as climactically, as bewitchingly, as shamelessly beautiful. In this House of Joy she was the *Ode to Joy*.

It was, of course, Margaret Ivanov, the evening's Scottish hostess, the Duke's friend. The cigarette no doubt signified that there was no reason for a heavenly phenomenon like her to conform to profane bourgeois convention.

There was a round of rapturous applause. Even the women joined in.

Robert looked at Margaret closely, his eyes focused on her ears.

No, Margaret was not totally naked, after all.

She wore Josephine's ruby earrings.

.   .   .

None of the guests waited for the dessert.

"There has been an earthquake," Robert said to Francesca. His bizarre behaviour—he seemed to be galvanized—was an entirely novel experience for her. "You must forgive me. Just give me your address and go home. You will hear from me."

He kissed her on the forehead and left, leaving her standing there totally puzzled, her mouth half open. By now, the dining room was empty. The waiters were clearing the tables.

The Duke of Hamilton, Boris and Margaret Ivanov, who had quickly put on an elegant, chaste, dark blue gown and was still wearing the earrings, sat down at one of the vacated tables. They had not had dinner yet. A waiter brought them the soup.

When Robert approached, clearly with something important on his mind, the Duke asked his two friends whether they would mind if he asked "the handsome jeweller from Frankfurt" to join them for a minute. Of course they did not mind in the least. Boris added that he, too, had had the pleasure of meeting Herr Koch. Margaret and Robert smiled at each other.

"Your Grace is very kind," Robert said. "I hope you have no objection if I ask Herr Ivanov an intriguing question."

The Duke nodded amiably.

"Do you remember the receipt for a pair of ruby earrings Ivan Turgenev left behind?"

Margaret automatically fingered "her" earrings.

"Of course."

"Well," Robert went on, "the interesting thing is that Herr Klammerer—I am sure you know him—told me only yesterday that some years ago they were duly returned to Turgenev in Paris."

"Oh, really?" Boris said. "No, I did not know that."

"You see, Herr Ivanov, they were precise copies of these earrings." He pointed to Margaret's. "Isn't that extraordinary?"

The rakish twelfth Duke cleared his throat.

"No, Herr Koch," he said. "It is not extraordinary at all. Frau Ivanov's earrings are genuine. They belong to my mother."

Robert's heart began beating.

"Oh William," Margaret cried, "that's not what you told me when you lent them to me."

"No, my dear, I did not. There was no need. Nor did I tell you that they used to belong to Empress Josephine." He paused. "There was no need to burden you with such unnecessary information."

"My old friend Mikhail Bakunin was right," Boris chuckled. "The aristocracy is rotten to the core."

"Not only the aristocracy," the Duke retorted with mock seriousness. He pointed to the ceiling. "Have you noticed that the hotel is rocking like a boat?"

They all laughed.

"You see," the Duke went on, "I was getting tired of my mother always talking about those boring old earrings. All my life I had to hear her about them. Of course I knew where they were. So one evening, after I had a few drinks, I simply went upstairs and took them. Just for the hell of it. I had no specific plans for them. One of these days I would return them. There was no hurry. I knew she would discover that they had gone, and that there would be a fuss. So much the better. Then, once you and Margaret were telling me about your plans for this evening's gala affair, it occurred to me that they would suit you perfectly, Margaret. And so they do."

Robert decided to be truthful and direct.

"Your Grace, I have come to Baden-Baden to see whether I had a chance to open a boutique here during the summer season."

"What a good idea," the Duke said. "My mother and I have said for years we need a first-class jeweller in this town. Mellorio, Ruthingen, Ludwig Weiler and Theodor Klammerer, who always has his nose in a book, they are no longer good enough."

"I was told Her Highness could be of the greatest help to me. Do you think you could arrange for me to get an introduction to her? And at the same time let me return the earrings on your behalf, to put her in a good mood?"

"Nothing would give me greater pleasure. You are just the type she likes, a suave, elegant Frenchman to the core, even if you have never set foot in France and probably don't know any irregular verbs. I'll mention you to her first thing in the morning. I assume you can be reached through our friend Louis Katzau. If you don't hear from me by five o'clock just call on our *Haushofmeister* and he will take you up to her. He may still have a beatific smile on his face when he relives his ecstasies with his Bavarian peasant beauty, but he will have most probably calmed down and sobered up by then. You can hand over the earrings to my mother and tell her I borrowed them for the Prince of Wales's friend Lady Charles Beresford when I found out that the poor lady had left her jewellery at home in London and felt naked without."

The Duke and Margaret beamed at each other. Boris Ivanov smiled indulgently.

"That's as good an explanation as any," he went on. "My mother is used to my little games. Just tell her I didn't want to bother her when she had so many other things on her mind. Yes, Her Koch, we need you in Baden-Baden."

With a radiant smile Margaret took off "her" rubies and handed them cheerfully to Robert.

· · ·

The next morning, Robert took one of the two emerald broaches he had brought along from Frankfurt from Fräulein Fröhlich's safe, put them in one of his green leather cases, wrapped the case, hired a carriage and took it to the address Francesca had given him. He did not ask the landlady whether Francesca was home.

On a note he wrote:

To Francesca —
In memory of an unforgettable night,
Robert Koch

Chapter 16

Robert was in a state of sublime bliss when he dropped in on Louis Katzau in his boutique, after having delivered the package, to announce the happy recovery of the Duchess's genuine rubies and describe in exquisite detail the events that took place last night in Louis's absence. Not a word was said about the time they had spent with Wanda and Francesca. There are certain things gentlemen do not discuss.

"Once I have the *brévet* in my hand," Robert declared, "you and I, and—why not?—Theo Klammerer, will be ready to have serious business discussions."

A *brévet* was the patent to appoint a person Special Jeweller to Her Highness, to closest thing to being *Hofjuwelier*, Court Jeweller.

"Let us not count our chickens," Louis responded, "before our eggs are fertilized. Since you are so French, as the Duke says, you must be familiar with the well-known fable by Lafontaine on this subject. Remember great ladies are capricious and unpredictable. The *brévet* will hinge entirely on the question whether you declare yourself as her second cousin at the beginning of the conversation, at the end, or have the strength to refrain from mentioning it altogether."

.   .   .

Robert's appointment was at six. The visitor who preceded him in the Duchess's reception room on the second floor
of the Palais Hamilton was the Mother Superior of the Lichtental
Monastery, who called on her every Tuesday afternoon. At seven
the Duchess's personal coachman, the Scot MacAustin, was
scheduled to take her along the Lichtentaler Allee in her open
carriage to the Final Banquet of the season in the Hotel
Stephanie-les-Bains, to conclude this summer's celebrations for
the twenty-fifth anniversary of the Iffezheim Races.

First, Robert returned Josephine's earrings. The old lady's
expressions of surprise and delight were more than adequate.

"My dear Herr Koch, I simply cannot tell you how vastly
relieved I am. Of course, I will make sure that you will have no
reason to regret your role as intermediary in this silly affair. I
simply could not bear the thought that a member of my staff
had taken the jewels, or that there had been a common, vulgar
break-in. As to the idea of having to go to the police—no, Herr
Koch, I could not do that. It never occurred to me, of course,
that, of all people, my son William would play such a trick on
me. He is so much like his father!

"Herr Koch, I do not want to burden you with my
family's history. No doubt after I am gone, someone will write
it. That will be the time to tell the extraordinary story of the
roundabout way Josephine's jewels came to my mother. That
will also be the occasion to give the reasons why I have come to
believe that the sad, tragic figure Kaspar Hauser was indeed my
brother, and to tell the tale of my—hm—difficult husband's entirely unnecessary death in Paris. I have never fully recovered
from the shock. In fact, ever since that sad day, I have had a
slight heart condition.

"Can you image, some one referred to me the other day
as a "Scottish princess"! The time is not far away when they
will call me Marie, Queen of Scots! I love my son dearly, and it
hurts me terribly whenever I am told of his inexcusable and
irresponsible carelessness in managing his affairs in Scotland.
Why is he never there? Why does he spend all his time at the

races and in disreputable company with former anarchists and women who are not his wife?

"William has always played these tricks on me. Let me tell you a story, Herr Koch. Everybody knows how fond I am of animals. Whenever I hear about dogs being used as draught animals to pull butcher-carts I buy them from their owner and add them to my own pack. One day, when William was about fifteen, he took my pack of dogs to the pavillion in the park during the Sunday afternoon concert. No one objects to the odd bark of individual, well-behaved dogs during a concert. That adds to the atmosphere. But on this occasion my wild pack was so noisy that the police had to intervene. The following week, William went to my butcher, bought a live calf and had him send me the bill. The following Sunday he decorated the calf with flowers and appeared with it in the park during the concert, proudly holding the reins There was the odd *moo* but, as far as I remember, it hardly interfered with the Strauss waltzes. He thought that was amusing. And last Christmas, his present to me was a shocking novel about a common whore, by this new French writer, Émile Zola.

"Herr Koch, I am an old woman, one of the rapidly disappearing relics from another age, living in a world in which I am less and less at home. That is the world of Alfred Krupp who visits me whenever he is in Baden-Baden, although I have the greatest reservations about him. In fact, I strongly disapprove of him. Still, I intend to introduce you to him because he may well decide to become a customer of yours. The founder of the family fortune, Friedrich Krupp, was an inventive speculator who served my grandfather Napoleon loyally. His son Alfred is known to the world as the *Kanonenkönig*. The so-called cannon king now employs fifty thousand workers in Essen and cares for nothing but money and power. He does not care for the finer things in life. He thinks that a relative of his wife's, the composer Max Bruch, is wasting his life in a meaningless pursuit. That is the barbarian world he lives in. If Bruch devoted his life to technology, he says, he might be of some use to mankind. Krupp pretends to be a great German patriot, but he would not hesitate to sell guns to Germany's enemies if it was profitable to him. He is absolutely without principles or scruples. If our Kaiser, or the people in the War Ministry, will not dance to his tune, he tells them that unless they do he will sell his company to France or emigrate to Russia. He keeps warning them that he can't live on German sales alone. Before the seven-week war against Austria in 1866, he sold guns to the Austrians and at the same time told Bismarck he was greatly concerned about Prussia's lack of preparedness for armed conflict. Of course he wanted to squeeze more contracts out of Berlin. When they did not advance enough money, he secretly accepted a loan from Paris. At the World Exhibition in 1867, Louis Napoleon awarded him a decoration for his services to France. You can imagine what real patriots like Moltke or Roon think of him. The other day someone showed me a sales brochure Krupp distributed in England pointing out that in the Russian-Turkish war of 1877–78 Krupp had supplied guns to both sides, and both sides had been very satisfied.

"Herr Koch, you are a young man, at the start of what I hope will be a splendid career. I can see that you are a man of taste, well equipped to make the best of your opportunities in the world that is now unfolding. There is no reason for you to find it as frightening as I do. I will not burden you with stories I hear from my friend the Kaiserin Augusta', about her brash and ambitious grandson Wilhelm, who is twenty-four and will one day be Kaiser Wilhelm the Second. He spends far too much time for her liking on the parade grounds of Potsdam and sounds like a bombastic drill sergeant when he speaks. The Prince of Wales is his uncle and tells me similar stories. Augusta says young Wilhelm can hardly wait to take over. By then I hope to be resting peacefully in the *Fürstenkapelle* in our monastery. How foolish he would be to pick another quarrel with France, or a new one with England, Germany's natural friend, or with Russia, after Bismarck's patient efforts to establish good relations with that huge country. We here in Baden-Baden have had the good fortune to make friends with Ivan Turgenev and so many other of Russia's worthiest citizens. Augusta says her grandson often speaks ill of his decent, modest, peace-loving father and especially of his mother, the daughter, as you must know, of Queen Victoria.

"Of course, I will introduce you to Augusta, but perhaps I will also have the chance to present you to another empress, or rather former empress, the Empress Eugénie, who occasionally visits me. I shall never forget the occasion when she stayed with me, in better days, nearly twenty years ago, when Grand Duke Friedrich and Grand Duchess Luise, Augusta's daughter, gave a reception for her at the Neue Schloss, a reception that Bismarck also attended. To think that five years later, after the Battle of Sedan, her husband was Bismarck's prisoner! It simply breaks one's heart. I went to see Louis Napoleon in Wilhelmshöhe, near Kassel. He was already very sick. I often wonder what would have happened if nearly fifty years ago I had accepted his offer to marry me. My mother would not hear of it. She was so proud of being the adopted daughter of Napoleon, but she regarded his nephew as nothing but a clumsy adventurer, unworthy of her daughter. Little did she know he would be Emperor of France for nearly twenty years, almost twice as long as his uncle! She wanted me to marry the Duke of Orléans, the elder son of King Louis-Philippe. That seemed a much better risk. And, looking back, as things looked at the time, he actually was!

"Please forgive me, Herr Koch. It is very rude of me to talk about myself in this way when I should concentrate on who among the crowned heads, or former crowned heads, or among the monarchs of industry I know, might benefit from making your acquaintance. When the Emperor of Brazil, Dom Pedro II and the Empress Teresa, will come again I will certainly present you to them. They were here in 1876 and stayed in the Europäische Hof. They have every intention of coming again.

"Herr Koch, there are many, many others.

"Before I ask my *Haushofmeister* to prepare the *brévet* for you, let me take a good look at you. From the moment I set eyes on you I had the uncanny sensation that your face seemed strangely familiar. Now I know what was in my mind. Has anybody ever told you that you bear an uncanny resemblance to one of the Bonaparte brothers—to Joseph? Louis? Lucien? Jérôme?"

"No, Your Highness," Robert replied, "I don't think anybody ever mentioned that. But I am deeply flattered that Your Highness should think so."

Postscript I

In due course, Robert Koch received charters from nearly all the German courts, and from the Prince of Wales, the King of Italy and the Tsar. There is no question that he came to some arrangement with Louis Katzau, but nothing specific is known about it, nor of his relations with Theodor Kammerer, Katzau's neighbour in Boutique Number Three. Kammerer is named Klammerer in this fiction since his character is entirely invented.

Robert Koch died in 1902, at the age of fifty, too soon to learn what members of the next generation of the Koch family discovered some twenty-five years later when they inspected his father's—Napoleon's putative love-child's—tombstone, near his legal parents Esther and Shmuel, in the Jewish cemetery in Stadtlengsfeld, not far from Jena. There they noted that the date of his birth was December 4, 1808, nearly twenty-six months after the Battle of Jena.

Robert Koch also died too soon to see his store move to one of the most sought-after locations in Frankfurt, the corner of the Kaiser Strasse and the Neue Mainzer Strasse. The building was designed by Paul Wallot, the original architect of the Reichstag. It was faithfully restored after being destroyed during the Second World War, and is today protected as a historic monument. Modelled on an Italian Renaissance Palazzo, it is now owned by the Robert Bosch Foundation and occupied by the bank Monte dei Paschi di Siena, founded in 1472.

Robert's successor was his younger brother Louis, who died in 1930, a compelling and ingratiating personality, prominent in the Jewish community, generous philanthropist remembered, above all, as the collector of musical autographs, including Bach's Kantata *Gott, wie dein Name*, Mozart's Singspiel *Der Schauspieldirektor*, Schubert's *Die Winterreise* and his last three piano sonatas, Beethoven's Diabelli Variations and Piano Sonata Opus 101, and Brahms's *Second Symphony*. Louis Koch also collected Napoleon's letters, including a love letter to Josephine, written during one of the Italian campaigns.

In 1938, when the firm had to be "aryanized," the Robert Bosch family acquired it and enabled it to survive in Frankfurt and Baden-Baden until 1986. Its last manager, Günter Greiling, today owns a distinguished jewellery store in Baden-Baden and is proud of being able to carry on the old tradition.

A year after Robert Koch's death, his grandson Rudolf Heilbrunn was born. He became a partner in the 1920s, even though his main interests were literary and scholarly. In 1938, he emigrated to Amsterdam. Four years later he was arrested and sent to the concentration camp Westerbork, Anna Frank's camp. He miraculously survived, returned to Germany after the war and died in July 1998 in Kaiserslautern, at the age of ninety-six.

In the camp, he managed to write his memoirs. One chapter contained his childhood memories of Baden-Baden. A few paragraphs were devoted to the Koch boutique:

> I still remember the name of the King of Siam who *pflichtgemäss* [dutifully] paid a visit. It was Chulalongkorn [1853–1910, the ninth son of King Mongku and remembered as a great modernizer who abolished slavery]. After he had gone, the manager telephoned grandmother and announced, in broad Baden dialect, "Frau Koch, we're sold out." This had never happened before in the history of the House of Koch. I was then told the full story. His Majesty had arrived in the boutique, equipped with a malacca cane. With it he not merely pointed to but actually touched every piece of jewellery exhibited in the store, saying things that the manager could not understand. He

asked the interpreter who accompanied the King what these gestures meant. "Every object His Majesty touched," the interpreter explained, "is to be considered sold. Please submit the account immediately." This was done, and the bill paid at once, in cash...

...I liked nothing better than to hide in a corner of the boutique to listen to the conversations of grown-ups. Once, I was a secret witness to the occasion when *Geheimrat* [Privy Counsellor] Alfred Krupp dropped in and modesty asked whether he could see "something interesting" [Alfred Krupp died in 1902; this must have been his son-in-law Gustav Krupp von Bohlen und Halbach]. Uncle Max [Robert's youngest son] showed him a pearl necklace, uttering at the same time the word "one," obviously intending to elicit the question "one what?" But Herr Krupp merely said, "Please put it in a leather case."

Uncle Max thought it only prudent to ask whether "one" meant "one million marks".

"But of course, my dear Herr Koch," the *Geheimrat* replied.

Postscript II

Louis Katzau died in 1928, at the age of eighty-eight, and is buried with his wife in the Jewish cemetery in Lichtental. They left no descendants.

"The king of all Methuselahs," the *Badische Presse* wrote in its obituary, "the last living witness of Baden-Baden's great days, crossed over into the eternal world of dreams, with all his memories of a society in which the alliance between the owner-ship of worldly possessions and the possession of spiritual culture was still self-evident."

He left behind a guest book in which, between 1885 and 1927, many of his friends and customers made entries, usually by simply signing their names but often also paying him reverent or irreverent tribute.

The location of the original is not known, but the *Stadtarchiv* of Baden-Baden has a copy and has kindly given permission to reproduce a few selected pages.

Baden-Baden *without* the always cheerful and pleasant M. L. Katzau – unthinkable!
Prince Hermann of Sachsen-Weimar

I share the opinion of Prince Hermann
Marie von Baden, Duchess of Hamilton

William Hamilton

Bade. 17 Juin 1895.

Bade sans Katzau serait inhabitable du reste les signatures antérieures, à la mienne prouvent que mon opinion et plus que justifié

Lord Charles Hamilton

Baden without Katzau would be uninhabitable. The previous signatures
prove that my opinion has been confirmed.
Lord Charles Hamilton

Countess Tassilo Festetics

Tassilo Festetics

Elisabeth

Baden 22. April 1888.

Empress Elisabeth of Austria-Hungary ("Sissi"), assassinated in Geneva (1854–1898)

Rudolf

Wien 23. Dec. 1888.

Crown Prince Rudolf of Habsburg (1858–1889), double suicide in Mayerling on January 30, 1888, with Baroness Marie Vetsera

Stephanie

Wien 24. Dec 1888.

Crown Princess Stephanie

Prince von Bülow, Reich Chancellor

Wilhelm, Prince of Prussia, later Kaiser Wilhelm II

Combien j'ai eu tort de ne pas aller plus tôt dans cette charmante ville de Baden-Baden, si abondante en promenades délicieuses! Combien j'ai eu tort de ne pas venir plus tôt serrer la main à monsieur Katzau, au milieu de ses belles ogandereis et présenter mes respectueux hommages à la gracieuse madame Katzau qui parle si bien le français! Je me promets du moins de revenir à Baden-Baden et de faire une nouvelle visite à Monsieur Katzau in l'illustre promenade

Anatole France

Baden-Baden 14 août 1913.

How wrong I was not to have visited earlier the charming
town of Baden-Baden with its abundantly delectable walks.
How wrong I was not to have shaken the hand of Monsieur
Katzau earlier in midst of his beautiful displays and
presented my compliments to the gracious Madame
Katzau who speaks such beautiful French. I promise
myself to return to Baden-Baden and to make another
visit to Monsieur Katzau in the illustrious Promenade.

Anatole France

Pietro Mascagni, 1863–1945, composer of Cavalleria Rusticana

Enrico Caruso

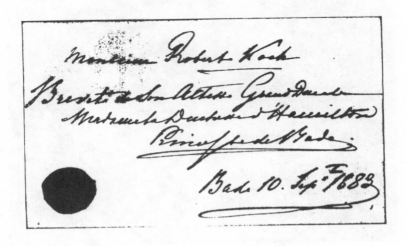

The "brévet" (See page 201)

AGMV Marquis

MEMBER OF SCABRINI MEDIA

Quebec, Canada
2001